22 Jamaican Short Stories

22 Jamaican Short Stories

A selection of prizewinning short stories
(originally published as Festival Literary Anthology in 1987)

First Edition 1987 (Festival Literary Anthology)
2nd Edition 1992

Reprint 2013
10 9 8 7 6 5 4

This is a work of fiction. names, characters, places and incidents either are the products of the author's imagination or are used fictitiously, and any resemblance to actual persons, living or dead, events or locales, is entirely coincidental.

All LMH Publishing Limited titles are available at special quantity discounts for bulk purchases for sales promotion, premiums, fund-raising, educational or institutional use.

Permission granted by Longman Group UK Limited to publish "The Love Orange" and "Ascot" by Olive Senior from Summer Lighting and Other Stories (Longman Caribbean Writers Series
1986).

Original book design by Kim Robinson

Published by LMH Publishing Limited
Suite 10-11, Sagicor Industrial Park
7 Norman Road
Kingston C.S.O., Jamaica
Tel.: (876) 938-0005; 938-0712
Fax: (876) 759-8752
Email: lmhbookpublishing@cwjamaica.com
Website: www.lmhpublishing.com

Printed in the USA

ISBN: 976-610-158-2

Contents

Editors' Note

From the first Edition

In the *Festival Literary Anthology* we have presented a number of short stories which since the inception of Jamaica's Annual Literary Competition have won gold and silver medals.

This anthology does not pretend to be a comprehensive collection of all gold and silver medal winners. It does, however, include all material which was made accessible to us by the Jamaica Cultural Development Commission.

It is our hope that future volumes will be able to supplement this first effort, not only by filling in whatever gaps exist within this collection but also by featuring other categories of work which may be as deserving of publication.

Kim Robinson
Leeta Hearne
June, 1987

Foreword

This anthology contains a selection from Gold and Silver Medal award winners in the Short Story (adult) category of the Festival Literary Competition over a period of some twenty years. It has long been the ambition of the Literary Committee to print the works of our talented writers, and it is with great pleasure that we present this publication.

The literary competition has for many years been overshadowed by the more spectacular popular music and exhibition arts. Indeed the use of abstract, subtle or analytical techniques of language must be suffused by the immediate impact of the song and dance aspect of Festival celebrations. However, despite the difficulties, shortage of sponsors and lack of publication over the years, an irrepressible expression of talent has surfaced through the literary competition, which will provide reading pleasure as well as an important historical document on what it was like to live in immediate post-Independence Jamaica.

Fortunately and significantly, this publication has come to fruition in the Centennial year of Marcus Garvey's birth, in which Jamaica also celebrates her twenty-fifth anniversary of Independence. In the expression of Garvey's insistent concept of black intellectual ability, we hope also to provide an indication of our nation's maturity at the quarter-century mark. Indigenous publishing is not only an important adjunct and a telling indicator of true independence, but what and how a nation publishes says much about its state of mental and social well-being. At age twenty-five, we are at last giving tangible recognition to our writers.

By insistence upon rigid – some might say 'harsh' – assessment criteria, we have succeeded in establishing a standard which needs no apologies as coming from the Third World. In 1985 we awarded a Silver Medal to Margaret Bernal's poem "Busha Graver's Saddle", which subsequently won the Gold Medal in the BBC's Commonwealth Literary Competition. Almost every successful Jamaican writer has come through this stringent system, and several, notably Trevor Rhone, Anthony McNeill, Dennis Scott, Michael Reckord, Charles Mills, and Olive Senior, first gained recognition through the Festival Literary Competition.

I must thank the many adjudicators, too numerous to mention by name, who kept the faith and worked without reward or recognition under very difficult conditions – year after frustrating year . . . . Thanks to the Festival Literary Officers Bari Johnson and Jean Breese for their enthusiasm and faith, to Humroy Whyte for his determined search for these manuscripts, and to Clover Thompson for her moral support. Thanks also to very many long-serving committee members and in particular to Tess Thomas and Rosalind MacLaughlin, without whose unflagging support and help, the Chairman might have given up the battle as lost. . . . Thanks to our editors Kim Robinson and Liz Hearne for their painstaking attention. Thanks to the Jamaica Library Service who have willingly and skilfully mounted our annual exhibitions for the encouragement of the winners. Thanks to Alcan Jamaica Limited, our sponsor from the outset, also to National Employers Mutual Insurance Company, who along with Alcan have generously increased the award prizes.

The Literary Committee, and indeed Jamaica, is indebted to the Shell Company (West Indies) Limited for funding the publication of this anthology.

Shirley Maynier Burke
Chairman
Literary Committee
Jamaica Cultural Development Commission

The Delinquents

by Arthur Scott

Gold, 1967

Fear followed him like a shadow. The fear had been with him since he left home and had been very intense in the dark. More than once, particularly when he was walking through the gully and, after, through the lumber yard, he had got the distinct sensation that he was being followed. But whenever he glanced in the direction he thought he saw someone, it was as if the person always managed to conceal himself in time.

When he came out on South Lane he was relieved to see, in the bright wash of the street light, the tall, slender figure of Johnny sitting on the bridge. Rupert thrust his hands deep into his pockets, approaching Johnny now with a little of his old confidence returning.

"What happen, Johnny?" he said.

"You not coming from you yard now?" Johnny asked.

"Yes, man."

"Then why you come all the way from down so?"

"I hear Whitey and him gang looking for me," Rupert said.

Johnny leaned and spat cleanly over the bridge. "Then you fraid for them?" he asked.

"You know is bout ten of them?" Rupert said angrily. "You know say them carry knife and me hear Whitey have gun."

Johnny came slowly off the bridge, hitching up his pants.

Rupert glanced keenly at him, a little startled and ashamed of his own vehemence.

They walked along the lane in silence. Rupert took his hand and felt the tender lump on his forehead. It was the size of a penny. He had got it at the Suede Shoes. At the usual Friday night dance a week ago. He had been there alone when he saw a girl in a tight black sweater sitting by herself. He had asked her for a dance and after a time he had thought that, because of how she swung her belly against him, it should be all right to try and get her across the broken-down wire fence and into the thick grass of the open land next door. He was going towards the door, an arm about her waist, when the girl was suddenly jerked away from him and the fellow who did it slapped her twice, quite hard. Then Rupert and the fellow, whom he subsequently learned was called Whitey, closed immediately. He had felt quite strong and sure of himself for he had been training with weights for over three months. They struggled violently, gripping each other closely. They had been so close together that he could smell the strong beer-smell on the other's breath. Then they had gone down heavily to the floor and Rupert broke away and brought his knee up and drove it hard between Whitey's legs so that he gasped hoarsely with pain. They stood up again and Whitey's face was a grimace of pure pain and he had one hand rubbing where he had been hurt. He braced himself as Whitey prepared to come at him again, then he saw that somebody had handed Whitey a beer bottle. There had been a moment when, twisting himself away from the descending bottle, he thought he had made it, and another moment when he did not quite know what had happened. Then he was on the floor, stupidly, on his hands and knees, when it dawned on him that the noise around him was the noise of people trying to get away because the police had arrived. He had climbed through a window and managed to make his way safely to the street.

Rupert and Johnny walked unhurriedly through the lane, passing between massed ramshackle buildings with their crazy broken-down fences. Presently they came to where the lane was bordered by open land and where there were no houses at all.

Johnny paused, and in the pale darkness Rupert made out the shape of what he had in his hand.

"Careful how you hold this thing, you hear, man," Johnny

cautioned.

Rupert held the gun gingerly as though afraid of it.

"Just hold it so. Don't do anything to it," Johnny said.

"Where you get it, Johnny?" Rupert asked. He held the gun in his hand, liking the curious thrill it gave him. It had been like the first time he had held a switch blade.

"I get it from a fellow off a boat," Johnny said.

"You can use it?" Rupert asked.

Johnny laughed, putting the gun back into his pocket. He wore a loose black shirt outside his pants, which covered the shape of the gun completely. Johnny was twenty-one. He was merely two years older than Rupert. Yet it was as though Johnny moved and lived in a world of men where life was really lived and was worth living. Rupert often thought of himself as existing on the drab periphery of Johnny's world and that he only managed to gain experience of this world because of his tenuous association with Johnny. Sometimes he was quite amazed at the extent of Johnny's knowledge and experience. For instance, Johnny said he knew how to use a metered telephone without using pennies and he also had a hundred ways of getting into a dance hall or theatre or watching a football match without once going into his pocket. Johnny often said he knew a lot of bad men and he also knew, he had said, where one or two of them were hiding from the police. Once he had shown Rupert a gold watch which he said had been given to him by a blonde American woman. Her husband, a Jamaican businessman, had gone to the United States on vacation. She had wanted Johnny to drive for her husband when he returned but Johnny had thought that would be too dangerous. He told Rupert that he knew all the sport houses in the island, and when he was driving for one of those rent-a-car businesses that catered to tourists he had driven a rich American man to one of those plush sport houses where you had to have a pass to enter and he, Johnny, had been the first Jamaican black man to have gone there. Some of the girls there, Johnny had said, you could see working in the day in the front section of the big offices downtown.

Rupert and Johnny walked around to the back of the gas station. Dicky, who was Johnny's friend, worked there as an attendant. They came upon Dicky by the sink. He was shirtless and was washing his face and hands with brown soap. He rinsed his mouth and spat loudly into the sink. It was obvious that

Dicky was in a nasty mood. They stood silently watching him while he began to curse, not loudly, but in a steady, intense manner. Then he ceased cursing and dried himself vigorously with a rag which he flung to the floor.

"What happen, Dicky?" Johnny asked.

"Mr. Mac no pay me off, sah. I feel like . . ." His voice ceased and he glared at them in a kind of baffled and unbearable anger. Then he tore a bright plaid shirt from a nail on the wall and put it on. "The man no say him doan like how me talk to him customers. Is what him wan' me fe do, eh, kiss them footbottom? I have a mind fe go inside and bust a chair 'pon him head."

"Play it cool, Dicky," Johnny said. "It don't make sense to do that."

"But is what else you can do wid a man like that?" Dicky said.

"Make we go up Suede Shoes an' drink a couple beers," Johnny said.

"But that too far, man. Make we go to Lennie instead," Rupert said.

"Look, guy. Whitey not troubling you if him see me with you," Johnny said.

"And we doan have fe walk," Dicky said. "I have a pal old Ford Prefect fe de night."

When, in the car, Johnny displayed the gun, Dicky did not appear to be impressed.

"Oh, is a thirty-eight," Dicky said. "Me had one last year and me threaten fe shoot a man, but me had fe sell it when the police them start look fa me."

Dicky suddenly swung the car hard to the left. "Me going cut through here," he said.

They were in the parking lot of a theatre, and Dicky was driving crazily in and out among the cars which were moving slowly into the street. He had almost gained the other road when, in swinging from behind a parked car, he crashed into another one. The car was large and quite new.

The driver of the car came out very quickly and stared at his wrinkled fender in a kind of shocked disbelief. He was obviously quite young. He was fair-skinned, clean-cut and well-dressed in a dark suit. A pretty girl was seated in the car. She stared out at them with round, frightened eyes.

"My old man is going to raise hell about this," the young

man said to himself. Then he turned suddenly upon them. "Do you admit liability?" he asked in cold fury.

"Admit what?" Dicky said.

"What you talking about, guy?" Johnny said.

"You want me to peel you tail out here tonight, guy?" Dicky said.

"I want your name," the young man said to Dicky.

"We don't have no name, guy."

"Come, David," the girl said in a thin, quavering voice. "Let us go."

The young man took a pen and notebook from his pocket. He walked towards their car, trying to read the licence disc.

"You don't hear the lady call you, guy," Rupert said. "Come David," he said, imitating the thin scared voice of the girl.

The young man hesitated. A shadow of fear flitted across his face. They stared at him stonily, a hostile and deep resentment uncoiling within them. It was easy to guess that he belonged to that class of people that got all the opportunities – they could tell that he had a good job in some big office uptown.

Rupert looked around. All the other cars had driven from the lot. They were alone there with the fellow. He removed his hand from his pocket, gently pressing the catch of the switchblade. It made a nice, clicking sound as the blade flicked free.

They doubled up with laughter as the young man drove hurriedly away.

"Man, them big American car is no good," Johnny said. "Look at this old car, man. All it have is a little sink on the grill."

At the Suede Shoes, a small group of people converged at the door. Rupert craned his head through the car window, staring at them. "See Whitey there, man," he said.

"Is all right. Take it easy," Johnny said.

Whitey and three other fellows, in a close little group, were leaving the Suede Shoes and were walking deliberately towards them.

Rupert felt a sudden and intense panic.

"Is him you mek beat you?" Dicky said.

Dicky's voice sounded loud enough for Whitey to hear. A curious mixture of anger and shame assailed Rupert. There was a violent pounding in his head and his mouth felt completely dry.

"What happen, Whitey?" Johnny said.

"Oh, is you, Johnny," Whitey said.

Whitey glanced at Rupert, scowling. He looked surly and uncomfortable. "You travelling wid this fellow, Johnny?" he asked, nodding his head in Rupert's direction.

"Yes," Johnny said. "I hear him an' you run into each other the other night."

"The guy no try tek way me woman."

"Is a misunderstanding. Whitey," Johnny said. "Him never realise she belong to anybody."

"Him never look like him want to know," Whitey said.

"Well him did find out soon enough," Johnny said, laughing.

They all laughed, Rupert tried to laugh too but his face would not respond.

"So why you don't call it quits, Whitey?" Johnny said. "The fellow never mean anything."

"Awright, Johnny," Whitey said. "As is your pal."

"You coming back to Suede Shoes later?" Johnny asked.

"No," Whitey said. He glanced back, scowling in the direction of the brightly lit building from where came the vibrant and compelling sound of a slow blues tune. "Man, them say me and me pals mustn't show we face in there again. Them say we create too much trouble. I wan' tell them, them doan see trouble yet. And them have one new guy as bouncer – a big black fellow – him was a heavyweight boxer one time. I going cut him up one day."

"You mean a man can't go where him want for a drink nowadays."

"I going see you, Johnny," Whitey said.

"Cool it, Whitey."

Whitey and his companions shuffled across the street and disappeared behind the grocery shop at the corner.

At the door of the Suede Shoes a small crowd clotted. A young boy who could not have been more than fifteen collected from the people who passed the door in single file. The boy glared constantly about him with hard, suspicious eyes, and he could curse as solidly as the men with whom he dealt.

"Where you going, man?" the boy said to a bearded fellow. "You t'ink you can come in here without money?"

"See you money here, man. You think me is a dam t'ief or what?"

"Hurry up an' pass through, man. You holding up everybody," the boy said belligerently.

"But this boy facety you know, man. Him wan' somebody whip him tail for him tonight."

"Whip what, man?" the boy said, glaring at the source of the voice. "Whip you father, you mean?"

"Come, bwoy. We doan have all night."

"Is sixpence more, man," the boy said. "Is what you trying to do?"

A man cursed and the boy cursed him back and a woman said, "But this bwoy don't have no respect fe woman at all."

Rupert paid his money and brushed irritably past the boy. He and Dicky entered the building. Johnny had not come in with them. For some reason Rupert felt moody. Something ugly was growing and intensifying inside of him. He spat arrogantly on the floor. "Make we have a beer, no?" he said to Dicky.

They sat at one of the tables beyond the dance floor, sipping beers. Dicky began to wink at a girl who sat with some men. Presently she rose and began to dance with a fellow in a red shirt. She kept looking around at Dicky.

Is what she looking at we so for? Rupert wondered angrily. She can't look someplace else? The ugliness was festering and it had become almost unbearable. He looked at Dicky with hatred. "Is pure jase ears woman here tonight," he said. "Mek we go someplace else."

"No, man. Make we stay here."

Rupert sat there, brooding. It began to dawn on him how often in the past he always had to be giving in to whatever Johnny and Dicky decided. He pondered on this for a while, recalling each occasion with great detail, feeling the violent mounting of tension within him.

Like a ghost, Johnny appeared suddenly among them.

"Where you was, guy?" Dicky asked.

Johnny sat slowly, stretching out his long legs. "I met a pal outside," he said. He placed the beer carefully on the table.

"I don't see no sense in staying here," Rupert said. "Make we go to Lennie, man."

"Make we cotch here for a while," Johnny said.

"Tek it easy, guy," Dicky said. "Whitey not coming back here tonight." Dicky was leaning back in the chair, a foot on the table, a wide, cynical smile upon his face.

Rupert slapped the beer from Dicky's hand. They both leaped violently to their feet, facing each other.

Johnny said, "Play it cool, Rupert. No sense in this, man."

Dicky cursed loudly. "Mek him stay," he said. "I going kill him here tonight."

"God blind me! Is what happening here?"

The speaker was Willy, the owner of Suede Shoes. Beside him was the boy who had been collecting and next to him was a big fellow with a battered face. The fellow wore a white T-shirt and he stood before them in a slight crouch, as a boxer stands.

"Is the fellow this?" Willy asked the boy, pointing to Johnny.

"Is him, yes," the boy said.

People had begun to converge about them.

"What you mean, man?" Johnny asked.

"You don't pay a damn to come in, man," the man said angrily. "You tell the boy that you just goin' inside to see somebody. How you can do a thing like that, man?"

"I can explain," Johnny said.

"Get out of here," Willy said. "I don't want you in here."

"Wait a little, man," Johnny said.

"Throw him out, Bigger," Willy said.

Bigger pushed Johnny violently. Johnny toppled across the table and fell awkwardly to the floor. He scrambled to his feet, his long legs straddling in all directions. Bigger pushed him again and this time he staggered backwards a few steps before he fell.

"Them is all troublemaker," a woman shouted. "Is that one start the fight the other night."

She pointed to Rupert.

"All of you get out," Willy said to Rupert and Dicky. "I don't want see any of you here again. The police them want to close down the place because of rowdy like you."

As they hurried to get away from Bigger, the three of them were momentarily wedged in the narrow doorway. Bigger came up swiftly and, from behind, he gave Rupert a hard thrust with his foot. The impetus hurled him against the others and they tumbled down the steps and fell to the ground.

The crowd laughed loudly.

Rupert's hand came in contact with something on the ground and when he gripped it he realised that the gun had fallen from Johnny's pocket. From the corner of his eye he saw Johnny and Dicky running towards the car. Bigger was coming quickly down the steps, walking towards him in a low crouch.

Rupert stood suddenly, pointing the gun.

Bigger stopped. He was motionless as a statue. His face, in the wash of light from the doorway, had that curious mask-like quality of intense fear.

There was a sudden screaming and shouting. People were running madly in all directions, like disturbed ants.

Then Rupert saw the gun in Willy's hand.

And before he could do anything at all, something struck him suddenly, with great force, in the chest. In an unbelievable sort of way it seemed to him that he was lying flat on his back.

He could hear many voices, confused and indistinct, as though shouting to him from a great distance. He could not understand what was being said. It was becoming difficult now to focus his attention on anything.

Then quite suddenly, just before it grew completely dark, he saw with the utmost clarity and intensity such as he had never known in all his life, the clear, unmistakable shape of the black hills against the silver sky and the moon a little above, incredibly huge and round and golden.

Less Than A Man

by Hugh Martin

Silver, 1968

Lefty fastened the last button on his pants and tightened the belt around his waist. He lifted his left hand and looked intently at it. The trace of a smile flickered for an instant across his face as he studied the three stubs that had once been his fingers. Only the hard, bitter look in his eyes betrayed the fact that there was no mirth in the smile; that there had been no mirth in him for a long, long time.

He lowered his hand and released a long bitter sigh. In school he was known as 'Lef-Han-Crab'. Now his left hand was almost of no use to him. A thumb and an index finger are quite useful – but they can't do everything.

He had never liked the nickname. He had had many fights on account of it. Later as he approached manhood it had been shortened and everyone had come to know him only as Lefty. Then he had grown accustomed to it. He had even got to like it.

But now . . . He shrugged and followed the warden into the office of the Prison Superintendent.

"Well, Brown," the Superintendent greeted him, "I see you are ready to leave us. Let us hope you don't come back. That might sound inhospitable but that's how it is here as you should know. The more we like our guests the less we want them to visit us. We like you, Brown, so rule that temper of yours and don't let us have to play host to you again. You have been well behaved and that is why you only spent six of the nine months of your sentence here.

"And one important thing, Brown, I know how you feel about the loss of your fingers. Don't believe that you are a cripple now. You may not be able to go back to cane-cutting but there are a number of other things you can do. You have only to look around and something will crop up in a short while."

Lefty listened quietly without really hearing. It was a trick he had developed while with the other prisoners. Their loud meaningless talk would be going on all around him and he would sit there, thinking – planning – unreached by them. He had come to realise that it was the only way to avoid being influenced by another's thoughts. It was the only way to retain one's own personality and not become an extension of someone else's ideals.

A man must be strong within himself or he cannot survive. In this place a man must have plans and goals or the life will become unbearable. He must have something to hold on to or he will become lost among the mass of mindless imbeciles who live only from one moment to the other and act only at the prompting of the strong. No, there is something outside for each man.

For one man there was the golden opportunity awaiting him to make a fresh go at life. For another there was that woman, strong, loving and faithful, waiting forever for his return. And for still another there was the sweet thought of revenge; revenge against the one responsible for his misery.

For Lefty there was no golden opportunity awaiting. There was no strong, loving woman. But there was sweet revenge. And it was this thought that had carried him through.

Half an hour later Lefty was on a bus bound for home. He sat near a window looking out of unseeing eyes. He was unaware of the person sitting next to him and of all the others in the bus. He did not see the other vehicles on the road. He paid no attention to the cattle grazing in the lush, verdant pastures of pangola grass, and when they stopped at Old Harbour he didn't notice the traditional vendors of fried fish and bammy.

But he surfaced from his stupor as the bus bumped its way

along the twisting Vere roads which divided the hundreds of acres of sugar cane. His eyes brightened as a surge of nostalgia swept through him. How he longed to feel the sun on his back as he grabbed the sweet stick and swung his machete again and again.

Grab, swish, slash. Grab, swish, slash.

Ah. But that was music to his ears – and rhythm for his body.

Then the brightness faded from his eyes and the old familiar hardness reappeared. Slowly he raised his left hand and looked at the three stumps. A blind fury seized him. His body shook and his eyes misted.

And through the mist he saw the stumps as they were seven months ago. And he watched himself re-enact the scene that had brought him this.

Lefty crept stealthily up behind Harry. As he neared him he dashed forward, grabbed his cap and made off with it laughing.

"Wha' de devil yuh nuh leave me alone, man?" Harry swore at him. "Bring back me cap, nuh. A big man like yuh still a gwaan like a bwoy."

Lefty doubled over with laughter as he stopped and pointed at Harry.

"Look on him head, man. Look on Harry head. Is a real stay-home trim dat. Ha hoi bwoy. Everybody tek a look."

Harry had had his hair cut the day before by an amateur. He was apparently conscious that a bad job had been done so this morning he had worn a cap for the first time since he started working on the estate.

Lefty had noticed it at lunch time and had been teasing Harry about it all afternoon. However, Harry had been on his guard so Lefty was unable to remove the cap. Now he had succeeded and his plan to torture Harry with ridicule had begun.

Harry dashed after him but he was waiting for it. He sprinted away with the cap in one hand and his machete in the other.

"Stop dat idiot fah me, Herbie," Harry called to a colleague ahead of them.

Herbie turned and held on to Lefty as the latter reached him but the speed was too great and they both went tumbling to the ground.

Herbie was the first to get up. He grabbed the cap and hurried to Harry with it. Then he turned and they both looked pityingly at Lefty as he rose to his feet.

"Dat bwoy will nevah grow up," declared Harry. "Him gwine gwaan until one day him really get hurt . . . Wait! What happen to yuh han', man?"

Lefty was holding his left hand out before him. On his face was a dazed expression of disbelief. His hand was a bloody mess. Two fingers were missing. A third was dangling ludicrously by a thin strip of skin. As they looked the skin slowly gave and it fell to join the other two. The machete, still wet with blood, was a few inches away from the severed fingers.

Lefty looked up and Harry and Herbie quailed before the rage and hatred that filled his eyes. He stepped back a few paces and stumbled over a stone. Still keeping his eyes on them he stooped and his right hand closed over the stone. He stood up, pulled his arm back and threw.

Now Lefty was not exactly ambidextrous. But he was very close to being so. He could use his less active hand better than most right-handers can use their left. There were times when, while cutting cane, he would shift his machete from his left to his right hand and would go on cutting where others would have stopped to rest.

Perhaps it was the lack of balance caused by his injury, or maybe it was because of his great passion, but his aim on this occasion was very bad indeed. He missed Herbie by a good two feet. It was only a pity that Harry was standing exactly two feet from Herbie.

Harry went down with the stone and when he sat up his face was covered with blood.

A crowd had now gathered and everybody stood stupefied. Then someone recovered and said: "Better carry dem up to de clinic. Dem a lose a whole heap of blood."

All the way to the clinic Lefty kept looking at the remains of his fingers without uttering a word. He said nothing while his hand was dressed and, when Corporal Kelly took him away, he was still silent. He kept glancing at the bandaged hand while the judge passed sentence on him and when the bandage was eventually removed a month later he said nothing.

He only looked down at the stumps that were once the instruments of his livelihood. His eyes misted and then cleared. Then they brightened with calculation and then dulled. And finally they hardened and remained so.

The bus came to a stop with a jolt and Lefty was brought

back to awareness of his surroundings. A man and a woman got off. Lefty got up just as the conductor buzzed the bus off. The driver swore at him but he got off without commenting. He stood looking around for some time then he walked up the parochial road leading to his home.

His mother came out of the kitchen with a spoon in her hand and watched as he approached. As he neared her, she recognised him fully and ran to meet him.

"Caleb, me bwoy! Caleb, yuh come home?" She was the only one who now called him by his proper name. She had always frowned on anyone she heard calling him 'Lefty' and had even promised to produce his 'age paper' to show that she had given him a good 'Bible name'.

She hugged him to her but he stood stiffly, looking down at his hands hanging uninterestedly at his sides.

"Yes, ah come," was all he said.

She released him and they walked up to the wattle and daub kitchen. Dinner was ready so she dished some out for him and watched him as he wolfed it down using his right hand with as much dexterity as he once used his left. She tried to make him talk but he said nothing. She avoided any mention of his fingers.

He finished eating and took up the machete that was leaning in a corner. He took a file from the top of the old safe beside the fireplace and he honed the machete for ten minutes. Then he stepped out.

His mother watched him silently, knowing it would make no difference what she said. The tears flowed freely from her eyes as he walked out of sight. She had failed both as mother and father. She would be as guilty as he would be for whatever he did today.

Lefty settled himself near the railway track. Herbie would pass there soon on his way home from the Estate. He was going to get a surprise this evening; one he would never forget — or remember for that matter.

Herbie wasn't long in coming. When he saw Lefty he paused momentarily then hurried up to him.

"Wha' happen, Lefty? Ah didn't know yuh was back. Bwoy, ah really glad fe see yuh. Ah nevah did get de chance fi tell yuh how sorry ah was about yuh hand."

"Ah going to kill yuh, Herbie," Lefty said, and Herbie saw that he meant it. "And yuh know why? Because yuh mek me less dan a man. Without me hand ah can't mek a living from the only thing ah can do. An' you is di cause of it."

Herbie felt the beads of perspiration gathering on his brow. He didn't want to die. Not in this way, at any rate. Yet if he must, there was something he had to say.

"Wait, Lefty. Yuh blaming me fah what yuh must blame yuhself. I didn't mek yuh less dan a man. Yuh was nevah a man. Every man pass through a number of stages in him life. Him was a baby, den a boy – den him reach a stage where him is neither man nor boy – den him become a man. Some people go through the stages quick, some slow. You, Lefty, is in de stage where yuh is neither man or bwoy. Yuh nevah come out a dat stage for all yuh thirty-five years. Yuh nevah grow up, Lefty, and dat is yuh main trouble . . ."

But Lefty wasn't listening. He lunged at Herbie and swung the machete. Herbie stepped back quickly and was spared. He heard the sound of a train in the distance and thought irrelevantly that it was some ten minutes late.

Lefty swung again but this time Herbie wasn't quick enough. He tripped and as he went down the machete bit into his thigh. Lefty towered over him. Herbie kicked out blindly and saw Lefty go sprawling across the track. He got up and tried to run but he fell again.

He looked back and saw that Lefty wasn't moving. The train was less than fifteen feet away. He crawled frantically towards the track but knew he could not make it. He watched the train pass.

Yes, he thought. Lefty was less than a man. As a corpse he didn't amount to much either.

The Young Trumpeter

by Ransford Smith

Silver, 1968

Johnny, the trumpeter, saw her first when they opened for two weeks at the Sea On Sky way up in the cool air of the Blue Mountains.

She had come in on the second night wearing a light green pants suit, her hair neatly cane-rowed and pulled sharply back from her wide forehead so that when you looked closely you saw the paleness of her skin where the hairline began. Pausing for a moment, she had looked meditatively at the bandstand; the overhead light shone fully on her intense face and he had seen the beautiful mould of her full lips, the flare of her nostrils, the dark glow of her skin, the pale crescent of her lipstick, then the light dimmed and she had been lost for a moment, and when the light shone fully again she was already seated and all he could see was the dark shadow she made sitting there, quietly nursing a drink, her fingers beating a rhythmic tattoo on the polished table top.

Johnny wondered about her – the sad look in her eyes; the melancholy of her sitting there. And instinctively he blew his trumpet for the girl in the green pants suit; blew like he had never blown before; blew until the guitar grew feeble and receded into the distance; and the organ faltered; and Troy the vocalist's voice cracked and nobody could keep pace with his trumpet anymore; and his eyes bugged and his lungs grew too big for his chest, and he steeled himself for the moment when they would explode like giant overblown balloons; and there was a tremendous roaring in his head as he played unceasingly on, and the room became an intimate cubicle in which only two people belonged, Johnny, the trumpeter, and the melancholy girl, her fingers keeping impeccable beat to the wailing of the inspired trumpet.

Then he could play no more and he stood there on the bandstand, drenched in sweat, his head hanging and his trumpet mute, listening to the roar of the crowd begin in the distance like the lonely clanging of the Kingston–Mo'Bay express of his youth, then growing closer, gathering momentum and intensity until it was right there sweeping past on the track before his excited eyes, and the noise of its wheels on the track, its shrieking engine, its passing, deafening, like a chorus of thunderclaps; and he could see the changing faces in the windows as it rushed by, then the express had surged past and there he remained standing alone by the track, with a great silence around him, and a great emptiness.

The express was no more, neither was the applause. He felt an overpowering loneliness within himself. For she had been missing from the kaleidoscope, the tangled faces flashing briefly before his eyes, their eyes gleaming with joy.

My God, she could at least have clapped once. She didn't have to rise from her seat and shout and scream or tear at her hair and clap until her hands grew red-hot and hurt. She didn't have to shout herself hoarse or work herself up into a frenzied ecstasy, so that the perspiration rolled down her face and spoilt the pretty crescent of her pale lipstick, because a young trumpeter had blown like a man possessed and for a moment it had seemed as if Louis Armstrong had come down out of heaven and had blown his trumpet out into the thin air of the Blue Mountains, seven thousand feet above the twinkling lights of Kingston.

But she could at least have rewarded him with a single handclap, he thought; a bringing together of those delicate hands for a fleeting moment. Not just sit there so icy cool and detached.

And he felt he had played in vain.

He watched now as she hurriedly paid her bill, her face slightly flushed by the gin and tonic she had had. A little smile that didn't reach her eyes and a tip for the waiter – and she was going through the door, pausing for a quick moment to look reflectively at the mural on the wall showing the blue of the sea touching the blue of the sky, painted so you never could tell where one began and the other ended and the fishes seemed to be swimming in the sky and the birds flying in the sea.

Overpowered by a sense of urgency, Johnny hurriedly left the bandstand, for he instinctively knew that he had to see her, speak to her.

By the time he pushed his way to the entrance, she was already seated in her car, an aging Triumph two-seater. Even from a distance he could see that she had now wrapped a pale chiffon scarf around her throat. It fell across her frail shoulders, shimmering and dancing playfully in the cool night wind. When he called out hoarsely, she looked back quickly and, for a lingering moment, a wistful half-smile of infinite warmth glowed on her lips, then flickered and died.

He stood there quietly watching the rear lights disappearing down the narrow road that spiralled like a giant staircase up the mountainside – watched until they were pinpoints in the dark, receding swifly into a blackness that finally enveloped all.

His eyes searched for her the following night, the next . . . and the next; and when she never did return to hear him play, the heart went out of his young trumpet.

And all that was left then was for the music critics to write sad, baffled obituaries to the career of the young trumpeter who had risen so swiftly to the mountain top – and then had fallen so suddenly.

The Exister

by Tessa Dow

Silver, 1969

Dora Olivetti walked out of the sixth form, and with an enormous sense of relief down the empty passage to the staff room. She would spend the remaining hour of school marking books so that at the end she would be quite free to forget about the whole business, especially the last forty minutes of humiliation. She knew that if only she could forget about her ridiculous height, the girls would too. Yet she was painfully aware that not only was she burdened with this deformity, but her general appearance was against her also. So what if they did call her Lofty, how could she expect to earn their approval with her plain face and the added insult of very short sight and very thick-lensed glasses. The ladies of the sixth set great store by physical beauty, being for the most part well endowed themselves, and having the gift of youth besides. It was not that they were intentionally cruel or rude, of course, it was just the fact of them being as they were, and giggling at what she was, with her deep earnestness about the literature of France. They had just finished exams, and it was the end of June, with two more weeks to go until the end of term. Earnest they could not be, not knowing what their results would be, or whether they were school leavers or not. They were in a mood of prolonged suspension, and it delighted them to play tricks or extract fun whenever the opportunity could be found. They could not know that Dora Olivetti was so unsure of herself that she dreaded their thoughtless efforts to create a little humour out of any little situation. What if they knew that sometimes her sleep was troubled with dreams of herself committing some act of violence against one or another of them, tearing their hair, or hitting them hard with a ruler? She really wanted to hurt them, to make some impression upon their invulnerable persons. But whenever a dream like this came to torment her, her actions were completely ineffectual, her victim would remain with untroubled countenance, to her mounting distress.

Four foot three, features crowded out by the thickest-lensed glasses, neat, upright figure, neatly dressed in anonymous-coloured clothing: she entered the staff room and made for her own position at the long table. Calm returned to her as she sat down quietly, and answered a greeting from her neighbour. Her fellow-teachers were a fairly uninspiring lot, pleasant, unhelpful, and rather self-centred. This gave Dora the chance she wanted for anonymity. The married ones were inclined to gossip amongst themselves, and there were snatches of conversation which inevitably reached her ears, and which she found shocking, filled as they were with intimate details of goings-on of husbands and children. It was an easy-going and rather quiet staff room. Dora found as a further barrier between herself and the others the fact that she came from one of the small islands, although she had not gone back after getting her diploma and degree. She had no friends there, and to her Jamaica was home, as much as any place represented that thing. In fact, brought up as she had been, as the protegee of an aunt who was completely dedicated to an odd religious sect, she had learned to value her own company, and to need to be solitary. This was a peaceful scene; Dora, going through a pile of test papers was aware of her heart lightening at the sound of the last bell. She arose immediately, gathering up her things and, murmuring goodbye, was the first to leave.

Her almost restored tranquillity was jolted at the sight of her car, which was old and unreliable. She prayed that it would get her home safely. Fear of a breakdown and having to appeal for help tormented her whenever she drove. Only last week it had happened, and her complete ignorance about a car's mechanism was matched by her total embarrassment as a man stopped his car and offered help.

"It may be the battery?" she suggested nervously. "It is kind of you to stop."

The man looked incredulously at it.

"Wrinch!" he exclaimed. "When last have you put water in it?"

He surveyed the corroded green thing with amazement. Dora had been almost paralysed with distress. Now, as she got into her dirty, battered car, she thought how lucky she had been. What if the next breakdown occurred in a less salubrious part of town? Dora was aware of the people down 'there', and of their wretched state of poverty and their hopelessness. But as an introvert, she could not detach herself long enough from her own problems to do more than briefly pity them, and then turn her back on a problem too hopeless to concern her. She pushed the thought of a breakdown to the back of her mind. She knew that she could afford to pay down on a new car if she denied herself the next holiday abroad. All her holidays were abroad, and all her money went on them. Since ninety percent of her life, the working part, was so unhappy, the holidays provided her with great escapes. She felt that she had to get away. She had travelled throughout the Caribbean and in Mexico, and planned to spend the next long summer holiday in America. These thoughts led her on to speculate as to whether she was bold enough to cope with America. What if something happened to her, or she got sick? Nobody would care, and she would leave no mourners. She would die, she went on thinking, like a cat or a dog: to be exclaimed over for an hour or two, and then be lost for ever in oblivion.

She drove home, which was a lodging with a small family in a quiet avenue away from the main road which led to the school. Here Dora had a pleasant room. She also had the respect that a lower middle-class family accords to one who has acquired the status of a teacher. As she entered the house, she would take off her shoes and go and lie on her bed. Both husband and wife were at work all day, and a good-natured but unkempt maid slept all afternoon, so that she could relax. She liked these people. As she lay on the bed, she would plan her next escape route, as it were, for the coming holiday. She seldom went out in the evenings, only occasionally seeing a film with the Smiths. Sometimes she would take them to see a local production of a play, or the dance company. No dinner dates for her, no picnics, no parties, no excursions to the north coast; nobody called her from one week to the next unless it was about work or suchlike. She longed in vain for someone with whom she could talk, not about her personal problems, of course, for they were complicated enough to make her realise that she would never bring them up for discussion with anyone, neither priest, nor doctor nor anyone. If only once in a while there was someone around who equally enjoyed literature, French literature preferably. They could discuss, for example, how the desperately poor in Kingston, in their placelessness in the society, were reminiscent of the folk in Zola's novels, in which poverty, the great demoraliser, drove them into dishonesty, cruelty, and crudeness. She would have liked to share with someone the humour and depths of Prevert; or to discuss the intellectuality and masculinity of the writings of Simone de Beauvoir. All this, alas, remained an unspoken dialogue going on in her head; something she forced herself to think about when the loneliness and despair threatened to overwhelm her.

The next day at school, Dora left behind a light-hearted fourth form and took her jangling nerves back to the staff room. Why, shè wondered, was she still teaching? Why did she allow herself to suffer so much in such an unrewarding job? She knew the answer. It was she who was the failure as a person, and she would always want to teach, no matter what humiliation it brought her. But why did she stay in this particular job? Money? But that was only useful as providing an antidote in the form of an escape abroad in the holidays in order to recover enough equilibrium to once again tackle her grim task. Why, in fact, did she stay in this land of violence, where daily the news was of murders, rapes and robberies? Might not this current wave of violence with its attendant pointless tragedies soon engulf and destroy her? Her chief, unspoken terror, after all, was of dying a shocking death, one lacking in dignity and meaning, and subject to a wider publicity than she had ever known or wanted in life. What sort of a place was this where the middle classes, while decrying the deeds of thugs, allowed their men to tote guns like schoolboys at play? Did none of them realise that anyone with a gun was a potential killer? She stayed here, she thought cautiously, because she really did not have anywhere else to go. Then also, she was an islander born, and the beauty of this island had power to move her. Where else would she find mountains so enchanting, which could vary their beauty according to the play of light and shade on their many peaks, and down their splendid valleys? Where else the bewitching variety of shades in the colour blue, deepening and lifting according to the time of day? These mountains could breathe peace to the torment within her. Moreover, Dora recognised that the people here were happier and kinder than she would probably find anywhere else. She sincerely liked them, and knew that it was her fault that she could not feel that they liked her in return.

Somehow an end came to the day, to the week, to the term. Free at last, she thought, as she left the dusty school compound; free to plan this holiday's escape and to go about collecting tickets, travel documents, and information. She was planning to leave in a few days for the States, and tomorrow she would go downtown to see the travel agent. She felt light-headed and light-hearted in anticipation, although at the back of it all, she wondered still whether she could cope with this ambitious holiday.

Leaving the hot, dusty school grounds, Dora inwardly rejoiced at the prospect of no teaching tomorrow. She got into the car. The heat was stifling as she reversed out and then wiped each sweating palm in turn on her dress. Her hair was wet also, and her clothing stuck to her as she drove on. Dust was irritating her eyes and making them water; her thick lenses were blurred. Then, out of nowhere, it seemed, a sports car was revving noisily alongside her as the driver overtook. It was a blind corner, and the truck coming in the opposite direction could not avoid collision with the sports car, which in turn was rammed into Dora's car. She swerved and ended up hard against a telegraph pole.

Later, Dora recalled people bending over her and being taken to hospital briefly, and the police questioning her. She awoke suddenly, thinking what a terrible dream she had just gone through, tried to sit up until a sharp pain seemed to be searing through her brain. She lay still, and anxiously tried to recall everything as it had happened. She felt less agitated when she realised that it had in no way been her fault. She was lucky to get away with bruises and a bad headache. Yet something was jarring her mind. She concentrated with difficulty, trying to discover what it was. Then it came back to her in a flash of anguish that the old car was well and truly finished off. Despite a little insurance money, she would not be able to buy a new car or a good second-hand one unless – unless she abandoned all hope of her holiday abroad. Knowing also that she would have to replace the car because of her job, a deep despondency settled upon her, nor was it in any way alleviated by the splitting headache. The situation offered no spark of hope. She began to wonder how despair could be a sin, since its presence lay upon the soul unmoving and immoveable; almost nothing availed to lift its all-pervasive gloom. Whenever in childhood this heavy despair settled upon her, she had always felt the need to walk, anywhere, so long as she could keep on going for hours on end, as though finally she would be able to shake it off. Her headache now made even the slightest movement painful. The future was a grey blank for Dora. It was just as blank for people living in an anonymous mass of humanity down the crowded environs of the Spanish Town Road. Dora was aware of this, and also that they were acquainted with despair; neither did they have a choice between a new car or a few weeks' holiday abroad. To a depressive, all things are not relative.

In time things sorted themselves out. The girls of the sixth got their results. Some passed and some did not. Most of them did a secretarial course, worked a while, and then got married. Dora Olivetti bought a second-hand Mini in fair condition, and a large part of the holiday still stretched ahead. America, of course, had to be shelved. Instead Dora found herself going for long drives through the island. It was a journey of discovery. She only now began to realise the full variety of the island's scenery, and to appreciate the island's fascinating history. She became absorbed in reading about the people and places she came to know. By the end of the holiday, when the last fiery days of August left everyone limp, Dora felt a kind of peace insulating her soul, so that she could actually consider the prospect of a new term, if not enthusiastically, at least with something approaching equilibrium.

Nevertheless, on the first day of term, she handed in her resignation to the Headmistress.

"Airletters, chicken breasts, rum, Harpic. That seems to be all. Can you think of anything else?"

"What about that new boutique that has opened up in

the Plaza? Shall we go and have a look?"

"Yes, I hear it's not bad at all. Who are you staring at?"

"Regardez la petite Mademoiselle Olivetti; elle a lavé les cheveux. Don't you remember her?"

"I didn't do French, but of course I remember her. I still feel that we didn't exactly help matters when she had that nervous breakdown. Is she still teaching?"

"She is going away next month. She has got a job teaching problem children. So I hear, anyway. I'm getting out of this thing, I'm as dry as a bone."

Two young ladies, heads loaded with ironmongery, snapped handbags shut on the pencils and old envelopes with which they had been communicating under the dryers.

Down on the waterfront, along the Spanish Town Road, and around the west side of town, nobody heard the news that Dora was leaving. News was always bad, whether it was of shootings or of thieveries. As for the girls of the hairdryers, they belonged to the most transient group of beings. Yesterday in the sixth, today just married, tomorrow regretting that that was life. Dora turned her back on them all.

She sailed from a banana port three days after the Christmas term ended. The boat was still loading when she embarked, but by five o'clock they were underway. She did not stand on deck with the other passengers, watching the island slowly receding. She was sitting on her bunk, dreaming of a small village in the Portland hills. It had been raining all afternoon as she drove, but by dusk it was over and all was quiet. Plants, trees, creepers and long grass, sated by the deluge, were gently dripping and stretching out leaves and stalks to air. The frog chorus had started, and the little valley was slowly filling up with the flashing winkies. Dora had gazed down the steep-sided slopes, and on an impulse she had cupped her hands to her mouth and called down the valley, "Dora!" The echo sent back its eerie answer. She got into her car and drove back to the city.

The Long Distance Swimmer Who Ran

by Noel D. Williams

Gold, 1970

His name is Theodore Maccacheer. Do you know him?

He lived in a one-room, tumbling-down hovel close to the bottom of the hills. That night he awoke, smelling the burning and fearing treachery. An oil drum used for rubbish near a house several yards away was ablaze, carelessly. In the house, he knew, there were ten people, crammed into one room. He imagined human limbs, bent, folded, twisted in postures of sleep. The fire would consume the house, he was sure; commit its treachery upon the darkness.

He sat on the floor and put on a pair of white, flashing yachting shoes. It was the month of August. A cold wind was tearing across the sky. The hills stood clenched in the darkness. Stillness. But for the sound of insects, unseen yet near.

And the treachery of fire.

Theodore Maccacheer stood at the door of his hovel. It was open, unhinged and falling away quite sick to death.

He looked at the blaze. The treachery streaked up his nostrils. The house would go quickly, would be reduced to dust and the dryness of the season. The cold wind whipped through the sky.

He turned from it, and was pelting through the darkness. His white yachting shoes flashed along the narrow track that led to the asphalt road. He ran, not very fast, feeling the thud, thud of the hard approving earth. He had left nothing behind. He owned nothing. He was travelling, he felt, across a vast sea. A swimmer across a vast sea.

Theodore Maccacheer was forty years old, as his limbs carried him along the track. Soon it would be dawn, unstoppable, coming up over the eastern hills.

The narrow dirt track came to an end quite suddenly, in the darkness of the month of August, pitching him out onto the asphalt road. His flashing, white yachting shoes made jarring contact with a new surface.

He turned from the direction of the Market Place and, keeping close to the grass verge, began walking towards the entrance of the Hospital. Across the road, beyond a green wire fence, were a number of tall buildings. He saw oblong squares of light, cars under sheds, private asphalt roads, a chain of electric lamps.

The road dipped slightly, crippling his gait. He would keep moving until his feet, worn through the soles of his shoes, felt the soft wetness of a new land; felt thick, lush grass, the bones of dead animals.

And soon, unquestionably and within a shorter time than he imagined, it would be dawn.

He stopped at the entrance to the Hospital, still on the other side of the road. A car turned through the gate, accelerated and picked him out with its headlight.

He was a shabby figure. His pants sagged, unstrapped at the waist, the crotch unbuttoned. His face was heat-battered, covered with a scraggly beard. He stood with both hands in his pockets. In the glare of the headlights, the yachting shoes that shod his feet flashed white, like a beam of light spitting off a knife blade.

The headlights impaled him against the darkness before sweeping away. The vehicle moved fast towards the Market Place, disappearing around a bend. Lost now, travelling to the city.

Theodore Maccacheer crossed the road to a gnarled tree at the entrance to the Hospital. The hands in his pockets were slowly swelling into tense bunched-up fists. The smell of treachery lingered around his nostrils.

Irrepressibly waves of morning light spilled over the top of the crouched hills.

* * *

He never knew when light tore down the house of darkness, hardly noticed the sharp outlines of the burning hills, the violence of dawn ripping through the land, stripping it of warmth, uncertainty, the fear and hope of waiting.

He was forty years old and the owner of a pair of white, flashing yachting shoes. He was standing under a tree, on the edge of a crevice caused by a great shift in the earth. A sharp light was streaming through. It kindled an old, drying bush fire inside his entrails.

Dawn. A car came round the bend from the Market Place, moving fast. Its headlights still on after a long journey through the night. It passed him as he stepped back onto the asphalt road. It missed hitting him. The driver screamed back obscenities, distorted in the wind.

See him there now. He has known, all his life, only the hardship of a swimmer upon the dry seabed. Day after day, arm over arm, he has smashed through giant waves. At times, exhausted, vision tired of the horizon's receding line, he would turn on his back and gaze above the hills to the heavens. He would contemplate the clouds, the tidal movement that left shadows on the earth.

Lying on his back would bring him close to death. He would panic, body slipping under by degrees, and begin to tread water. To run, for movement; some sort of assertion kept him alive.

See him there now.

The waves have begun to swell. They threaten to lift his small craft right out of the sea and throw it far into burning space.

The day is building up a heat momentum.

Traffic has appeared upon the asphalt road. The grey bus is on the run. It sweeps around the bend at the Market Place, travelling fast. It stops just ten yards away from where he stands. The driver, youthful, handkerchief between neck and collar to block the pressing heat, grips the huge wheel with both hands. The bus beats up the air, air brakes release the pressure. It roars down to the village at the bottom of the hill.

And the day swells into a heat momentum.

He does not sense it, arm over arm through the bigness of waves. He is peeling off strips of bark from the tree. Now and then he surprises a lizard, its marble eyeballs watchful, motionless. He looks at a poster nailed onto the tree. Knowing, for sure now, the old, drying bush fire spreading within.

But wait. See him there? He has moved.

The waves have picked him up, he is walking towards the Market Place. The pavement is narrow and cracked, stones and pebbles wait to trap the ankle. There are craters hacked out by the sun and the rain and feet marching toward tomorrow.

Arm over arm, he flings forward. Debris is floating past his eyes, looking straight ahead.

Heat-battered, perspiring faces; the sharp clash of colour on drab clothing; the turbulence of perfume trailing after an over-dressed young girl, whom he does not see and would not desire; young men, veined muscles, talking querulously, rushing with empty hands to claim the land's denial; women moving slowly under imminent, pregnant frocks; and frequently a child stumbling behind, looking back at something perceived, slapped into tears and hauled on.

He comes within yards of the bend that leads beyond the Market Place to the main road. This road runs to the city. But he has turned and is walking back.

Do not marvel at his aimlessness, his drifting, empty purpose. In a vast sea, a swimmer who has travelled long and far sees only a horizon line and vast ranging space. His body bobs like a coconut, felled from a tree. The sun chops at his brown skull.

Meanwhile the face of the hill is burning in the season's heat. He gazes at its biblical features, ten yards away from a bus shed.

People have begun to assemble. The bus is charging up the slope from the village at the bottom of the hill. It tears around the corner, beating up the air. They load on. The bus stop is vacant, the wind blows emptily through the street. People gather again, one by one, waiting until they die. The bus picks them up, takes them around the bend, to the main road and further to the city.

The sea is everywhere, in the asphalt street, in the hammer of the heat, in the tension and sudden haste of the lizard moving up the tree to the dark growth of branches, eyeballs wide and watchful. Again he knows the drying bush fire within, sees through reddened eyes the rising tide urging him (he would not resist now) to float on his back, drift around the bend to the city.

Under the bus shed the fire is so terrifying, people wait

outside. A boy, lifting one end of his pants, pisses through the green wire fence. Ten yards apart an English priest is smiling at the hills, at the face of the day, at the smell of passing sweat.

In his hand, held carelessly, is a blue airletter. It might be snatched from his thin wrist at any moment by a swift, uplifting wind. A woman rushes out of the Hospital gates. She is pregnant. She consults a black handbag.

After three minutes, the bus not yet in sight, a small group approaches, dressed for ceremony. Two men look stern and rebellious in black suits. One is smoking. His blotched cheeks sink in to the bone as he inhales. There are three women with them. They wear white dresses, long to the ankles, and squint through steel-rimmed glasses at the continuous traffic. Unceasingly, they use tiny handkerchiefs to dab their faces, heat-wounded.

They glance at him, but do not understand his indifference to it, to the stone-throwing temper of the sun. Why is he looking at them like that?

They make sombre remarks to each other while the day burns, the heat lashing away.

"The *whole* family gone dead, you see? The house burn up while they all sleeping. They so far behind God back, nobody could know when it happen . . ."

The bus has come up, locked tight by air brakes. The doors swing open. They push, shove, scrambling up. He has stumbled on the steps, but it moves off.

"Me hear say the smallest one escape. Run outside when he smell the smoke. But like him gone lost. They don't find him yet . . ."

The vehicle is travelling fast. He looks through the square space of the window, at the English priest still standing at the spot, smiling at the day.

"The Lord works in strange ways. We cannot tell his purpose. All we can do is thank Him for sparing our lives."

Coming around the bend, tyres humming, it barely misses a man on a cycle going in the opposite direction wearing long, matted locks. A Rastafarian. He disappears as the bus sweeps around the bend and prepares to submerge into the hot regions of the city.

"It hot like hell in here," says an old man next to him, his grey hair cut close to the skull.
people crowd on. Body to body, wedged tight in the passage,

innumerable hands – wearing rings, a bandage, a soiled glove – gripping the handrail, greasy from the fire of sweating palms. Another bus passes, going in the opposite direction. He sees for a brief minute, while the drivers honk at each other, eyes peering through the thick haze from black faces.

He looks away. The man next to him cranes forward, recognising someone.

The bus has stopped again, motor running. Across the street, vast, sprawling low buildings, with oblongs of glass filled with dissolving images and reflections. The showcases of stores, the posture of mannequins, wax faces frozen following the eye with expensive, mocking allure. He can no longer see the sky. It is blocked out now by huge posters and billboards, carrying outsize faces.

When the bus moves again, it takes another bend, gears grinding, and dips. Its descent is now along a narrow road. He can see the hills again, not the green, biblical features of early morning. There are jagged rocks and hewn out regions.

Another stop. More waiting. His eyes fall on a youth standing at the corner of a street that peels off from the main road. Inside his private knowledge suddenly flares. The youth is bracing a lamp post, his feet crossed; he is pulling fiercely at a cigarette, a cool slow motion of hands to lips, a sullen, fixed stare behind dark glasses, his face wreathed in flames.

Their eyes meet, and sparks fly from a collision of private knowledge.

The bus will not move off. The doors have not closed. A few people attempting to get on are caught in the doorway. The bell rings. The conductress is angry, curses the black faces, the smiling arrogant teeth.

And suddenly his back feels heavy on the bed of the sea. He is sinking again. The youth outside takes a final long pull at the cigarette, then flicks the butt end at his window, eyes smoking with contempt, the bush fire of the victim's hate. Sinking by degrees, unable now to float, he knows he must get off.

He shoulders through the throng in the passageway, treading feet on the floor, shuffling forward, the smell of travel and the bush fire trailing in his wake.

His progress is aggressive, without apology. It is taking time. The bus, quite suddenly, jerks and moves off. He freezes,

He does not answer. At the back of the bus, hunched up

tight in a corner, he does not answer.

There is confusion at the door. The bus conductress looks harassed, exchanging coins for tickets; her hair askew under the cap; her face wet and puffed, sagging with strain. People keep piling into the bus. Its motor is running. It will soon loop around the Square, dip and travel fast down the main road, following the wire strung above on poles that line the route to the city.

"When it move off, it wouldn't be so bad again. Though the bus so pack up, the air can't even circulate . . ."

Outside drab buildings leaning on each other, in slow stages of collapse. The heat bouncing off rust-zinc fences, off bare heads, the littered asphalt Square. He can see past knots of lounging youths into the dark regions beyond open doors.

Near the market the people scatter upon the land like litter dropped from a passing ship. The smell of rotting fruit, the odour of a urinal, quite close somewhere. Through a gap that leads to a dark passage, he can see planks of wood, thrown away things, a man close to the fence, feet apart, relieving himself. Music spills out of a bar.

"You going right through? To Kingston?"

He does not answer. The sea is everywhere. The drying bush fire inside is his only knowledge. Words are banished.

Bells. The release of air brakes, a slight convulsion throwing many off balance, and the bus is in motion, gears shifting, moving, now, fast.

From where he sits it is impossible to see far ahead. He is following the wires on the poles overhead. On the road, running parallel to the main street, houses are stacked side by side. His eyes take in the view dimly through the glass window. A man on a motorcycle races alongside the bus but falls back.

Strapped behind him is a large box. The sky is empty, uncompromisingly silent.

After a while the man next to him switches on a tiny transistor. It crackles, making distorted sounds – a voice with an urgent, happy message – which brings a smile to the man's face, separating his lips to reveal discoloured teeth.

It would not disturb him. He would not object. He clung to his vision of the sea, of the tide and the waves fishing on the other side of the glass window.

At various points along the road, the bus stops and more stranded in the passageway.

Riding faster now, the bus digs deeper into the seabed of the city. They pass through narrow streets. He stoops once, catching a glimpse of a zinc fence over which faces peer, heads wrapped in coloured scarves. Slowing down, then picking up again, the motor racing into gear, the air brakes in lock and release, the bus churns through a gauntlet of shops; the pavement is filled with swimming faces.

The moment the bus stops he flings himself forward. His white, flashing yachting shoes cut a vicious path, his soil-soaked body cleaves through the centre of the passage. He reaches the door, where three steps dip to the asphalt street. He starts down, trips and is flung into the vast, roaring city.

* * *

It is the month of December. Near the end of the year. The pleasant confusion in the city at this time. Slow, continuous hum of traffic, people milling through King Street. There are many tourists.

You walk past the big stores, and music – soft, chiming, familiar melodies – filters through the air. You breathe deeply, inhaling a strange excitement, a buoyant feeling of mingling, stepping aside, pausing to look at things with other people.

Overhead, far above the roofs of buildings, a fickle afternoon. Clouds shift, patches of blue filling out the sky again. It is a quarter past one. It may rain again a few hours later.

The season is everywhere, tumultuous in the city, splendid over the hills, streaking through the countryside.

There are so many children in the streets. Policemen, in pairs, stride slowly by, chat to each other, give directions to a woman weighed down with gift-wrapped parcels.

There is a commotion around the bend. Does your heart beat faster?

Something has happened, the street is grinding to a halt. A few people point in the direction of the Post Office. The policemen are running back, hands to their hips. So many things happen at this time of the year.

A crowd is swinging into King Street. At the intersection traffic has come to a stop. It seems they have held someone, the fellow with hands pinioned behind his back, in the centre of the crowd. Clerks from a large store nearby have heard the commotion and look out through the windows on the second floor.

They come closer. The man's face is covered in blood. A man in a grey suit keeps striking him with a walking stick.

He is screaming something to the clerks above, repeating the word 'criminal' over and over. The crowd shrieks. Children are running ahead to look at him.

As they pass, it is difficult to see his face. He is an old man. He shuffles forward, the howling mob heavy on his back. The feet are dancing, the feet are marching up the street. Wait. Among the moving legs, close to the asphalt – the flash, of white yachting shoes. The man with the bleeding face.

Do you know him?

Judah Come

by Phoebe Chang

Silver, 1970

Ras Judah felt the bright noon sun hot and burning against his cheeks. His shoulders soaked the rags covering them with wet perspiration, his hand clammy on his walking stick, his feet burning and sore in his sandals, and his hair itchy under his wool tam. But most of all his mouth and tongue and throat felt dry and dusty like the road stretched out ahead of him. And his stomach weak with emptiness.

But his eyes looked straight ahead and his head was held high and full of meditations. When he walked his steps were firm and even, and the lower part of his body seemed to glide. He was looking ahead with steady brown eyes and the blackness of his face gleamed in the sun. Five ringlets of wiry hair stuck out of his red and green tam and above his proud face in all His glory was pinned the image of The Most High Emperor — Haile Selassie I.

"I will be true to you." Music and words lifted his spirits while his mouth tasted as dusty as the road clouds stirred by the passing cars.

Ras Judah had begun walking on Spanish Town Road in the cool of morning and now he was approaching the Matilda's Corner intersection on Hope Road. "Glory unto the most high God, sing praises, unto His name, Jah. Even as the faithful shepherd did lead his sheep to safe ground before the storm, so shall I lead I people out of Babylon before the destruction of the Temple of Idols. So come up hither, Judah, and let I show thee things which must be hereafter, I and my comforter." He fondly rubbed his walking stick.

Judah had walked nearly a quarter mile during this last meditation and felt the dust biting his throat and his lips crack with heat. He paused. He looked up a driveway and beyond a neatly trimmed hedge he saw an oasis of green. Rolling lawns, a Buick in the carport. But what caught Judah's attention was the shade spread out by a sprawling mango tree in front of the house. The cool green soft grass opened up before him as he passed through the open gate, and he was sure he saw an orange-red mango hiding in the green leaves of the tree.

The shade brought visions of the Garden of Eden to the mind of the locksman and he gave thanks to the Creator for the splendours of life and for allowing him to partake thereof. "For I an' I shall be like a tree that is planted by the rivers of water that bringeth forth fruit in due season. I an' I lock also shall not wither and whatsoever I doeth shall prosper."

Looking through her kitchen window, Mrs. Wilson watched this intrusion with horror. She must have left the gate open when her husband went to work this morning. She would have to try to get another maid. She couldn't remember everything.

She was annoyed with herself and finished washing the plate in her hand. She looked up to see the Rastafarian still under her mango tree. She slowly realised the situation. She bit her lip in panic. Suddenly she wished she could vomit. But nothing seemed to be there to come up. Even her legs seemed hollow.

She held the wet dishrag dripping in her hand as if she were frozen. She watched the Rastafarian through the window as if she were part of the house itself.

Ras Judah was gently poking his walking stick into the foliage.

"Now's my chance," she thought. "I'll sneak away and telephone the police." She moved stealthily as if the black man's eyes were following her.

Breathlessly she explained her position to the emergency operator. Then slowly she returned to her place before the sink and window. Her eyes fixed on the bearded face. He was seated comfortably under the tree sucking the last juice from the mango seed.

"In the times of the ancients it used to be that Man did walk in fear of I, the true living God, and did honour and obey I laws. And in these times the land of Ethiopia did prosper."

Mrs. Wilson mechanically began to rub the dishes with the dishrag again, only her hands moving. She thought of playing the game of statues as a child during school recess.

"If I can just maintain composure. Just go on as if nothing unusual is happening until the police come." Over and over again Mrs. Wilson repeated and repeated this dictum, only interspersed with pleas for the police to come charging down the driveway – swords in air like T.V. cavalry.

"Great kingdoms did wax and wane and wax again even as the setting sun does rise the next day. And men ruled over all these kingdoms and man prospered and grew wise." Ras Judah paused in his meditations to look around his newly found Garden of Eden. Then Ras Judah felt a natural urge and stood up to respond.

"What is this? No! Unbelievable!" Mrs. Wilson's eyes were deceiving her. "What desecration, what insolence, what bestiality! Right in my own yard like a dog! My own front yard, my own mango tree! The neighbour's dogs are enough nuisance, but this is nakedness!"

Mrs. Wilson acted in fury. Letting go of the dishrag she ran out the kitchen door and around the house. "There's just so far a person can be pushed, just so much a person can put up with. This is my house, my lawn, my tree – ."

Mrs. Wilson wasn't sure when she stopped thinking these thoughts and began yelling.

Ras Judah looked down on her with calm as he replaced his instrument of watering. It was as if a buzzing mosquito had interrupted his meditations.

Mrs. Wilson looked up at the beard, the blackness of Ras Judah's face, the whiteness around his calm, staring brown eyes, and the five ringlets of hair standing against the blue cloudless sky.

"Love, sister," Ras Judah pronounced in a blessed tone.

Mrs. Wilson thought again of what she had seen him do. "Where do you think you are? A dog in the park letting himself go freely?"

"I am always in God's park," a sonorous deep voice rolled.

"Oh," Mrs. Wilson drew herself up tall with biting sarcasm. "I had not been informed. The grass is still bare in spots and the fruit trees slow to bear – I would have expected more."

"No more, no less. It is His Will," the deep voice rumbled.

"Now see here – out. Out and off my property. If you think you can just –"

Beyond the five stiff ringed curls Mrs. Wilson saw the cavalry advancing down the driveway in the form of a police car and two policemen in the front seat. And just in time as she wasn't quite sure how she was going to finish her threat.

Ras Judah turned to face the police. "The days of Babylon have come," he called. "Being certain of their leaders, being filled with conceit and wicked desires, did see fit to denounce God, and make a mockery of I laws, and the people being no more than clay in the hands of the officials did listen to these blasphemous teachings and were filled with the Spirit of Evil and did lust after such things as money and women and strong drink."

One policeman stuck his billy stick into Ras Judah's side. Mrs. Wilson winced. Maybe that wasn't quite necessary. After all he hadn't really been violent. Perhaps he meant no harm. He might have gone away by himself. But the police were already doing him that service as they led him to the police car.

Then Mrs. Wilson saw his walking stick in the grass. She picked it up. It felt light in her hands and she knew she would keep it.

The world seemed to be in its place again. Mrs. Wilson would telephone her friend, Mavis, and tell her about her adventure and recount it again at the dinner table for her husband.

She looked up again and watched the police remove Ras Judah by gripping his arms and dragging his feet on the grass.

Ras Judah looked up to the sky. "And they became unworthy of being the Children of God and I saw fit to deliver them up into the hands of the pagan Philistines as due punishment."

Mrs. Wilson felt limp with relief as she watched. Then the same policeman stuck his club into the side of Ras Judah. She didn't know what to do. Should she call out to the retreating policeman?

But now the three figures slowed down. The policemen were keeping step with the bearded man who was walking with measured steps, head held high, the five ringlets spread out in the breeze.

"Almost regal," thought Mrs. Wilson.

His voice called out to the sun and the sky. "Behold I people have served long enough, and have come to know humility once more. And I will show them that I, Ras Tafari, am Alpha and Omega, the first and last, that which was, and is, and is to come. I shall free I people from the hands of Babylon. The time has come for the harvest to be reaped, for debts to be paid. Let the doors be bolted and the windows shuttered."

The last exclamation coincided with the policeman shutting the car doors and then driving up the driveway. The car turned left and carried Ras Judah further up the road he had been travelling that morning.

"Come together all ye prophets and apostles of truth. Call thy people from out of Babylon, for none shall be spared. Now shall the hills be levelled and the mighty shall crash when I pass judgement. For they have built their seats on the hill-tops from whence they rule I people with an iron hand. But their seats shall fall and their hilltops be made again into dust and their iron chains broken. I am the Lord thy God and death to all who heed not. Selah."

The Call of Soul

by Michael Reckord

Silver, 1970

About two o'clock in the morning, the last of the white people left the party.

No, not quite; my wife was still with us. But, you know, after two years I've come to regard June as different. To me she's, well, colourless. With her, nowadays, I just don't think about colour. Except at a party like this — a black party. Here she stands out, and the rest of us feel slightly uncomfortable; as I guess nearly every Negro feels around a white person in this society.

At two a.m., after four hours laughing and chatting with other black people, the white society seems very far away. After the fourth or fifth drink your defences relax. You get tired of the Beatles, the Stones and even Bob Dylan. Not that they aren't saying something, but you long for Soul music, black music. And you want any white people still around to leave — even if one of them is your wife — for Soul doesn't feel right with white people near you.

I knew that was what Joe, our host, was thinking as he headed for the record player as the last white couple walked out the door. Joe took off the Pet Clark LP, slipped it into its jacket and put it with other records on the left side of the player. He took out a couple from the right side stack, then glanced at my wife. Immediately, his eyes flickered to me and he grinned sheepishly.

He's my best friend and I knew he didn't want me to feel that June wasn't wanted, but he knew the records wouldn't sound right with her there. The others, two couples and two girls, one of them Joe's girlfriend, weren't looking at June, but I knew they were thinking the same thing. Hell, I was thinking it.

Joe took out two more albums and started examining them, giving me time to do what I had to do. The stoppage of the music had brought near-silence to the room. Only one couple was talking and their voices were low. Others were eating or drinking. One girl in a bright red mini-dress was washing glasses at the sink. All were waiting for the second act.

June and I were by the window trying to catch some of the breeze blowing into the warm room. Mid-July in Ottawa can be hot as hell – as hot as the plains of St. Elizabeth, Jamaica, any time of the year. I know; I'm from St. Elizabeth.

"Darling," I said, "it's late. Why don't you run up and get your beauty sleep? I'll join you in a little while."

June smiled slightly. "If my beauty's gone, sleep won't bring it back. Do I look awful?"

"Love, you're the prettiest thing for miles." She was too. She's one of the most beautiful girls I've ever seen and I'm damn lucky to have her. "But," I said, "we want you to keep pretty."

"Okay, Louis. But don't . . ." Pain, quickly veiled, leaped into her eyes. "Don't be too long."

I took her arm and guided her gently to the door. "I won't. Promise." I watched her walk to the elevator. We lived three floors above Joe's flat. The hurt in June's eyes stayed with me as I turned back into the room. I heard hurt too, in the voice of 'The Genius' as he began wailing out *Georgia*. Thinking about June, I poured myself another Scotch and water and, glass in hand, walked toward the chocolate-coloured girl in the red dress.

I love my wife. I think I always will, whatever may happen – though I hope to God we never part – for June's a very lovable girl. When first I saw her five-foot-six, 37-25-37 figure, her flawless complexion, classical features and blonde hair and green eyes, I wanted her – wanted her as any man would want her; wanted her as any black man would want to possess a woman who represents the cream of the white race. When I got to know her, I *loved* her.

I met her at the opening of an exhibition of her paintings, her second exhibition since she graduated from the Banff School of Fine Arts. The display was put on in the lobby of the high school where I taught and I glimpsed it as I was leaving for home, wondering how the hell I'd spend the evening. The glimpse I had of the colours intrigued me and I decided I'd return later for a closer look.

The paintings were good. With very little form to them, their impact came almost exclusively from their unusual colours; every colour I'd ever seen and some that I'd not. Here colours swirled together in a whirlpool, there they stood apart. Some colours blended into each other, some provided shocking contrast to others. I was glad I'd taken the trouble to go back and see them. I was more glad, though, when I met June.

She was wearing a full-skirted green dress that matched her eyes, and her shoulder-length hair shone under the lights like the sun. Like a good hostess, she was moving from one group of people to another, paying as much attention to the casually dressed, hippie types as to the over-dressed. As she was leaving a group near me I spoke.

"That's my favourite." I nodded toward a rectangular painting which showed a black vertical area on the left merging so gradually that no definite line of change could be seen, into other colours and eventually into white.

She stopped and smiled. "Oh, why?"

"It shows that, in spite of what people say, black can become white. There's hope for my people yet."

The smile began to fade, but she caught it in time. "That's one interpretation. But couldn't it show that black and white are parts of the same continuum, parts of the same whole?"

"You don't mean equal parts, do you?"

"How do you judge equality? Is a red rose equal to a white one?"

"Depends on which one you ask. What do *you* say?"

"I say the world would be pretty drab with flowers, or anything else, of only one colour."

"You know, I like your kind of talk. May I have the opportunity to talk with you again?"

"Maybe. The exhibition lasts for a week, and I'll be here every day trying to sell some of the stuff. Now, if you'll excuse me. Some friends of mine just walked in."

"I'll be here every day too," I said as she turned away. She turned her head, an eyebrow raised in surprise. "I work here," I added.

"Oh." She left. I like to think she looked a little disappointed when she realised I hadn't been flattering her. Still, I was at the exhibition every day and I talked to her more and more each day. When the exhibition closed, I took her to the movies. She wouldn't go to bed with me that night, nor on any of the subsequent nights I dated her. After a while I stopped propositioning her and started proposing. Two months after we met, she accepted me. A month later we got married.

It has been a good marriage, very good as marriages go. I've learned to regard June, most of the time, not as a white woman but as a woman; and I've grown to look at white persons I meet every day as persons, most of the time. But once in a while, at a black party, at two o' clock in the morning, I feel again as I'd grown up feeling – that black people are different beings from white people. And I feel once again the pull of my own kind. So, I ditch my white wife and approach a black woman.

"Hi," I said to the girl in the fiery red mini-dress. "I'm Louis."

"Not Armstrong?" she smiled.

"No, though I'm told there is a resemblance."

"Well, the colour is about right, and the pearly white teeth. But you're better looking."

"Thanks. What're you having . . . ?"

"Edith. Rum."

"Rum it is, Edith." I poured a drink from a bottle at her elbow. "Know where this rum's from?"

"Yes. Jamaica."

"You from the West Indies?"

"No, but I know Jamaican rum. I'm from New York. You?"

"Jamaica. This rum could've come from the parish I was born in."

"Your wife?"

"She's Canadian."

"Why did she leave the party?"

"She's tired. But I'm not. Finish your drink and let's dance."

We both drank up and danced to a sizzling James Brown LP. Then we drank some more and danced slow and close to the music of the Drifters. And when we were very warm, from the liquor, from dancing and from the heat of the room, she showed me the Boogaloo and the Funky, and I showed her how to Reggae and Rock Steady; and more and more we mellowed toward each other – just as the other couples in the room were mellowing toward each other.

About three a.m. one couple left. The rest of us sat around listening to the music, murmuring to our partners. Then the other couple went away, leaving Joe, his girl, Edith and me. Joe and his girlfriend started some heavy necking and soon he put on a stack of records and, with a nod to me, went into the bedroom with the girl. Edith and I were sitting close together on the sofa. I moved even closer, then kissed her.

Edith regarded me gravely and asked, "Why are you doing this?"

"I could ask you the same question."

"No. I have no husband, I get lonely in this city. But you have a wife."

"A white wife."

"So. White women have the same things black women have."

"There's a difference."

"Sure. Blackness."

"No," I said. "Negritude."

"What's that?"

"That's what makes the difference. It can't be explained, except that it springs from the black history, the black culture, the black colour."

"I think the difference is in your mind."

"It may be. I've thought of that. But it's there. And that's why I'm doing this."

We made frenzied love to the sounds of the incredible Jimmy Smith. Afterward, looking at Edith's black skin touching my own, I felt contented, as if I'd come home after a long journey. At least that's how one part of me felt. Deeper down, I realised I had another home; and suddenly I wanted June beside me.

Edith took her clothes to the bathroom. I dressed and sat on the sofa waiting on her, hoping she'd hurry. When she came out I took her to the door, touched my lips to her cheek and said: "Good night. And thanks. It's been fun."

She smiled and walked down the corridor. I headed for the elevator.

I let myself into the apartment quietly and peeped into the

bedroom. June was in bed. After a quick shower, I joined her. By the light of the moon I looked at her pale, innocent, sleeping face and the golden hair around it. A white arm lay outside the covers. I eased myself onto the bed and gently kissed June's shoulder.

I love you, I thought. And I was hoping that she would teach our children to regard themselves not as different from other people, but as parts of the same continuum, parts of the same whole.

Pole

by Dennis Scott

Silver, 1970

I don't know how long it is really, I mean I try to count the steps all the time, but something always happens. My mind wanders, or I start to thinking about how I'll walk right past the telephone operator this morning, and don't even say hello — the one that straightens her hair and is always touching herself when the men are around, like she was squeezing the skin a little. Some days it's like you can smell her. Touching, touching. One day I got as far as five hundred and three, just by where the guango tree leans out over the fence, and then four dogs came out of the bushes. The bitch was in heat, and the bulls were falling all over each other to get to her, and squealing. I had to cross the road to get away from them, it was terrible, man, and then I forgot all about counting for a while. But I haven't given up.

The other way is short, you see. It goes straight down the Avenue, that takes you to the Terminus, it's shorter; but there are always the two girls in their green uniforms waiting for a lift. They stare at me when I walk past and I can feel my ears burning long after I pass them. Actually, sometimes I'm sure they don't really see me at all, when I'm late and have to hurry that way, not really, don't notice my shoes or my old-fashioned tie or the little tears in the pocket of my shirt, they're probably talking about the date they had last night or the gossip at the office – but suppose they're actually whispering about me? Suppose they're giggling about the way my arms dangle, my mouth that Arnie says looks twice too big for my face? When I pass them I know my walk gets funny, jerky. I take the longer route.

This morning Arnie has the day off. It's Saturday, and he's slept late so that we leave at the same time. He's going into town to walk around, and later he'll be drinking with the men from the factory. Arnold is very popular. He's Union delegate. Now he's walking with me, bouncy. At the gate.

"Why you go this way, man? It longer, you know." He starts straight down the Avenue. "Besides, we going pass them two chick that work at the Bank. Pair o' nice thing, you know them?" I don't answer. He hitches up his trousers and grins.

Arnold rents a room in the boarding house where I live. It used to belong to a politician, in the days when this was a well-to-do place just on the edge of town. Now the house is full of people, two Cubans, a student, us; a dressmaker lives and works in half of it. Sometimes I hear her in Arnold's room in the early morning. They wake me up sometimes, laughing.

The poui tree at the corner is blooming, bright yellow. Arnold whistles a little under his breath. Dust is coming away from his sneakers in little puffs. It's a narrow road, and when a car passes we step up onto the bank. Whenever that happens I remind myself to dust off my shoes with a handkerchief before I get to the office. Mr. Weekes is very particular about the office staff, even though the pay is so low. Cheap white man! Sweat is forming already behind my ears. It's going to be a bitch of a day.

The girls are just coming out of the house where they live, the brassieres are showing through the thin shirts they have on. All of a sudden I feel like my pants are too tight for me, the way I did once on the bus standing close to a fat smelly woman. Nothing that you could see, mind you, but if I thought about it I'd get stiff as wood.

One of them is wearing nail polish the colour of the bougainvillea at the gate. A Public Service man has climbed up close to the top of the pole opposite, he's stretching up towards the wires. I cross over, looking at him, looking interested in what he's doing. Arnie stares at the girls, bold, and slows down. He pats his hair in the shiny window of the van. Then he looks up the pole to where the man is hanging below the wires, working very seriously.

"Come nuh, Arnie." I say it quietly. He frowns at me, shrugs. He looks at the girls, sort of nods as though he isn't sure he knows them, but thinks he might. One of them returns the look and says something to her friend. The friend looks at her watch like she's been waiting a long time.

Suddenly, there is a little cough from the top of the pole. At the same time there's a slight sizzling sound, like water on a live coal, and then a pair of heavy pliers comes clattering down, bouncing off the spikes on the pole, and it falls beside Arnie.

He says "Rahtid!" I look up quickly. The linesman is arching back like half of a C away from the pole. He's only held up there by his belt now. His feet are sticking out from the other side and his hands are fisted out behind him, pointing straight down in heavy black gloves.

"He touch a wire!" Arnie says in an awed voice.

"Look!" "Oh mi god!" One of them has dropped her bag. The sweat stings my eyes. A bright blue sky. The car zooms past us, left-hand drive Chevy with a poodle on the back shelf.

"We have to get him down," says Arnie loudly. "The belt look as if it going to slip any minute. Miss, call the police. Call an ambulance."

The girls twitch. One of them runs off back inside the house, clattering on the concrete pathway. Her bottom is swaying in the tight uniform. The other one looks at her watch and then she looks at us. All of a sudden I remember the way their faces look, those women that go to the pictures alone. When you sit down beside them it's like that. Not sure, but waiting. I am always afraid, though. Suppose they call out. Suppose they came and turned the flashlights on me? What then. So I never do anything.

"Both of us have to go up," Arnie is saying. "You have to hold him while I loosen the belt."

"The current . . ."

"Him not touching no wire! Gwan up, man." His eyes shine. The girl is taking it all in, squinting her eyes in the glare. I feel her. He turns to her.

"Better call the police, too," he says again. He wraps a handkerchief round his hand. The girl doesn't move, just glances down the road, then back at us.

"You going to climb up and bring him down," she says, not

really asking or giving any opinion. She's got bumpy knees, this one.

"You coming with me or not?" I move like a puppet towards the foot of the pole, not answering him. He leans against the van and strips off his pussboots and the green socks to match his shirt. Then I am climbing slowly. He tugs me from behind.

"Hold still, you going break you blasted neck in those shoes." He pulls off the loafers, I hear them hit the ground. The metal spikes on the wood are cold, even though the sweat is soaking my collar already; it's funny, you never think how hard it is to climb straight up like that.

We're near the top now, the man's hands are just a few inches from my head. His head hangs back looking straight up into the sky.

"Go on higher. Get on a level." He's excited, his voice sounds higher than usual, very clear.

"He's dead."

"How you mean, dead? Suppose he's just suffering from shock? Is shock! Just suppose, you going leave him up here?"

"We should have a ladder, we have to wait for the police, you need a ladder."

"After we get up here already?"

"Artificial respiration, that's what you supposed to do. The quicker the better."

"What?"

The girl who was telephoning runs back out, I hear her. She gasps, staring up at us. I feel very brave. Arnie is very good at making decisions.

"Go right up," he says. I climb another two rungs, counting automatically. Nine. Ten. Now I'm looking down at the man's face, I'm touching him. His face is surprised. There's a slight breeze now, but the sun is very hot. I tighten my hands on the spikes, crouch against the wood so there's a big space between my head and the first set of wires. The belt has left a scuff mark where the man slipped down the pole, it looks ugly and whitish like a scar. His crotch is jammed up against the pole. All of a sudden I think about what it must feel like to be pressed up against it like that. If you're conscious, that is.

"Step on my shoulders," says Arnie.

"They trying to take him down," from below. I stare at the streak of something yellow, like paint on the man's brown shirt. It matches the sharp pencil that sticks out of his breast pocket. I move my right foot a little, feeling the smooth spike under my socks.

"Careful. All right, go ahead." I feel for Arnie with my feet, trying to see down. Then one foot shifts, my weight tilts over a bit, it's on him now. My stomach cramps up, but I don't make a sound. I want to piss. Arnie grunts as he takes up the strain.

"All right," I say. "What now?"

"See if his heart is beating." I want to say, don't be a blasted fool, he's dead, he's dead, and the sun is right in my eyes. I lean over carefully. I'm squinting against the glare.

"I can't reach him, Arnie, it's too far."

"Hurry, nuh! I getting cramp." A little further, and my hand is on his chest. He seems to move a little, in slow motion, and the head turns all the way over to the other side, on his long thin neck. But the way it looks, he's going to fall, I know it. Before I can stop myself I'm holding his shirt, and the head swings a little slowly backwards and forwards, like a hanged man. All loose. I know I am going to be sick.

I vomit dry towards the ground. Past the limp, stiff face.

"Jesus," says Arnie. I'm holding on too tight. I look at my hands. The knuckles are damp and grey. After a long while Arnie says, "All right. All right, come down."

We shift over, very slowly. My feet are on the spikes again, both of them. I hear him going carefully down the pole, and after a bit I relax my hands enough to follow him.

"Artificial respiration," he says. One girl nods quickly; her eyes are wide open. The one with the handbag holds on to it tightly, licking her lips and frowning a little. "He's dead."

"Maybe." He shrugs. My socks are dirty, I'm thinking and wishing I could do something about it. I lift a foot, and brush at the sole. It doesn't help. The girls are staring at me. I wipe my hands on my handkerchief. I know what they're looking at. My mouth. I wipe it. I wipe it, with the back of my hand. I get my shoes, looking at the road. Then I sit down in the shadow of the van, trying to put them on. My fingers are clumsy.

Arnie says, "How you feel, boy?"

A black Buick pulls up. The girls go quickly to the door. One of them holds back and says, "They're coming. I called the police. They said to wait." I am thinking what it would be like to force myself between her legs, and make her call out with the pain. As the car starts away I see they're talking very fast to the driver, and looking back at me. My mouth is salt, and sweet, and bitter from the vomit bile. My shoulders hurt. I wonder how long before the ambulance gets here, or something. Monday morning I'm going to have to go the long way, as usual. But I'm going to count it next time. That way I'll know for sure how far it is.

Journey To The Exterior

by Charles W. Mills

Silver, 1971

Outside, the heat; all life and motion repealed by a totalitarian sun. Inside, cool; the air-conditioner humming to itself as it performed its sentry's duty. Through the green glass louvres, closed against the flies, the boy on the couch could see the gardener asleep under a tree. Officially, the latter's lunch break had ended at least forty minutes ago. But he remained prostrate, as if the empty bottle by his hand had contained embalming fluid rather than beer. Wait till my mother wakes up, the boy thought, not really with anticipation so much as detachment.

The record player clicked off. He riffled desultorily through the stack of LP's beside him, thinking that it was really time he bought some new records. Perhaps over the weekend he and Denny could go down to the record shop at Liguanea, the one which had been advertising the fresh shipment from America. And oh yes – he had to tell Denny about the 45 he'd heard on the Miami station the night before. It had really been something else.

Eventually he put on another record and settled back to listen. Coincident with the opening lines of the music came the grate of a window being pulled down in another part of the house. He winced, reflex appreciating the import of the noise before conscious analysis.

"Winston!" The voice disembowelled the languorous atmosphere. He turned automatically to the window. The gardener still lay comatose in the shade, oblivious of his discovery.

"Winston! Get off your damn backside, boy! You think I'm paying you to sprawl off on my lawn? You think you're in your damn pigsty at home?"

Winston was just sitting up, dimly aware of some disturbance in his environment but hazy with sleep, not yet able to locate it. He looked uncertainly around, rubbing his eyes. Another lacerative volley from the window awakened him to his position. He stumbled to his feet, stammering "Yes, ma'am" as he made a quick, guilty hunt for the lawn mower. With the thanksgiving of a drowning man chancing upon a lifebelt, he grabbed the handle and began to push it frenziedly backwards and forwards through the green, unfortunately through the same section he had already cut. A further outburst pointed this out and he jerked the mower to the uncut area, tripping over his feet in his haste to escape. Satisfied, the lady of the house withdrew.

A few minutes later she came into the living room. "Oh, hello, Philip, darling. I didn't know you were back from school."

"Yes, Mum," he said, lifting his face up dutifully to receive his kiss. He wished his mother wouldn't go on treating him like a primary schooler when he had entered the sixth this year. "I heard you shouting at Winston."

She shrugged irritatedly, dismissing the subject. "Oh, those people. Unless you know how to treat them they won't do an hour's straight work for you." She smiled at him, affection momentarily softening the stern, martial contours of her face. "You're looking a bit pale. I'll fix you some cocoa to drink."

"No, Mum. I'm feeling OK –"

"Now, son," she interrupted, calmly steamrolling over his objections. "You know you're not a healthy person. Just lie there and rest." She went into the kitchen.

"Yes, Mum," he said softly, talking to the air. He supposed that she knew best, as usual. Following orders, he relaxed and tried to resume his interrupted listening. But the clatter of the lawn mower prevented him. Howling from peak to peak, the noise continually teetered on an almost demoniac intensity. He looked outside. The gardener was performing his task with imploded violence, viciously dragging the machine over the grass, heedless of the miniature barrage of pebbles that spattered his chest in its wake.

* * *

"What you thought of it?"

"I don't know."

"You didn't buy one?"

"No."

"Why not?"

"Why should I?"

It was Friday afternoon and they were waiting outside the school gates. Philip had wondered about his friend, who had been alternately silent and irascible for the whole afternoon. Now it seemed that even these last innocent inquiries were going to be seized upon as a *casus belli.* Shifting his books to a more comfortable position under his arm, Philip tried to placate him.

"Oh, come on, Denny. What he was saying was no big thing." He looked appealingly at the other.

"It was shit! It was pure shit!" He was startled by the vehemence of his friend's tone. Denny's face was flushed and red beneath the thatch of blond hair. "And you – you were just lapping it up with the rest of them!"

"But I –" Philip began, completely bewildered. He could get no further. The other had started to gesticulate wildly, appearing almost on the verge of hysteria.

"How could you even *listen* to someone like that? You saw his hair? Like a – like a damned dust mop! Like a *Rastafarian*!" Mingled hurt and outrage made his voice brittle, seeming about to snap at any moment. "Black power! Black pride! What's the use of – of having a national motto saying 'Out of many, one people' when you have people like that? And they're all communists! My father told me and he knows. They expect you to eat with your maid – or your gardener – Like a . . . a . . ." He choked on his words, unable to imagine a simile that would do even remote justice to the concept.

"And you – you're supposed to be my friend! All the rest – I know what they call me behind my back . . . They think I don't know but I do – a . . . a . . . *pork!* But I thought you were different! And you're really just the same! You're all alike, just as my father said." Blowing his nose in his handkerchief he stumbled off down the road where, Philip saw, his father's chauffeur had just driven up.

The man started to get out to open the door, but a tearfully imperious command returned him to his seat. The big limousine hummed away, Philip still staring in bafflement after it.

Now what had that been all about? Crossing the road to his bus stop, Philip shook his head in dismayed incomprehension. He opened his folder and took out the source of their dispute. It was a thin, typewritten pamphlet, flying at its masthead a strange title which he vaguely supposed might be African in origin. Inside was a motley collection of articles, poems and caricatures, the word 'black' seeming to serve as a common cement for them all. The vendor, a UWI student with a great corona of hair, like a golliwog nurtured on electric shocks, had looked at him strangely when he went to buy.

"A weh you name, bredda?"

"Davidson." He had suppressed his automatic irritation at the barbarous parody of the Queen's English. Once, in the far-off days when his brother still brought his friends to the house, he had wondered why they invariably spoke so badly. In other people it might have been attributable to ignorance or a bad upbringing, but he knew his brother could speak English as well as he could. Only later did he begin to suspect that it had been a ploy, deliberately designed to infuriate his mother. In which it had certainly succeeded.

"You 'ave a bredda up so?" The query was accompanied with a jerk of the hand in the general direction of the campus.

He had said yes, cowardice overcoming an impulse to reply, "I beg your pardon?"

"Yeah . . . Yuh favour 'im slight-like. Not plenty, you know . . . but slight." Then magnanimously ignoring the coins in his outstretched hand, the student had said, "Fe love of your bredda, den," and given him a free copy. Now, sweating in the oven of noonday, he regretted the whole episode. On Monday he supposed he would have to try to convince Denny that no personal slight had been intended. It was ironic that his brother, even by proxy, still managed to affect his life – and adversely at that. Almost inseparable in their childhood, they had gradually drifted apart for reasons that Philip had somehow never bothered to analyse. Nowadays, on the rare occasions they met, Alex always seemed to have some jibe for him, whether oblique or direct. "The old lady start use the bleaching cream on you yet, man?" or "The old man still checking the t'ing in Harbour View?" (His stiff declaration of ignorance of the entire subject had been met with uproarious laughter.) or "So how's life in the ivory tower, man?"

And always, running strangely contrapuntal to the taunts, there had been that frightening bright hunger at the back of his eyes, that unexpressed plea for something Philip could not identify. He had first noticed it one Sunday evening, when his brother had come home drunk from a protracted week-end. Sprawled on the couch, Alex had apparently felt the urge to talk. So Philip had been commandeered as an audience, albeit a reluctant one, primly averting his nose from the rum-soaked intimacies.

"When I tell you, man – the old lady wasn't expecting me, you know? Boy, your big brother barely made it! I just – sort of slipped through somewhere." A ribald snicker. "And when I entered the world – she found I'd slipped back as well! A gene must have drawn reverse along the way! So when the old man looking for the cream in his coffee – as his mother doubtless reminded him on her deathbed – the poor guy nuh find dem serve him a drink even blacker than himself! What a t'ing, eh!" He gave a conclusive hiccup and looked at Philip, The mockery slowly drained out of his face as he did so and when he spoke again his voice was soberly contemplative. "But you now . . . You came out all right, man. The old lady was in seventh heaven . . ."

And Philip had been forced to turn away from the remote unacknowledged realisation that haunted those eyes. The next day his brother was missing again.

Remembering, Philip sighed in exasperation. Why did he have to drink so much and cause everyone so much trouble! And why should he, Philip, receive the blame for – He guillotined the rest of the thought, a sudden discomfort making him oust the whole subject from his mind. Anyway, the bus was coming.

Three quarters of an hour later, he turned in through the driveway of his house. The gardener was working on the bougainvillea hedge that screened the yard from the road outside. Quickening his stride to escape the heat, Philip's sweaty grip on his folder slipped and the pamphlet fell to the ground. He bent to pick it up. The gardener had heard the noise and when Philip straightened up he saw him looking his way. Why he's so young, the boy realised suddenly: hardly older than I am. The impromptu scrutiny he had given the other's face now made it impossible to just turn away and continue inside. Feeling a bit foolish, Philip said, "Hi." The gardener eyed him warily, then grunted. Embarrassed, he hurried down the pathway and through the doors. A wave of refrigerated air greeted him, re-establishing the authority of civilisation.

Later he drifted idly through the house, searching for occupation. The tentative record safari would now, of course, have to be postponed. With uncharacteristic sourness, he wondered why the role of peacemaker always seemed to devolve on his shoulders. In common with Philip's mother, Denny appeared to possess an almost instinctive expertise at making him feel guilty. Perhaps this was why they got on so well together? He reproached himself for the disloyalty and looked out of the living room window. His mother was standing out there, having decided to supervise the cutting of the hedge. Faint outbursts of sarcasm were filtered through the air conditioner's hum, like the distant crackle of musketry. For the first time he noticed the jumble of aluminium chairs by the wall; evidently guests were expected.

His mother was moving away, presumably having delivered the *coup de grace*. A few moments later she came in through the kitchen.

"Sweetheart."

"Mum."

Mother and son kissed. She was obviously in a hurry, for she swept on without the usual sinister prophecies about his health. He heard her opening drawers in her room. Then she reappeared, handbag on her arm. "Philip. Make sure you remind your father about the cocktail party we're having. And – as we both know how he forgets these little things – that the guest of honour is Mr. Chiswick." She sailed out, voice still hovering in her wake, like the Cheshire Cat's smile. "I'm going up the road to Mrs. Whitman." A last postscript from the garage. "And keep an eye on that damned boy."

"Yes," he said. These conversations with the air were becoming disconcerting. And who was Mr. Chiswick? The name was unfamiliar, so it probably belonged to a recently imported rather than local nabob; snared by his mother as a potential booster of her husband's career. After a vigorous take-off, his father's trajectory in the world was slowly levelling off, like a rocket with insufficient fuel, and gradually falling prey to the gravitational pull of his surroundings. The conflict this had engendered had resulted in the conscription of Philip to his mother's side, fighter in an as yet undeclared guerilla war. So far his contribution had demanded only the passive recipience of the "*Entre nous,* darling, we both know" sort of comment. He hoped that no more active a role was scheduled for him. Already his father was looking with suspicion and resentment at the expressions of theatrical resignation thrown in his son's direction. He felt again the momentary surge of irritation for the part foisted on him. Why did people always seem to assume so much where he was concerned?

Restlessly, he glanced at the lawn, where the assigned object of his surveillance was now stacking chairs. As Philip watched him, he was immediately reminded of Denny's hysterical accusation. Was Winston, then, one of the 'sufferers' mentioned by the student? Somehow he had never regarded him in that particular light before, accepting his presence or absence as a function of the arbitrary household alchemy whereby milk bottles appeared on Tuesdays and Fridays and bread loaves on Mondays and Thursdays. The 'sufferers', that broad, amorphous conglomerate so dear to his brother's heart, had always in his mind been safely confined to their natural habitat. This was, of course, the antipodean West Kingston, so notorious in myth and fable (Here There Be Dragons); a remote, exotic jungle where criminals and Rastafarians spent the hours not devoted to mutual slaughter in the smoking of ganja. The thought that Winston, camouflaged as a gardener, might really all the time have been an outrider from this flamboyant frontier land gave him a thrill in which delight vied with trepidation, like discovering a unicorn among your gardenias.

He stood watching for a few more minutes; then, suddenly decisive, he went into the kitchen and opened the refrigerator. A pyramid of beer bottles had been erected in the freezer, doubtless in anticipation of the coming party. Decapitating this monument, Philip headed through the garage door, holding his offering by the neck. He walked over the lawn towards the tree against which Winston was leaning. The gardener's back was turned to him.

"I thought you might –" Philip stopped as the other, taken unawares, jumped away from the tree and whirled around. Automatically he made a step backwards. Close up, he could see that his estimate of the gardener's youth had not been mistaken. The face now mobilised for attack before him was that of a boy of nineteen at most. Philip hoisted the beer bottle again, trying to emphasise the nonbelligerent nature of his mission. "I just thought you might like something to drink," he repeated. The sentence seemed to fall flat and implausible, once uttered. He could almost see it lying on the ground between them, like a stage prop which has collapsed through insufficient support. In the lengthening silence the sun had begun to pound at his temple. His mouth, still etched with its manic rictus, felt like a dusty museum exhibit, displaying for an apathetic audience some fossilised specimen from the Palaeozoic Era. Desperate to break the stasis, he held out the beer bottle. Winston looked at it suspiciously, like a judge being presented with a questionable exhibit, but made no move to touch it. With great concentration, Philip opened his mouth to speak. He felt dimly that unless he said something now, he would never be able to move again, but be mummified for ever in the cloying golden syrup around him. "It's all right," he said haltingly. The words were difficult to grasp properly, as if he were engraving jewellery in the gloves of a construction worker. "My father said I could have one." He waited, unable now to do anything more.

The gardener took the beer bottle. He gave Philip the hesitant understudy of a smile.

* * *

The new shirt – last week's find at Liguanea; the bell-bottoms – just returned from the dry-cleaner; the boots – brought back from America by his father on his special request. Hair – good hair – given the final fastidious touch. A last approving look in the mirror. Explanation to his mother while she invigilated over the sculpting of the *hors d'oeuvres*, then away through the gate, heart pounding with the intoxication of revolt, exultantly tasting again the lie he had just spoken, the first real lie he had ever told his mother.

Winston was waiting at the corner of the avenue. They set off together, the gardener walking too rapidly for Philip, so that he had to struggle to keep up. He was panting slightly by the time they reached the bus stop. Leaning with relief on the metal wall of the shelter, he glanced at Winston who, hands in pockets, was idly pacing the concrete floor, showing no sign of exertion.

Vaguely annoyed, he asked, "What was that frantic pace for, man?"

The other stopped his aimless circling and turned watchfully in Philip's direction, eyes cautious. "Wha'?"

"What happen?" Phillip laughed. "You don't speak English? All right, never mind."

His good humour returned. How simple these people were really! His mother's bullying tactics were so unnecessary. All you had to do was to be kind to them. He was suddenly flooded with a feeling of warmth and protectiveness for his companion, still staring uncomprehendingly at him. Just to prove that he felt there was no difference between them, he determined to be especially solicitous and friendly.

The bus arrived and they climbed aboard. It was crowded, so that when they finally got seats and he could look out of a window, they were far away from the surburban districts of his comfortable, regulated orbit. But the unfamiliarity only served to further stimulate his mounting sense of adventure and recklessness. "Where's that?" or "What is this place called?" or "What's the name of that club?" he would ask, receiving monosyllabic answers from his taciturn companion. "I feel like a tourist," he said suddenly, laughing, turning to Winston. The other smiled stiffly and Philip froze, thinking that for a moment he had ambushed some other emotion on that stolid, inexpressive face: a half-glimpsed flash of something strangely like . . . contempt? No, of course not. He turned back to the window, laughing at himself for having even briefly harboured such a ridiculous notion.

Several stops afterwards, Winston spoke. "Ring de bell."

"We're getting off here?"

"So what else yuh t'ink ah ask yuh for?"

Philip gaped, momentarily flabbergasted. He was still gaping when the other kissed his teeth and stretched across to pull the string himself, bouncing Philip in the process. The bus screeched to a halt and they got off. It was cold outside. Small, close-set houses squatted along a road strewn with rubbish. Philip had intended to ask "Is this West Kingston?" but now he no longer wished to. The earlier effervescence of his mood had somehow bubbled away in the last few minutes, leaving him curiously flat and leaden. He followed the silent figure ahead of him, trying to shut his ears to the finality he heard in the departing roar of the bus. Already he felt like a spaceman marooned on an alien planet, watching his last link with light, warmth and familiarity swallowed by the dark. What had motivated him to embark on this idiotic quest? He cursed his own glibness, traitorously responsible for the impending, self-requested visit to a 'blues dance'.

Down a seemingly endless succession of anonymous lanes they walked, back alley opening into back alley like a maze for abnormally advanced rats. Philip toiled onwards behind his guide, continually stumbling into the giant potholes that mined the road – all of which were presciently avoided by Winston. Eventually they stopped. He thought he heard something.

"Is that it?" he asked, loathing himself for the querulous tenor that framed the question.

The other turned from his contemplation of the distance. "Yeah, we deh 'bout now. Come." He began to walk quickly in the direction of the sounds, a scout guided by an aural trail, blazed on the air. Philip hurried after him. Though he was sure that they were going towards the music, the volume, instead of getting louder, seemed to ebb and increase in an arbitrary fashion, almost as if some scrambling pattern had been imposed on it for purposes of obfuscation. Their arrival at the scene of the dance took place with a jerk, a quantum leap through the space-time continuum of the dingy streets. One minute Philip was foundering in an indeterminate no-man's-land of shadow and rubble, certain only of the ground beneath his feet; the next he was following Winston down a gravel driveway towards a large, box-like building, from whose mouth light and music belched. Crowds of people were surging about the entrance. The women's dresses were a chaos of reds and yellows but the men, he noticed, mostly wore the same unprepossessing T-shirt and dungaree garb as Winston.

As they approached the door, eyes began to rotate towards them. Thinking that his own contrasting costume was winning admiration, Philip felt pride inflate his chest, like the first inrush of helium into a balloon. (Only when they came closer did he read the expressions aright.) Blood storming to his face, he tried to look only at the ground, meanwhile screaming a silent appeal to Winston to walk faster, faster, faster so that he could escape inside the hall. Two hundred years later, the sweaty hand of the gatekeeper appeared in his downwardly-directed field of vision and with thanksgiving he thrust a two-dollar note into it, before, heedless of change, rushing away into the tolerant darkness.

The room was claustrophobic with people. Temporarily night blind, Philip was jostled from couple to cursing couple until he reached the safety of a wall. There he relaxed and began trying to orientate himself. Like a great beast, the sound system crouched at the far end of the hall. A few lounging men, silhouetted in the red light of a naked bulb, ministered to its needs. The beat thumped at Philip's skull, overriding his individuality, seeming to invade the citadel of the brain itself. Subjugated by the music, the atmosphere was alternately contracting and expanding around him, like the walls of a giant's heart.

Winston found him dancing with a woman in a violent red dress. He synchronised his movements with the tidal shifts of the dancers and shouted something in Philip's ear.

"What?"

"A sey if yuh wan' a spliff?"

"What's that?"

"Rass, man! Yuh not a Jamaican?"

Discomfited by the exchange, even though he saw Winston's grin, and embarrassed by the overt interest of his partner, Philip abruptly ceded the last taboos. As Winston was about to merge back into the crowd, he shouted, "Awright den. Gimme one nuh." The other's grin extended itself to an almost impossible width. Winking, he left.

Philip turned back to the woman and they resumed dancing. "Damn you, mother," he whispered, with apparent irrelevance.

"Wh'appen?"

"Cho. Nutting, man."

* * *

He was in church. They were all together in a church.

They sang:

"Let the naked be clothed
Let the blind be led
Let the hungry be fed
And the aged protected."

Winston was in the church too. But for some reason Winston

wanted to pull him off the ceiling. He did not mind Winston's being in the church. He thought, in fact, that it was quite wonderful that they should be in a church together. But why was Winston insisting on pulling him off the ceiling?

They sang. He sang.

"Lord, deliver us
Lord, deliver us."

They were all one, *We are all one*, he thought.

Winston had gone away, which was good, for there was not much space on the ceiling and now his brother was up there too. His brother was reading something from a paper, looking rebukingly at Philip from time to time.

"– That while your panegyrics over the cruder manifestations and artifacts of a sub-culture would be acceptable, or even commendable, in an anthropologist, they hardly seem appropriate when voiced by a university student. In fact, this almost ribald insistence on –"

But I never actually said that.

But you wrote it down.

But I never wrote to you.

No, you never did.

But I couldn't . . . Mother wouldn't have approved.

It's all right. You don't have to feel guilty.

Why should I feel guilty? I've never done anything.

No, nothing, never, never, never . . .

His brother was gone. I must confess, thought Philip dully. I must confess my sins. The high priest will absolve me.

The high priest was beginning the litany.

V: You gave I King James Version
R: King James was a white man
V: You gave I dangerous weapons
R: To kill I, the black man
V: Black man get up, stan' up on 'im foot
R: And give black God the glory.

They sang together. He sang.

"So bring back Maccabee Version
That God gave to the black man
Give back King James Version
That belongs to the white man."

He was to be made clean. He must receive the sacrament to be absolved.

Winston was back again, trying to pull him off the ceiling.

Winston was saying something.

"Yuh wan' some curry goat and rice? And some rum?"

He did not understand what Winston was saying. "I must wait for the sacrament," he told him.

"All right. Wait here." Winston disappeared. He returned a few minutes later. "Come nuh, man."

Winston had brought the sacrament. He would now be absolved by Winston, the acolyte. He suffered himself to be led off the ceiling.

They sat down. He waited. Winston looked at him impatiently. "Eat the t'ing nuh, man." He lifted a fragment off the plate and put it in Philip's mouth.

The body of my Lord Jesus Christ.

Philip chewed and swallowed. He waited. Seeing him motionless, Winston grew concerned. "Yuh all right, man? Have a little rum." He lifted the paper cup to Philip's mouth.

The blood of my Lord Jesus Christ.

Philip drank. "I am absolved," he said, looking at Winston.

"Yuh can eat now, den?"

"Yes." He began to eat.

* * *

No more time, no more space, no more partitions between the here and the not-here, the I and the not-I, the now and the not-now. The universe had contracted to the room – the room had expanded to the universe. His mind was a breached castle, overrun by a horde of anarchic images. The pentagram of sight, sound, taste, smell, touch spun faster, blurred into a circle. He/they/we sang. He/they/we danced. He/they/we breathed. At the top of the room their heart throbbed like a great dynamo, cycling and re-cycling the tension, building to the point of detonation.

Someone had broken step. Their collective rhythm faltered, fragmented into random, individual spasms of movement. The crowd was beginning to mill around confusedly. Drifting back to earth, Philip abruptly felt his body crystallise around him again. Almost immediately he was pushed hard against a wall. The source of disturbance was ploughing its way through the crowd, creating little eddies and whirlpools of reaction. Philip craned his head, trying to see what was happening. A line of muffled curses, like a trail of damp gunpowder, was sputtering towards him. Suddenly afraid, he groped for the shelter of the wall, but the space behind him had already been filled. Somebody turned on a lamp. A figure was disgorged into the taut circle of light.

It was a policeman.

And there were others all around. Pouring in through a door at the end of the hall. (He saw truncheons raised and the first bodies beginning to go down.) There was a shot and a brief scream. The crowd started to panic, hopelessly attempting to rush through the narrow exit. Someone ran past him with blood on his face. Still unable to really comprehend what was happening, Philip had not moved. Not to *him*. This could not be happening to *him*. It must be a game. What was he doing here? Who was he? He was confused. The policeman. He would ask the policeman. The policeman would understand, would clear up the mystery. The policeman would explain what he was doing here, tell him who he was.

He stepped into the light. "Officer! I –"

The policeman turned.

And so it was that Philip got his answer; there, in the last few seconds while he watched ten pounds of hardwood begin its terrible acceleration towards his head and realised that in the bleak landscape of the war zone there is no longer time for such ambiguities as 'games'.

We are all one, he thought numbly.

Lord deliver us.

See Dem Come

by Hazel Campbell

Silver, 1972

The two old women sat at the table in the middle of the room, working. There were piles of letters to be sorted, entered in a book and filed.

Daphne came from a back room, walked over to the table and took her seat. She wasn't anxious even to appear to be working. So many stupid letters to be sorted and punched and then placed on the hook in the big book. More letters in the letter-box to be stamped and taken to Post Office in the sun hot. Such a bother. Not worth the ten dollars a week, she thought.

One of the old women started to speak.

"The young, young bwoy! What a shame! Lawd! An you can bet the parents never even know whey him de!"

The other old woman sighed and went on punching holes in the letters, importantly.

"The young bwoy that get shot this morning," the first old woman explained, catching Daphne's eye before she looked swiftly away.

"High school bwoy at that. Ma'am! If the police never reach in time! The poor woman! God only know what dem was gwine do her!"

Stupid woman. Stupid old woman, Daphne thought. Why

you don't shut up. Maybe you'd like the young boy to be doing 'God only knows what' to you . . . Nobody would . . .

"Him dead?" the other old woman interrupted her thoughts.

"No. Him in hospital. Have a seat, sir," the first old woman said to a man who had entered the building, asked for Mr. John Ferron and been quietly waiting for an answer. "A believe somebody in there wid him!"

Can't even take the trouble to find out, Daphne thought. Them suppose to be teaching she and that stupid girl, Lena, all about the work so them could tek over from them, but all them doing was jealously guarding their job. Won't admit them too old to carry on.

"Hanover Street Baptist have one lovely service last night you see." The other woman began her story.

Oh, shut up! Oonu can't work widout talk! Thank God the man at the Embassy say that she would hear from them in another month or so . . . Away from all this . . . America! Away from these old . . . A buzzer sounded.

The first old woman had gone to knock at Mr. John Ferron's door to find out if he would see the man who was waiting.

"Him not there. Him soon come back. Wait a little," she said in the direction of the client who had asked for him.

"Coming," she grumbled at the buzzer and looked meaningfully at Daphne as she shuffled to the other door.

Daphne kissed her teeth and walked over to the clerk's desk to pick up a pile of letters which she had to stamp and enter in the mail book.

A man and a woman entered the office.

"Is Mr. Ferron in?" the man asked.

"Mr. Paul or Mr. John?" the old woman at the desk asked.

"Oh! I didn't know there were two."

"Father and son," the old woman said proudly as if she was responsible for this fact.

"P.L. Ferron."

"Mr. Paul. That's the father. Tek a seat."

He is handsome, Daphne thought. And such a nice voice. A pity men like him didn't look at her except for one thing. Them look at her and see only a maid who only good to . . . But she gwine show them. Is only that she didn't get a chance. When her mother died she had to leave school and work, but America next month, maybe. March the latest.

She wasn't no maid either, not like them old crow. Them two

old crow.

Start working wid Ferron and Ferron for two-and-six a week. Would believe is them mek the business grow if you hear them talk. Talk, that's all them do. Hanover Street Baptist Church. Wonder what else them know 'pon Hanover Street.

Sighing wearily, Daphne took up the bundle of letters and prepared to leave the room.

The first old woman rocked her way across the room.

"But Molly, you ever see anything like that Daphne? She hear the buzzer and wouldn't even look up, much less answer it."

"She mus' be don't work wid Ferron and Ferron. You no know how dem young people stay dese days? Don't want work. Short frock and money and boy fren'. That's all!"

"Who fe pile a things dis?"

"The girl from Casey's. She come in while you was talking to Miss Norma."

"Oh. I was just gwine throw dem off. Come, missis," she called to the girl from Casey's who had just entered the room. "Move you tings mek me get on wid the work."

"You can see how old the servants are," the man was saying to the woman. "Many of these lawyers and solicitors find that it doesn't pay them to move. They're so well established in a particular spot. So they modernise the buildings as much as possible and pass on business from generation to generation. See how modern the facade is, but notice how the old woodwork inside has been preserved. Look at the hand carving on those stairs. Everywhere cool and dim and musty with age. Look at the panelling in this room. This must have been the hall!"

"Can you imagine them?" his companion murmured dreamily. "The family gathered. Stern papa smoking in the corner. Maybe he wouldn't have been smoking in the presence of the ladies all crinolined and bonnetted. Did they wear bonnets in the house? Maybe Louisa – all the girls were named Louisa, weren't they? – would be listening eagerly for the clip-clop of the horse on the cobblestones which would mean that her lover, Mr. Bennett, no, Mr. Bennett sounds like an old man – Mr. Bogle – no, he was a runaway slave, right?"

"You need to go back to school," he told her dryly. "You've got no sense of history."

He looked at her closely and wondered again if he wasn't

making a mistake rushing to divorce his wife to marry her.

Who him calling old servant. Why, them wasn't servants at all, not even office maids really. Them didn't scrub floor or anything like that. A little light dusting and carrying water for Mr. John and Mr. Paul and look how much paper work them had to do. She couldn't even read the name on this envelope M-O-S-E.

"Molly, see if you can mek out dis name."

"Moore. Dat don't belong to Ferron and Ferron. Put it back in the letter-box. That young bwoy won't even read the envelope dem."

"Maybe him can't read."

"Postman can't read? Missis! Tek a seat, ma'am. All dese people before you."

Daphne came back into the room with a pile of letters. Some were to be delivered by hand. She had to be careful. As she reached for the satchel in which she carried them, her hand bounced over the INFORMATION sign.

Information! Christ! These old crow couldn't tell nobody nothin 'bout nothin except 'bout Hanover Street Baptist Church an' who dead an' bury an' in hospital. Look how that Jane face light up when she see the one arm woman come into the room. She boun' to ask her how it happen. She live on dead flesh, on rotten flesh. Old crow, John crow, Jane crow, Molly crow.

"Daphne, why you don't hurry up? You should go to Post an' come back aready."

"Miss Jones was talking to me," Daphne answered sullenly.

Show off. For the benefit of the clients. Them expect her to call them Miss, too. To show respect. But she wouldn't call them nothin'. She wouldn't call them name at all. Miss Jane Crow, Miss Molly Crow. Watch them a look 'pon the one arm woman.

See the carrion eaters come.

See them come.

Dum, dum.

That was poetry, yes. Like that poetry her Rasta boyfriend tek her to hear the other night at the library. Him like things like that. An' sometime him talk like him reading poetry too . . . Maybe when she went to America she would go to school, night school. Plenty opportunity in America . . .

Daphne placed her satchel under her arm and walked out

through the door.

"I wonder why that young woman looks so angry," the man commented.

"Maybe Mr. Bogle didn't come. There wasn't any clip-clop on cobblestones, nor gentle knocking at the door," his companion answered, still dreaming.

Birthday Drive

by Norma Hamilton

Silver, 1972

Mr. Shaw fretration about him future now dat di war over prove unnecessary. Whole heap a new job open up ina Jamaica. Him find himself wid more money dan him never did have ina him whole life. Him decide to go ina business, open up a hardware store. Di business doing well. Him stop wuk fi people an when him not looking after di business him doing real estate. Real estate big-big in Jamaica now dat some black people a-get money enough fi buy house. Mr. Shaw him boasty like cock chicken. Him buy two car. One big one fi show an one little one fi do him business wid. Him buy a refrigerator, di fus one ina Clacton. Him buy electric stove. Him put telephone ina him house.

Mrs. Shaw boast off pon di woodman. "I won't be needing wood any more. My husband bought me an electric stove." And pon di ice-man, "Don't bother to drop any more ice. We have a refrigerator now." Both a dem gie Mrs. Shaw bad looks and wen di electricity cut off, which happen at least once a month widout warning, dem woulda never sell Mrs. Shaw any a dem products. Dem cuss her off di fus time she ask dem.

"Go use yu fridge," di ice-man tell her. "A woulda never sell yu a piece a ice even if yu was dropping dung from tirst. A was a-set fi yu people wid unoo fridge for me know say that electricity not a constant ting ina Jamaica."

"Those people too ignorant," Mrs. Shaw say. "Ignorant and bad-mind. That's why Chinee do better than Nayga anyday."

One of Mr. Shaw favourite occupation was to take the family for drive round Clacton in him new American big car. Him always a-drive roun Clacton slow-slow, so mek sure dat all di neighbours can see him ina di car. Is one ting dat not Mr. Shaw line, an dat is driving motor car. Him always a-drive di little car ina di middle road an di Merican car pon di right han side a di road instead of pon di lef. Dere was scarcely a day dat Mr. Shaw an di oder drivers pon di road not in a big argument. Him wife nag him everytime she go driving wid him. She tink is her duty to warn him gainst all dangers, real an imagine. Dis annoy di hell outa Mr. Shaw.

"I been driving twenty years now an never in accident yet," was him favourite reply to her.

Sandra was sprawling her long self pon her green-tile verandah pon her birthday when Mr. Shaw hustle from out di drawing room an say to her, "Yu waan go fi a birthday drive, Miss Sandra?"

She jump up quick-quick an say, "Yes Papa."

Mr. Shaw hustle back ina di drawing room an shout out at Mrs. Shaw, "Yu want go fi a drive, Miss Marina?"

Mrs. Shaw hesitate. Sandra coulda see dat she was a consider if she shoulda stay at home an be bore or go wid Mr. Shaw an suffer from too much excitement.

"I gwine buy ice cream and patty on di way back," Mr. Shaw tell her. Mrs. Shaw still no answer so him get vex so kiss him teet.

"Yu never waan go nowhere yet. Yu is a pain."

"All right," Mrs. Shaw say. She know say dat Mr. Shaw a-go mek her life miserable if she refuse fi go.

"Where di boys?" Mr. Shaw ask.

"Dem down the road playing cricket," Sandra say.

"Mek dem stan. A doan have no time to waste pon dem. Go dress quick-quick, Miss Sandra."

Mr. Shaw sidung in di drawing room an wait bout five minutes. Him get up, walk out pon di front verandah, walk back inside di drawing room an shout, "Yu ready, Miss Marina?"

"Don't rush mi, Howard," Mrs. Shaw say.

"A was ongly asking if yu ready, puss."

"If you going start rushing me just let me know and I won't

bother with it."

"But who was rushing you, puss?"

"You rush all your workmen until they don't even have time to blink dem eye and when you come home, you trying to do the same thing in you house."

Mr. Shaw sigh and sit down for another five minutes then him say to Sandra, "Miss Sandra, you not ready yet?"

"Coming, Papa," Sandra answer.

"Stop coming and come, madam," Mr. Shaw say. Sandra done dressing and Mr. Shaw tell her to go sit in the small car. Him get ina di car too an start blow di horn.

"What's the matter with this man, eh?" Mrs. Shaw ask.

"Come on," Mr. Shaw say. "Miss Sandra an me ready."

"Jesus Christ," Mrs. Shaw say. Then when she realise what she just say, she say, "Yu see how yu making me sin mi soul?"

Them continue sparring like dat fi bout ten minutes after which Mrs. Shaw come out so sit in di front seat a di car beside her husband. Mr. Shaw start driving di car an since is di small car him driving Mrs. Shaw say to him, "Yu driving in di middle of di road, Howard."

"Stop nagging me, Miss Marina."

Mr. Shaw kiss him teeth.

"Stop! Yu going hit dat car!"

Mr. Shaw slam him brakes hard an it gie off a loud screech an stop near-near a car dat fly past him cross di road. Di car driving behine Mr. Shaw almost run ina him car-back.

"Yu see how yu mek dat car almost smash up mi back, Miss Marina?"

"But if yu didn't stop yu would have hit the other car."

"Twas my right of way. Who tell him could try beat mi to it? Would have serve him bloody right if a mash up him car."

Mr. Shaw see one of him friends crossing di street so him rest Mrs. Shaw. Him drive up near di man an bawl out, "Obie, yu son of a bitch, come ya."

"Mr. Shaw!" exclaim Mrs. Shaw. "Don't you dare swear in front of your girl-chile." But Mr. Shaw was not the only person swearing. All the people who driving back a him cussing like hell and blowing dem horn. Mr. Shaw ignore dem. Him get out of him car slow-slow an lean on di car-side so talk to Obie. Di people get tired a cussing an drive off. Den Sandra see one American monstrosity of a car a sweep dung pon her. Mrs. Shaw see it too an fe her face tun chalkwhite. Mr. Shaw don't bat an eyelid. Just when Sandra sure di car gwine smash dem an she clutching her rosary, trying to pray an tink bout all di bad tings dem dat she ever do ina her life, di monstrosity car-brakes screech and she feel di car she ina jerk an she see dat di monstrosity stop so close it touch di car bumper.

One good-looking black man wid a cool-cool complexion jump from out di monstrosity. Him shirt immaculate-white an di crease ina him pants dem razor-sharp. Him shoes shine till yu can see yu face ina dem. Him look like one a dem big-shot civil servant man who walk roun wid towel an always washing dem hands an talking wid Oxford accent when poor black people a look service. Di way di time hot him must bathe bout three time a day fi look so cool.

"You are creating a traffic hazard," him say to Mr. Shaw.

"Mind yu bloody business," Mr. Shaw tell him. "A should sue yu fe dent mi bumper."

"Look, old chap, my car measures twenty-two feet, how much does that little bug of yours measure?"

Mr. Shaw open him mout an not a soun come outa it. Him speechless at di outrage a smady outbraggadocioing him. Him so shock dat him low di man fi tek out pipe an light i' an start smoke i' before him get back him composure. Him den decide say di best course is fi ignore di man and gwan talk to Obie.

"Here's my card," the man say. (Him card prove dat him is a solicitor and have him business address on it.) "I'd like to have your business card, if somebody like you can own a business."

"The only time you will ever see the money I mek is when you see it write dung pon paper," Mr. Shaw tell him. Obie bid Mr. Shaw goodbye and lef so Mr. Shaw have no oder alternative but to concentrate pon di facety man.

"Your name an address so I can sue yu sir," di man tell Mr. Shaw. Mr. Shaw gwan ina him car an slam di door. Him start up him engine.

"Your name and address please, sir," say di man again.

Mr. Shaw say to him, "Stan dey in front a mi car, yu ugly black monkey yu. Stan dey front a mi car see if a doan mash yu."

Di man tek out pad an pencil an start copy dung Mr. Shaw licence number. Mr. Shaw aim him car at di man an start drive. Di man continue writing. Mrs. Shaw a-beg Mr. Shaw fi stop drive di car an acting like a fool. "Howard," she bawling out. "Howard. Stop. Stop. Stop I say." Di man leap outa di way just when she an Sandra sure dat Mr. Shaw done mash him. Him leap faster dan any acrobat. Mr. Shaw laugh.

"Tink him wouldn't move. Di man fool."

Di man start cussing Mr. Shaw some real ole raw-chaw Jamaica bad-wod dem an him Oxford accent gone like kite. Mr. Shaw speed off lef him.

"Yu hear di language him using, Miss Marina? Him lose him speaksy-spokiness fast, eh?"

Mrs. Shaw say, "One of these days you going get youself in bad trouble, Howard Shaw. Just mark my words."

Mr. Shaw start drive fast-fast and then slow down all of a sudden an then again without warning him start up a fast driving.

"Drive at a even pace, Howard."

"Look here, Miss Marina, if yu say one more wod bout mi driving a going put yu out di car."

"Awright. I won't say another word. You too rude and crude. Not even if I see death coming will I say a word to warn yu bout it an have yu insult mi wid yu sharp tongue."

Mrs. Shaw swallow her spit hard an roll her pretty eye to heaven for strength to bear her up under her great burden. Mr. Shaw look ina him rear-view mirror an notice one car a follow him real close.

"Wat dat woman a-stick onto mi tail for?" him ask an start drive fast-fast. Di woman drive fast-fast too. Him slow dung. Di woman behine him slow dung too. When Mr. Shaw reach one stop an go sign she draw longside him so push her head from her car an say to him, "You damn fool. You must have bought your licence."

"Damn woman driver," Mr. Shaw say to her as if dat is enough of a curse an shoulda shut her up. But di woman doan tink so for she her mout still strong.

"Stupid goat," she call out to Mr. Shaw an wid dat song she speed off ina cloud a dust. But she mek a big mistake if she tink Mr. Shaw gwine mek her get di las wod even though she is a woman. Him follow her, man. Him follow her all over Kingston till him ketch up wid her.

"Gwey," him tell her. "Yu ugly ting yu. If ugliness was a crime yu would have been hang long time." Di poor woman tun grey unda her tan colour skin and gasp . . .

"Oh God. It was a evil day when all sort of riff-raff Jamaicans like you start earning enough money to buy car."

"Look pon yu how yu dry an wizen. All di substance gone from yu. No man no want yu, yu dry-up ole bag," him tell her an lef her wid eye-wata a drop fram her yeye. Mrs. Shaw was a-hide her face ina shame but Mr. Howard Shaw a-drive in a cloud of triumph for him know is not a easy ting fi out-argue an silence a woman. Him start sing. Him sing till him reach St. Andrew an come out so look pon di house dem dere an di lights a Kingston a twinkle below him an him can hardly see di sea.

Moonrise

by Charles W. Mills

Silver, 1972

The hut has obviously been abandoned for years now. Left to the wind and rain, it sags ever closer to the ground from which it was once raised. Eventually the hillside will reclaim its own. Towards that day the walls fold, the floorboards rot and the roof leaks. Dark puddles of water accumulate in the corners and grass and weeds push their way up through the floor.

To all this I am indifferent. I sit on the weathered steps and look at the city in the plain below. It is night and the city is a constellation of colours. Whites, yellows, blues and reds burn against the darkness. The others stay in one place. But the reds flicker. The reds move. Now they are here, now they are gone, now they have reappeared over there. The reds are fires. In the morning, as on all the other past mornings, a thick pall of smoke will hang over the city.

And I am here waiting, waiting for my time to come.

Why am I doing this? Listen, and I will tell you. Listen to this strange and extravagant tale.

It goes back a long way, of course, like all these stories. Centuries and more. But I think I could start with the moan. The moan had woken me up, a low-pitched, infinitely mournful sound that came twice again while I was still trying fuzzily to separate dream from reality. Shaking my head, I sat up in a tangle of bedclothes. A full moon was shining through the window, investing everything in the room with a calm, unnatural luminosity. Shivering slightly, I strained my ears towards the main body of the house. There were only the creaks and groans of the building shifting restlessly about on its foundations. Then the sound returned, now on a louder, more insistent note. With an involuntary start of fright, I recognised my father's voice.

What is he doing now? I cowered against the wall, trembling apprehensively. I was thirteen years old and terrified of my father. Heart pounding, I waited, frozen, for the procession of the slow, heavy footsteps towards my door.

It sometimes seemed as if I had been waiting for them all my life. My father was a silent, brooding man, a man whom the world had misused. He had returned triumphantly from England in the postwar years, prosperous, and with an English wife. He had rapidly obtained control of a thriving local business and begun plans for its expansion. Everything had seemed to be going his way. Then somehow it had all collapsed. My mother had left him, for reasons that were never made clear to me. The business had suffered a setback which had been enlarged to disaster by his resulting distraction. And suddenly my father found himself forced to sell the mansion and change his whole way of life. We had to move to the ramshackle old two-storey house in its decaying neighbourhood that was all that remained of the family property.

So he retreated into a private world, a world that could not be touched by the sordidness of his surroundings. I was forbidden to play with any of the neighbourhood children. Although I do not even think he saw them, nor their brawling, noisy parents, our neighbours, who jeered when he passed in the street. All he lived for each day was the hour when he could return to his library, there to forget himself in one or other of the dozen of cheap Everyman editions that made up his treasured collection of the English classics. And, as I later discovered, to write poetry.

For my father was a poet and this was why he beat me. I did not recognise this terrible connection until I was ten. Up to that time all I knew was that the postman would come, bearing a long, thick air-mail envelope. There would be an interval of about ten minutes. Then the frightening tread up the stairs would begin and my father would be standing there, his black face remote and inaccessible, the strap twitching slightly in his hands. Sometimes I would beg him to tell me why. Sometimes I would steel myself to an equal silence. But it made no difference. No matter what I did, the strap descended with the same merciless power.

Till one day, driven mad by desperation, I intercepted the postman, tore open the envelope and found myself the baffled possessor of a two-page poem on the beauties of 'A Winter's Night in London'.

It had been rejected, like all the other poems I intercepted and clandestinely burnt in those crazy years. They were all similar in content – 'Trafalgar Square Revisited' and 'A Caribbean Othello' are two other titles that stick in my mind; they were all sent to magazines with London addresses; they were all, as even I could tell, very bad; and they were all sent back with neat, standardised rejection slips that did not even have a human hand on them to soften the blow.

But what can it have to do with me? I asked myself in terror, when I had first recovered from the shock. *What?*

And always as I circled the room wildly, looking for an answer, there was no reply but the steps themselves, coming up the staircase, telling me that another letter had slipped through.

And now these moans. What did they mean? Fearfully, I waited. But the minutes went by and I heard no footsteps. Gaining a little courage, I slipped out of bed and tiptoed nervously out to the landing. The bedroom light was on, but he was not in there. I listened in the darkness. The sound that floated up to me seemed to come from the downstairs bathroom.

I descended the stairs. Timidly, I knocked on the door.

"Papa?"

His voice was low. "Is that you, Leo?"

I told him yes.

"Well, listen to me good, boy." In a calm tone, my father told me that he saw no further point in living and so had decided to kill himself with the .38 revolver that he kept in the bathroom cabinet to discourage thieves. However, he thought it was only proper that I should be informed beforehand of this decision, hence he was doing so.

I listened with horrified disbelief. It could not be true. But my father was completely matter-of-fact about it. Crying unashamedly, I went into a frenzy of incoherent pleas. I beat on the door. I wrenched the door-handle fruitlessly back and forth. Eventually sheer exhaustion brought me to a halt. As I lay sobbing against the door, my father said something in an odd, faraway voice.,

"Perhaps . . . there is one thing you can do. On my desk there is a new poem. If you could . . . read it to me . . ."

If I could? I was ready to do anything. I rushed into the library and grabbed the sheets there off the desk. Running back, I began to read hurriedly, stumbling over words I had never seen before.

"And where now, then, thou
O great ship that listed
Through the savage waves enow
To carry the lion to far shores misted."

After the first five verses I paused for breath.

"I can't hear you!" came my father's shout through the door. I was puzzled by this. We had been hearing each other quite easily before. But there was no time to question anything. I flew to the back door, unlatched it and ran out into the yard. In the moonlight it looked strange and dreamlike, the dark bulks of the trees towering above, the ground bleached beneath my feet. A peculiar sense of peace descended on me. For suddenly I felt that I too was a part of this hallucinatory landscape. A pyjama-clad ghost, drifting across . . . I stubbed my toe on a tree-root and was brought back to reality. Halting, I looked at the papers in my hand, seeing them truly for the first time. What was I really doing here? Had I begun to accept this sort of madness?

Then my father called again. I hurried to a spot beneath the bathroom window and went on reciting. But my brief moment of oneness had passed. I was self-conscious and agitated. Why in God's name was he making me do this? And the night was so still.

"Is wha' a go on down deh so?"

I looked up. My cheeks began to burn with embarrassment. A startled woman, head covered in curlers, was staring at us through the window of an adjacent house. In a frenzy to have it over and done with, I began to read faster and faster, skipping whole verses, gabbling lines together. I finished in a jumble of unintelligible words. "That's all," I whispered thankfully through the window. There was no answer from within. "That's all!" I repeated desperately. A noisy fumbling at the medicine cabinet door commenced. I wanted to scream with frustration. Numbly, I started over. By now the audience had grown to a sizeable crowd of men, women and small children, all shouting encouragement from the fence. The full moon shone down brightly on us all. Why, I asked myself in my innocence, why are we doing this?

Because it was all wrong and nobody would admit it. The years went by in the same unrelenting confusion. I grew up. I won a scholarship. My father told me I was going to Oxford or Cambridge. I told him I was going to the University of the West Indies. It was the first time I had opposed him and for several days he was too stunned to speak. Before he could recover I had packed my bags and fled up to the Mona campus. It was there that my awakening to the realities of the other world first took place.

I had been peripherally aware of it for a long time, of course. I had always vaguely realised that not everybody lived as we did. But most of the fragments I picked up – from conversations overheard in the street, from casual references made at school – were so completely discordant with my own experience of life that I had automatically rejected them. I was a solitary child, with an experience sharply curtailed by my father. I listened to him on the rare occasions he spoke, I read his books, I read the *Gleaner*. And none of these prepared me for what I saw: for the cardboard shacks, festering in the sun, for the people scavenging through the garbage heaps for food, for the stench of rot and decay that hung over everything, for the naked, pot-bellied children who were slowly dying of malnutrition, and above all for the commonplace, accepted barbarity of the police. It had been there all the time and I had never seen it. Yet everybody else seemed to take it for granted.

"But none of it . . . *shows*," I said stupidly. That was what had affected me most of all, the idea that this sub-world could have been in existence all my life without there being the slightest indication of its presence on the radio, television or newspapers. I was trying to explain this to a medical student named McIntyre, one of the leaders of the campus movement which had arranged the tour. He tended to be more tolerant of my ignorance than the others, probably because his o[illegible] history was not all that dissimilar. The son of a wealthy [illegible] ance executive, he had dropped out of his Beverly Hills home after coming to the university and was now living with a woman in August Town. His renunciation had been total, extending to the way he spoke.

"What show on de surface an' what dem seh doan 'ave any-t'ing to do wit' reality, yuh know. But it dere if yuh know whe fe look." He gave me a yellowing collection of newspaper cuttings. They were *Star* stories for the last three years, covering the shooting of criminals by police. "De criminal always shoot fust, yuh know. Sometime count up fe me how many criminal dead. An' how many policeman even wound."

I did. The statistics were frightening.

That weekend I went home to have a confrontation with my father. I was confidently angry, determined that he should now give me a complete explanation of everything. Without ceremony, I thrust McIntyre's collection at him. He seemed taken aback.

"What . . . is this?"

I wondered why he still bothered with the pose of ignorance. In a few brief words I explained the situation, then sat back and waited. But still he pretended not to understand. I began to grow uneasy.

"But what do you want me to say? A few criminals have been killed. Would you prefer that the police were killed? And what does it have to do with me?"

I told myself that he was mocking me, deliberately missing the point. He must know that it was really his poetry I was asking about. And yet I could feel my conviction beginning to wither away. Was I on the wrong track?

"Your hair is getting too long."

I mumbled something about an assignment to finish and rushed back to campus.

But I could not turn back now. I joined the movement. I knew the extent of my naivety and so I laboured to educate myself. Sometimes McIntyre would talk to me about the things I h[illegible]een. He would ask me how I thought they could [illegible]

[illegible]n?" I asked tentatively, for this was an election [illegible]______ get in?" But McIntyre snorted contemp-[illegible]

[illegible]n den yuh jus' 'ave a new set of samfie-man. [illegible]ge in dis country since 1944?"

"A third party, then?" I was trying hard to understand, to ask questions that were intelligent.

"Dat better," he encouraged me. "But t'ird party crash plenty time before. Who yuh gwine get fe lead it?"

This question threw me completely. I could only hazard a wild guess. "You?"

McIntyre turned away in despair. Obviously I still had a long way to go.

Over the next few months I worked doubly hard in the movement.

Then one night at about ten o'clock McIntyre came to my room.

I could see he didn't want to talk. He gestured and I followed him silently down to the Hall parking lot. We drove down to George VI Park, stopping on East Race Course. McIntyre expelled his breath in a low whistle. He turned to me. "Yuh 'member what we did talk 'bout once, Leo? Bout de t'ird party?"

I nodded eagerly.

"Well, we come 'ere fe get de leader of de party."

"Here?" I looked blankly at him, then round at the deserted streets, expecting someone to spring suddenly out of the darkness. "Who?"

"Marcus Garvey."

Marcus Garvey. I felt myself reel backwards in the seat, as from a physical blow. It was happening again. And I had thought I was making progress . . . "But Garvey is dead," I said gingerly.

"We goin' to bring him back," replied McIntyre simply. "Yuh doan see, Leo? Dis is de only way fe beat dem, to bring back a man who we *know* de people will follow, an' at de same time a man who we *know* not gwine sell we out." His face came closer. "Is a long time ah been working on it, yuh know. All ah did want was a book like dis fe de final detail dem." He held up a mildewed leather volume. "Obeah. A frien' smuggle it een fe me."

It was a joke, I thought bitterly. Or some sort of test. I looked accusingly at McIntyre, waiting for him to admit it. But the car was silent. McIntyre stared back at me. In the pale light his eyes were growing impatient. He was serious, I realised slowly, as a hollow sensation began ballooning upwards from my stomach. He was serious about this. And he was impatient with me, impatient that I was so slow to understand.

Suddenly I was reminded of something. I looked up – and shrank back from the face of the full moon, rising above the trees. So it was here too. Was that part of the answer? I thought back to other nights, other lunacies.

I got out of the car.

Carrying the pickaxes, we walked over to the shrine. We unearthed the casket at about two-thirty. Then McIntyre motioned me away and I obeyed mutely, stumbling through the piles of broken concrete. I sat down on one of the remaining points of the star and rested my head in my hands, too weary to think. Out of the corners of my eyes I could see McIntyre moving ritualistically about the casket.

Then there was a flash and the earth sighed. I fell to the ground. Vaguely against my ear I caught a disappearing rumble of drums. For a moment I blacked out.

Then McIntyre was bending over me. And there was another figure, silhouetted against the sky.

We took him back to the yard in August Town. At first he was like a man in a trance, unable to speak or to understand anything. But McIntyre's woman brewed a pot of coffee and McIntyre talked patiently to him and gradually he began to come round. By dawn he was weakly asking for breakfast. The two of them rushed to prepare it for him, both grinning like lunatics. They hardly heard me when I said I had to go.

I went back to my room in hall and sat on my bed. I felt I should try to think about what we had done, to work out all the implications. But in the middle of framing my first question, I fell asleep.

The story broke the next day:

GARVEY ALIVE!

Thousands flock to August Town to see miracle

There was a picture of Garvey in the middle of a cheering crowd. McIntyre's exultant face was somewhere in the background.

Then it all began. The radio and television interviews. The editorials. The newspaper columns. The telegrams of congratulation. The invitations to address meetings and open functions. All against the rising tumult of the people's jubilation. It should have been perfect: everything we had ever hoped for. But something was wrong. Something kept nagging at me, something I couldn't quite put a finger on. It was connected with what McIntyre had said to me once. I kept searching through the news, not knowing what I was looking for. Once or twice I tried to go to the house in August Town to talk to him. But the crowds were always too great.

Still I was uneasy. I seemed to be waiting for something, something that didn't seem to be coming.

Then, one day –

"Security Police, eeh?" said McIntyre thoughtfully. "So is wha' dem do?"

"They told my father that they had a search warrant. That they were looking for guns, ganja, subversive literature . . . things like that." I paused for breath. I had run most of the way here. "Then they just – went into his bedroom and started!"

"An' what dem find?"

I hesitated. "A folder . . . of his poems."

"An'?"

I looked in growing dismay at him. What was wrong with McIntyre? Didn't he realise how serious this was? Impatiently, I told him the rest of the fantastic story my father had given me on the phone: that the superintendent had read the first two poems, apologised profusely to my father and immediately sent the men away. That the two of them had then apparently spent the rest of the evening drinking tea and reminiscing about life in the mother country, where the superintendent had served some time during the war. I didn't bother to mention my father's angry demand to know what I had been doing that involved the police.

"So what are you going to *do*?" In spite of my efforts, my voice had risen to a shout.

"So is what yuh *wan'* me fe do?" he shouted back at me, seeming to be as astonished at my agitation as I was at his lack of it. "If dem come, dem come! Me cyan do nutten 'bout it! Might get a few licks, but dat is all. De place clean." Suddenly he made a step towards me, looking with amazement at my bewildered expression. "Den wait . . . Yuh didn' realise dem woulda come? You mean yuh *still* – "

Abruptly he broke off. He stood motionless, listening to something. I listened too. A sudden uproar had broken out in the yard below. Angry shouts were rising to the window.

With a sense of fatalism, I realised that the police had arrived.

"Well, dem come," McIntyre was saying briskly. He gave the

room a quick, sweeping glance. "Now jus' res' cool an' doan bodder answer dem back." He looked swiftly around again, as if reassuring himself. Then for the second time he seemed to freeze. His face changed colour. "Lawd God," he whispered, staring at the bookcase. Confused, I followed his gaze. "Me figet – "

A thunderous knocking began at the door.

I could see McIntyre take one desperate breath. He launched himself across the bed and began to scrabble frantically at something in the bookcase.

"Hold him!" The door burst open. The room was full of policemen. I was grabbed roughly and pinned against the wall. I tried to look around and caught a glimpse of flailing limbs before my head was wrenched back to the front. Sweating with fear, I held myself rigid. The policemen were struggling with McIntyre. I heard a sharp curse. Then a voice said, "So 'im bad? Jus' let me – Mmmhm!" There was a characteristic, dull *thok* and the struggling ceased. In the sudden silence somebody was panting loudly.

"All right. Check dat one." The voice was more leisurely now. As rough hands began to move down my body, I looked steadily at a patch of peeling paint six inches before me, trying to control my trembling. *The book,* I thought. *It must be the obeah book. But didn't McIntyre tell me he'd* – ? I was gripped by the shoulders, my hands pinioned behind me and turned around.

"So you bringing subversive literature into the island," said a stout man in khaki. He was leafing slowly through a book in his hand. The superintendent, I thought emptily. I looked cautiously around the room for McIntyre. He was propped up at the far end of the room, a thin trickle of blood running down one temple. His face was carefully blank.

"Yuh not answering me, boy?" There was menace in the tone now. I looked helplessly from one to another of them. My mouth felt like sandpaper. What in God's name did he expect me to say? The book . . . I glanced vacantly at it – and then stopped breathing. It was impossible.

I re-read the title, *Philosophy and Opinions of* –

"That's Garvey's book," I said incredulously. I felt like a sleepwalker jerked awake. "Our National Hero. You were going to arrest him for having *Garvey's Book.*" It was too absurd, too unsurpassably ridiculous. I began to laugh, softly at first and then hysterically. They stared uncomprehendingly at me. "You don't understand?" I said harshly. I tried to get control of my voice. "You don't understand? Mac! Explain it to them for me!" I turned to him.

Then I stood rigid with shock.

McIntyre was staring at me with the same expression as the police.

"No," I heard a voice saying feebly. "No." But it sounded far away and unconnected with me. Just as everything else suddenly started to become faraway. McIntyre smiled crookedly at me, with sadness and a little pity in his face. The superintendent gesturing and a man starting to move towards me. Then right after that Mr. Garvey coming in and the superintendent beginning to talk a lot and saluting and bowing and backing out of the room with his men. And Mr. Garvey and McIntyre laughing together.

And then a long time after that McIntyre came over to me and put his hand on my shoulder.

"Me did t'ink you unnerstan' by now, Leo, man. Me really did t'ink so. But yuh see even dem 'ave limits, yuh know? Even fe dem, dem 'ave some t'ing dem cyan do."

I got up stiffly and went over to the window. I watched the police car drive away.

It was to be the culminating event, the grand climax of the most extraordinary month in the island's history. McIntyre was everywhere at once, determined that each last detail should be worked out to perfection. He spoke confidently to me, whenever he had the time, of thirty thousand police. I listened without enthusiasm. It seemed that I was never really going to understand what was happening.

But he was wrong about the crowds. There must have been fifty thousand people in and around the Stadium when I got there. I managed to squeeze into the grandstand on a special pass he had given me. By that time the fence around the cycle track had been breached. People were being forced through to escape the relentless pressure of the crowd outside, pouring in an ever-increasing tide over the athletics track and on to the football field. A sea of humanity spread over the ground.

Two hours before schedule Garvey suddenly appeared. A swelling ocean's roar greeted him, a great booming sound that went on and on, reverberating back and forth between the massed banks of people.

Then he raised his arms and in an instant there was silence.

He began to speak and from the beginning his control was absolute. Poised at the centre of the huge bowl of light, he lifted an arm and they were silent; he spoke a sentence and they hummed with approval; he shouted a question to the heavens and they gave back a thunder of denial.

"– And so," he was saying, "after much consideration I have decided to reform my party under the new name of the People's Freedom Party, and do hereby announce my candidacy in the forthcoming –"

Then the roar overtook him.

I woke up to the sound of somebody knocking. Groggily, I pushed myself upright. My father again, with his poems . . . No, that was a long time ago. Through bleary eyes, I registered the familiar outlines of my room in hall. My head felt as though it were enswathed in cotton wool.

I looked at my watch. Three o'clock in the morning. Just two hours since I returned from the celebrations in the streets.

The knocking came louder. And now there was a girl's voice too.

"Leo! Leo! Wake up!"

I went to the door. It was McIntyre's woman. I caught one glimpse of her face, irrevocably shattered like an old crystal. Then she collapsed in my arms. Numbly, I listened to the fragmented sentences: McIntyre shot by the police, Mr. Garvey arrested, martial law about to be declared, a squad probably on their way here by now . .

"Mr. Garvey arrested?" I said stupidly. "But they can't . . ." My voice trailed off. Over her shoulder it stared at me, the brooding silver face. A remote, chill light lay over us. And suddenly all the pieces fitted together and for the first time I truly understood. "Yes . . . Of course they can . . ."

She was sobbing. "Dem jus' shoot 'im, Leo . . . Oh God, dem jus' shoot 'im . . ."

"He didn't understand," I told her sadly. "He thought that there was a place where they had to stop. That was what puzzled me. Why he should believe that once they had started there should be any limit at all . . ." She went on crying, not hearing me. Gently, I disengaged myself, telling her that I had to go now. Through the tears she seemed to nod.

I knew what I had to do now. I dragged on some clothes and ran up to the hospital, where taxis are parked all night. We drove to a certain place, where I found something, then raced down through the empty streets to my father's house. I let myself in and went up to the room. In a few minutes I had packed an old haversack with as many things as I thought I could carry. Hoisting it over my shoulder, I started downstairs.

My father was standing halfway up the staircase. He had some sheets of paper in his hand.

We stared at each other. In the silence I began to hear a faint sound, growing rapidly louder as we stood there.

Before he could speak, I said calmly, "Listen. Do you hear that noise?"

He hesitated, disconcerted by my manner. Halting on the stairs, he listened to the noise. which was now at our front gate. "It sounds like a police siren," he said slowly.

"It is the police superintendent," I told him authoritatively. "What do you think he's come for?"

He seemed to falter under my gaze, becoming even less sure of himself. "To hear – me read my poem?" I said nothing. "I remember he was a cultured man." Abruptly he went into the library.

I unlatched the back door and stepped into the yard. As I started towards the back fence my father's voice began to declaim powerfully from the front verandah. I could hear the angry voices of the police raised against his. But he only ignored them and spoke louder. Suddenly a mocking sentence rang out. "But dis man a try wuk obeah pon we!"

Simultaneously there was a shot. My father stopped in mid-sentence.

I dropped to the floor of the gully behind our yard and began to run up it.

Now here I am, in the hut.

Here in the mountains time passes more slowly. The sun wheels across the sky by day, the stars by night. There is time to think, to meditate upon things in general. There is time to gain insight into the workings of the universe.

There is also time to read and understand books, or rather one book in particular.

For the moon has me now, as it has all those others. The

moon is in my blood, driving me on, making me a party to our common insanity. And when the time comes for me to go down again into the city they will recognise that I am one of them now, one who has finally been initiated. Even in the moment that I gather the people to say the words that will raise up those other dead so that they too can join our terrible game.

The Man With the Red Shoes

by Charles W. Mills

Gold, 1973

This was the story. Flying down from some island a thousand miles to the north-west, driving all the long, twisting way to the capital, they had come to see the Festival. This they both agreed on: they, the man and the woman both, the husband and wife, the two lovers, hating, loving, destroying, trying to save each other, they agreed on this. It seemed that the man was an artist. Once, in fact – years ago – he had been described as a most promising young artist. They had both been young and confident then, secure in their conviction that the world had to open up each time they knocked. Now the man was not so young any more, nor so promising, and knowing it. And of course the woman was older too, and, looking in the mirror, she resented this, as women will. The Festival began on the twentieth. Somehow there had been a mix-up, a mix-up with the invitations. The man had not received his. It had been sent late. It had been sent to somebody else. It had not been sent at all. It was not certain. Nothing was certain. Perhaps they were thinking of this, the man and the woman, as they came out of the taxi to greet their landlady.

Their landlady was an old woman, a squat black figure, face cobwebbed with wrinkles, patting her hair in an ancient, chuckling coquetry. The man and the woman, however, seemed oddly ageless, neither young nor old, their faces waiting for something, some decision to be made as they turned inquiringly toward each other in the sun. The man – or perhaps the woman – said something. The other nodded. The Indian taxi-driver waved from the window of his cab. They ascended the wooden stairway behind their landlady. The woman looked back suddenly, as if she had lost something. The house waited to receive them, dreaming on its concrete legs, staring out over the ocean. The house swallowed them silently and then stood waiting. The taxi drove away. The sun shone down on the empty garden.

Somewhere in the long night, somewhere on the white sea of the sheets, the man tossed and dreamed. He dreamed that there was a knocking at the door. When he went to open it a man was standing there, a man with red shoes. The man said, "Third door down the corridor. On your left."

"What?" he asked; but the man had already gone. A cold breeze whistled down the corridor. He shut the door quickly, before he could catch a chill.

When he told the woman about it, she frowned absently. "Red shoes? Oh, yes," she said suddenly. "That reminds me, I gave your watch away yesterday, you know." Shifting her head on the pillow, she turned to him with an expression he had never seen on her face before, a faintly mocking smile. "In town. To a man with red shoes."

He said nothing. The sheets of the bed were cold. He wondered if there was a blanket anywhere in the room. After a time he got up and went barefooted over to a closet in the corner. He was about to open it when he noticed that the room was getting lighter. Stepping to the window, he pulled aside the curtains and looked up at a pale, waiting sky in which shoals of tiny, pink-edged clouds floated. Their room faced the east; morning had come. Automatically, he glanced at his watch. His wrist was bare. Suddenly he realised what the woman had said.

For a moment he stood motionless. Slowly, incredulously, anger grew in him. The woman had calmly taken his watch and given it to a complete stranger. And he had accepted the news with an equal detachment. What had he been thinking of? Had he been asleep? "Why did you do that?" he demanded, whirling around. There was no answer. The woman was asleep. He went over to the bed and began to shake her roughly. She lifted a blurred, antipathetic face.

And your face is so innocent, too, he thought viciously, as she looked inquiringly at him. Softly, laying the trap, he said, "You seem to know a lot about him."

It was her turn to shrug. "He's an old friend. I knew him quite well a long time ago . . . Then recently I saw him again. That's all." Her eyes suddenly became challenging. "When we go out *somebody* has to talk to people. *Both* of us can't be sitting in the corner drinking."

"No, my dear, of course not . . . So we'll move in with Jim, then. I suppose you can be relied upon to make the rental arrangements?"

The slap took him by surprise, a crisp, stinging blow that rocked his head to the side. He rubbed his cheek automatically, too amazed to be angry; she had never done anything remotely like that before. Her face was set and wooden; the eyes smouldered. "I'm tired," she said clearly. "I'm tired of that sort of crap." For a moment tension flared between them. Then the man picked up a towel and went through the door.

It was still dark. He shuffled slowly down the corridor. Their room was at the easternmost end of the house. At the opposite end lay the bathroom, connected by the long passage which ran like a tunnel through the entire length of the building. All the doors on the left were closed; their landlady, Mrs. Ricketts, had told them yesterday that they were the only guests she had at the present. On the right was the single, curtain-hung door to the dining-room. A pale, weary light came from it. As he walked carefully through the gloom, his cheek still smarting from the blow, he suddenly remembered his dream and began negligently to count the doors on his left. But from their bedroom he could only find two more. There was no third door.

"Your wife sick?" Mrs. Ricketts asked him sympathetically after breakfast. She had said nothing to him during the meal, only bustled in and out of the dining room, carrying plates. But when she had seen him remain at the table she had come to join him.

"Not really," he said. He smiled at her to show that no snub was intended. The old woman was good company, if a bit inquisitive. And right now he didn't have the slightest desire to have any conversation with his wife. Christ, he thought angrily, remembering, she must really take him for a fool.

"You come for the Festival?"

"Yes."

"What?" she asked in irritation.
"Why did you do that?"
"Do *what*?"
"Give my watch to the man."
"What man? You don't have a watch. What are you talking about?"

He could see the hostility in his own face reflected in hers. But she was right, he realised slowly, as he stared at her. He didn't have a watch. What had made him think he had one? He must have dreamed that too, lying here, waiting for the long night to end. The watch and a man with red shoes. Silently, he turned away and sat down on the other side of the bed. He began to feel self-consciously for his slippers, aware that she was watching him.

"By the way." Her voice was too casual. "When are we leaving?"

He pretended not to understand. "Leaving where?"

From the corner of his eye he could see her sit up, startled. Didn't expect that, eh? he thought, beginning an involved, unnecessary search for his left slipper. The woman said sharply, "You said you were going to see the Director today."

"I changed my mind."

"When?" she asked suspiciously.

He shrugged. Actually he knew very well when he had taken the decision: in the last two minutes. "They've decided not to invite me," he said, with specious carelessness. "I'm not going to go and beg them for accommodations."

"All right." There was a tic above her left eye; a sign, he knew, that she was trying to control her anger. With reluctant admiration, he watched it disappear. "Wait – I know," she said, as if to herself.

"What?"

"Listen." She looked up at him. "I have a friend who lives in town. Someone I was expecting to see at the conferences."

"Male, of course," he said, with heavy irony.

She gestured impatiently, brushing the comment aside. "You know I don't get along with women. Anyway, look. Jim – my friend – has some contacts with the Festival people. He could find out for us. About the invitation. Maybe he could even put us up," she added suddenly, as if it had just struck her. "It'd be much closer to where everything is happening. And he has a guest room."

"You been married long?"

He nodded. Good-naturedly, he watched her studying him. No shyness about her, certainly, he thought. Stifling a yawn, he glanced around. Sunlight was drifting in through a white lace curtain. In the still air dust-motes hovered motionless. He felt he could sit here forever. His eyes wandered back to his landlady. She was wearing a dress patterned with pink roses; her head was resting on her hands, looking straight at him. Something about her intentness, some animal quality, teased his memory distantly. Like an iguana, he realised vaguely. The same heavy folds of skin under the neck, the same unblinking eyes. He started. "Sorry. What did you say?"

"Said I wouldn't mind going myself . . . I ain't been in town for a long time . . ." Her voice was a soft, reminiscing drone. "You gets old . . . You don't go nowhere no more. . . Ain't it so?" Carried along by her voice, he nodded. She smiled at him, a startling flash of ivory in the black face. What a lot of teeth she had. Of course, though, they were false. ". . . Since my husband used to take me."

"Your husband?" he echoed vaguely. The sunlight and Mrs. Ricketts' voice were making him feel sleepy.

". . . That was a real saga-boy . . . When that man got dressed to take you to town . . . put on his suit and his dancing shoes . . ." Drowsily, he nodded his head, not listening, looking at her eyes. Black and glittering, like two pebbles polished by the sea, rapt in their private vision . . . by the sea . . . sea . . . sea-wall . . . "Sorry," he said. "I'm falling asleep."

". . . Said that afterwards we'd go down by the sea-wall . . . after the dance, you know . . . on a Saturday night the whole town would be there. But you gets old . . . first you's young . . . then you's old . . . then you's dead . . . Ain't it so?"

Startled, he jerked upright. The old woman was poking him in the side, face split by a wide grin. How long had he been sitting there? He looked in confusion at her expectant face. Apparently she was asking him some question. "Oh, yes," he said thoughtlessly.

There was a high, shrill burst of sound. Several seconds passed before he recognised that his landlady, her mocking agate eyes staring at him, was laughing. Puzzled, but unresisting, he joined in, wondering what he had given his assent to.

The sea-wall ran parallel to the far side of the road, a concrete embankment overlooking the ocean. Clumsily, cursing steadily, he manoeuvred the aluminium tripod and easel on top of it, then the bag of paints, then scrambled up himself. "Shit!" He was in a bad temper already and the heat was making it worse. Before the woman had left to go into town they had had the scene he had half-feared, half-hoped for. He had been snide and sarcastic, as was his style, while she had just been unaffectedly furious, as was hers ("Do you know why you really want to stay here? Because you're ashamed to face your friends! Because neither you nor they can remember when is the last time you did anything even a tourist would look at!").

All right, bitch, he thought savagely. Let us see. He jumped down to the other side. The tide was out. He found a firm patch of ground and set up the easel and tripod. Glancing up, he saw with satisfaction that his subjects, a man and woman he had first glimpsed down the road, were still there. They were standing, talking, at the edge of the long concrete pier that ran at right angles to the embankment down the beach and into the ocean. The man was throwing stones into the water. He began to sketch them quickly. When he had a rough likeness he pulled the watercolours out of the bag and started to paint. To right and left, as far as he could see, there was no sign of anyone. Behind him, the long, dominating sweep of the sea-wall cut off all contact with the city. It was as if they were in a separate, isolated world, a world with no evidence of life but the two hallucinatory figures on the pier. Above, the burning vault of the sky, in front, the grey ocean, behind, the empty sands; and at their meeting-point, opposing their leaden, oppressive power, the man and the woman. He felt the old, almost forgotten excitement as the composition came together in his mind. It would be a good picture. He was sure of it. The paints ran into each other, colour blurring into shimmering colour. It was getting hotter all the time: a steady, directionless heat, beating down from all parts of the metallic sky. He could feel his shirt sticking to his back, feel the warm serpent-slide of the sweat down his face. He worked harder, wiping his forehead, squinting against the glare. Heat waves were beginning to rise from the sand . . . He looked up again. The couple had gone. Dissolved into the haze some time while he was working. He turned to the paper to see what he had painted . . . the crumbling pier, the opaque sky, the deserted ocean, all harsh in the dreadful light, as he had intended . . . The pier was empty. The couple were not there either.

"Mrs. Ricketts?" He knocked rapidly on the door. From inside he could hear a chair scrape on the floor. Then the slow, dragging footsteps approached the door. Hurry up, he thought.

"I's coming . . . I's coming." The door opened. Mrs. Ricketts appeared, beaming as she saw him. "You got a nice picture . . .?" she began. Then she noticed his face and exclaimed, "What's wrong? What's happened?"

"Nothing," he said brusquely. He didn't want to be drawn into any long explanations. "I was too long in the sun." Suddenly, after coming in, he had decided that he should go and find the woman. "Tell me, has my wife come back yet?"

"I ain't seen her," said the old woman shortly. It was obvious that she was not going to be put off as easily as that. "Now what happened? Sunstroke?" She took a decisive hold of his arm. "Better come and sit down for a while."

"Mrs. Ricketts –"

"Come and sit *down*."

What a stubborn old woman she was. But he didn't want to hurt her feelings. He let himself be led through the door. Besides, it would only be for a few minutes; then he could go and find his wife. It was cool and dark inside after the burning sands. The old woman took him to a chair and waddled out. From the kitchen came sounds of ice being prised out of a tray. He let his eyes wander listlessly over the room: closet, religious prints, artificial flowers, a dresser covered with items: china statuettes, glass jars filled with hairpins, an atomiser, bottles of cosmetics, spools of thread, an old photograph in a glass frame . . . He shut his eyes wearily. Just a little bit longer. Then he would go.

"Hold this."

Something cold on his forehead. He lifted his hand and felt a bag of ice cubes. Gratefully, he slumped back in the chair. He could feel himself relaxing, his consciousness sinking slowly down into the darkness. Wait. Unease flickered briefly like a candle flame. Something he had to remember. It was receding from him. It was gone. He sank down further. No. Again. Wait. Something he had to do. His wife. Yes. His wife. Effortfully, he opened his eyes.

Mrs. Ricketts' black lidless gaze was fixed on him.

He staggered to his feet, staring. Her face seemed to shift and change. In a surprised voice she said, "What's wrong, mister?"

"The key," he said, covering up. "You said you'd get the room key for us."

"Oh, yes." She pursed her lips, her eyes speculative. Turning around, she went to the dresser and rummaged around for a while. She handed it to him silently. He mumbled something and walked quickly, unsteadily, to the door. As he left he could feel her eyes on him.

This was a wooden city, he thought. He was walking briskly through the festive crowds that thronged up and down the tree-shaded walkways of the main streets. It was early afternoon, the sun beginning to slant diagonally through the golden air. Exhilarated, he stopped and looked around. His wife had been right. When he found her he would unhesitatingly admit it. They could move tomorrow. Or today. Ahead of him, a circle of people had converged around the bright, reverberant company of a steel band. The notes rippled metallically out. He listened, then went over to join the growing crowd. Eight young men in glowing orange shirts, hunchbacked with concentration, eyes intent on the intricate, weaving dance of their sticks. People were beginning to sing along with the calypso tune. Smiles flashed and glittered, hands clapped, heads tossed on a sea of dashikis. Picking up the chanted words, he began to sing too.

Suddenly, on the other side of the crowd, he caught sight of his wife's face. She was laughing vivaciously, head thrown back, body shaking with delight. A man was whispering something into her ear.

He stood rigid for a few moments, staring at them. Then he began to push his way through the crowd, not caring if he stepped on anybody. People gave way reluctantly. He was almost through to the edge when he tripped and fell heavily against someone. The man swore viciously and tried to pull him back. Roughly, he tore away, nearly overbalancing into somebody else. For a moment he paused, disoriented. At the same time the music stopped. People began to drift away.

Cursing silently, he looked around for his wife and the man. Nowhere in the dispersing crowd could he see them. He broke into a quick, indecisive trot; then halted, feeling foolish. His eyes darted in frustration from figure to figure. Ahead of him a couple were turning the corner into a side street. At the man's feet there was a flash of colour.

Red shoes.

The man! he thought, transfixed. So she had lied to him.

Then he was running after them. Somewhere horns blew, tyres screeched. Heedless, he sprinted furiously around the corner. He heard the fragment of a sentence – "second door, on your left" – before they turned round.

The woman was not his wife.

"Who –?" he had begun. Then stopped, speechless. They were looking inquiringly at him. The man wore a flamboyant orange shirt. A faint, almost imperceptible contempt seemed to hover in his face for a moment. Ignoring him, he looked at the girl. She smiled back, amiably but without recognition. She bore no resemblance to his wife.

"What's the problem, man?" asked the man in the orange shirt.

"I – thought you were somebody else," he said, after a while. Where had he seen the girl before? The man shrugged disdainfully, took the girl's arm. They were turning, about to walk on. He looked down at the ground. Red shoes. The same ones. "Wait!" They stopped again, the man's face beginning to tighten. He stepped decisively towards them.

"So you came at last." Footsteps behind him. He turned in surprise to see his wife, smiling gaily. "I've got news, darling, news. Just listen – wait, what's wrong?"

"Know him?" he asked coldly, gesturing towards the man. He was watching her face closely, looking for the betraying reaction. But her eyes travelled blankly down the street. Wheeling, he saw that the couple had taken the opportunity to depart; he just glimpsed the girl's pink dress disappearing into a building.

The woman was shaking him. "What's wrong with you? What are you looking at?"

"Nothing," he said. "Nothing." Suddenly he grabbed her roughly by the shoulders and stared into her face. *Who are you?* he thought. *I keep thinking you're somebody else. Or somebody else is you.* Her face wavered and blurred under his gaze. Everything was melting and dissolving. "What's *wrong* with you?" she was asking, struggling in his grip. Just as suddenly he let her go. "Nothing," he said. "I'm feeling sick. Let's go and sit down." They walked across the road. Things returned to focus. They had sat down in an outdoor restaurant attached to a hotel. A few bright flags, celebrating the Festival, flapped along a string stretched overhead.

She was saying something. He turned. "I said I saw Jim this morning. He's spoken to the Director. He says they have a place for us. We can move tomorrow. I told you it was all a mistake. He says everything has been handled very inefficiently. Cables weren't sent out on time. That sort of thing. Lots of other people weren't officially invited either."

He said nothing. She leaned eagerly over the table towards him. "Don't you see, darling? They did invite you after all. It was just the usual bungling."

For a moment, poised, he gazed at her, pulled towards the radiant, excited face, with its buoyant corona of hair, vivid in the afternoon sunlight. Then a shadow rose up before him. The eyes turned sardonic, the smile mocking. She was laughing at him. He felt his breath beginning to come faster. "So Jim just arranged everything, eh?" he said harshly. His control of his voice was going. He felt himself becoming hysterical. "Well, isn't that wonderful? Now should I bother to thank him? Or have you thanked him already?"

He stared desperately at her. She had lowered her head, as if examining something in her lap. One hand scrawled aimlessly on the table. When she raised her eyes, her face was defeated. "What do you want of me?" she asked softly.

The man, he thought emptily. The man with the red shoes.

Somewhere in the long night there was a knocking at the door.

He knocked at the door. "Mrs. Ricketts!"

The wrinkled face appeared in less time than usual. It was as if she had been expecting him. He said sharply, "Have you seen my wife?"

The old woman shook her head. She seemed amused.

"You must have seen her," he insisted angrily. Damn the woman! She was hiding something. He was sure of it. "I overslept. I just got up. And she was gone. You sure she didn't leave a message with you?"

"I ain't seen her," she said imperturbably.

He stared in frustration at the dumpy, self-assured figure.

The old woman appeared to be trying to hide a smile. Where could his wife have gone to? Without saying anything more, he turned and went back across the dining room. As he pushed through the curtain he heard his landlady's mocking voice: "Maybe she gone out by the sea-wall." Ignoring the comment, he went through the open door of their room. He had started to untie his dressing gown when it struck him.

They were in the wrong room.

His gown fell unnoticed to the floor. He walked quickly to the open doorway and into the corridor.

They were no longer at the far end. The room they had spent their first night in was now to the right of them.

Slowly, disbelievingly, he went to the door. He tried it. It was locked.

Third door down the corridor. On your left.

In a sudden frenzy he ran down the corridor, frantically counting. But there were only three doors, as he had noticed from the first morning. Third door from the first room meant four rooms. Where was the fourth?

Where was his wife?

"Mrs. Ricketts!" he shouted. By God, he would make the old woman explain. Not waiting for an answer, he strode through the dining room and began to pound on her door. It had not been closed. At his first few blows it swung gently open. He pushed inside and looked feverishly around. The old woman was not there. On the dresser something caught his eye. It was the picture of Mrs. Ricketts in her youth.

For a long second he stared at the face of the girl in the pink dress.

Then he dashed back to his room and began savagely to pull on some clothes.

Outside, the light struck him like a physical blow. The sun exploded on the zinc roofs, burst like shrapnel on the cars' windshields, drove splinters of white fire towards him. He shut his eyes in automatic reaction, realising with horror that it was even later than he had thought. A break came in the traffic and he ran across the road. Fingers scrabbling on the concrete, he pulled himself up the embankment and on top of the sea-wall.

He shaded his eyes and looked out over the mud flats. The glare made it difficult to see. Waves of heated air shimmered up from the grey sand, distorting perspectives, forming mirages.

When he went back to the house he badly needed a drink. He went into the kitchen and poured himself some water from the fridge. After that he stood for a long time, leaning on the counter, pillowing his face in his hands. He was trying to concentrate on something important, but he couldn't remember what it was. The burning white after-image of the outside still scorched his eyelids.Feeling curiously light-headed, he tried to remember what he had been doing out on the sands. As he stood there the sound of water splashing in a tub came to him. He looked up. The kitchen door had been left ajar. It opened on a rickety wooden stairway which descended into the backyard of the house .

Leaving the glass in the sink, he went over to the door and looked outside. A woman was down there, wringing clothes out over a washbasin and then hanging them on a line. When he called out, she looked up and smiled at him.

He stared at her. Suddenly he remembered. His wife. He had been looking for his wife. With relief, he stepped out on to the landing. "I've been looking for you."

She smiled again, an odd, oblique smile. "Have you?"

"Yes." He descended the staircase and walked shakily across the grass to her. She watched him as he came, unblinking in the sunlight, little drops of water glistening on her hands. He put his arms around her. "You smell of soap."

"Yes," she said, her glossy black eyes looking at him. For a moment he wondered why she was washing clothes. But the moment passed. Out in the sun the feeling of dizziness had returned. He felt things changing under his eyes, wavering, slipping away. "I was worried about you," he said uncertainly.

"Were you?" she replied, laughing slightly now, with her odd lizard eyes, touching him.

"Yes," he said emptily, knowing, knowing now, and knowing also that it was too late. The grass was soft and warm in the sun, green and luxuriant as they rolled slowly over. But when he reached for her breasts he shuddered, for they were withered and dry.

He woke up . . . and looked directly into a dying orange sun, a sky the colour of copper . . . *The western window . . . He was in the third room.* . . The house was empty. He knew it even before he ran despairingly out. His wife was gone . . . As he had dreamed, before he woke . . . Or had he dreamed? Or had he woken? . . . He shouted, a protesting, inarticulate sound . . . and ran down into the front yard. Huge purple clouds, supported by pillars of light, hung like curtains across the sky. Bloated and ponderous, the sun was sinking in an angry red smoke. He slammed the gate and looked wildly up and down the road. How long to wait for a bus? *No time. Too much time had gone already.* He began to run down the grass verge, slowing to a jerky walk whenever he got out of breath, then running again, walking, running . . . till he stopped, gasping, feeling the remorseless bite of a stitch in his side. He closed his fingers around it savagely, trying to squeeze it out of existence. Above, the light was slowly draining out of the sky, following the sun. He hobbled forward, the pain like an iron claw below his ribcage. To his right the sea-wall suddenly veered away as the road turned in towards the heart of the city. For a moment he wondered where he was going. Then realised that he knew . . . *Before the sun goes down,* he thought hopelessly. *Before the sun goes down.*

Then the streetlamps flicked on, two columns of blue mercury flame, and he knew it was too late. He went on mechanically, past the choked canals, the silent trees, into the city; the nightclubs just opening, whores fluttering like bright moths in their yellow doorways, the patrolling policemen, the first limers cruising up the night. The pain in his side had gone now, but he didn't hurry any more.

When he got to the street he turned up it. No lights were visible in the building. As he started up the stone staircase a man came through the door. The man was walking in a slow, leisurely way, whistling to himself. He did not seem surprised to see him. As they passed, the man said, "First door down the corridor. On your left."

He had turned his head away so that he would not see the man's face. As he went through the door he could hear the other's footsteps going down the street.

Inside the building it was quite cold. The corridor stretched away into the darkness before him. A yellow oblong of light shone faintly in the distance.

He began to walk.

When he reached the room the woman was lying on the bed, staring through the window. The sheets were rumpled and dishevelled. She turned as he came in, then looked away.

He sat on a wooden chair by the bed. Neither of them said

anything.

After a while she pointed through the window. "It's morning."

He looked at the high pink clouds. "Yes."

She glanced at his arm. "And you've got your watch back."

He had not noticed. "Yes," he said slowly, looking at his wrist. "The twentieth."

"The Festival," she said, as if to herself. "The Festival begins today."

He said nothing. After a long while he touched her shoulder gently. His voice was half-hoping. "Does – it matter?"

For answer she began to cry softly into the pillow. "Oh, God," she sobbed. "Oh, God." When he tried to put his arms around her she turned away. Sinking back into the chair, he began to look through the window. Now it was all over, he thought. Yes, now it was all over. But how strange it was all the same, he thought in amazement, still trying to understand it. Now you are young. Now you are old. And in the midst of his dreaming sleep he had not even seen it happen.

Child of Darkening Humour

by Noel D. Williams

Gold, 1973

Mrs. Beverly Segree (her husband had died in a spectacular crash, she had informed a vacationing American at the beauty parlour a few hours ago, and her little boy was approaching fourteen and quite a prodigy) almost collapsed from laughter one evening, minutes before Mrs. Hart and her husband finally left. She had been preparing to go out (it was her birthday) to dinner with the Doctor, and then the playhouse, and had welcomed the Harts graciously, hoping to suggest (as she had learnt to with difficult people and complainants at the Tourist Office) that the timing of their visit was distressingly wrong. While Mr. Hart was parked placidly before the television, a picture of the courtroom composure he had worked hard to master (the pipe-smoking lawyer, ingeniously detecting false evidence), Mrs. Hart had slipped off and was perched on the pink spread of the large bed, talking vociferously. She was relating at that very moment, while Mrs. Segree skipped from bathroom to dressing mirror pausing only at the hushed point before the climax of a scandalous disclosure, an incident circulating in talk relay among the men and women of the University community. About a foreign lecturer in Physics and a city prostitute. "My dear, it is quite frightening sometimes, the things that go on up there. You'd never believe it. The man was led to believe she was a medical student . . ." Mrs. Segree had interrupted, suddenly serious-faced, and shouted to Gran in the living room to listen for the Doctor's car. He was not a very patient man. He announced his arrival by giving three short blasts on the horn, and waited, the motor still running, for her to join him outside. Once in an inexplicable rage he drove off and left her standing, well-dressed and fumbling with the latch of the gate. She had stayed in Montego Bay (where her office was located) for over a month and a half before coming home to Gran and her boy and the neighbours who must have forgotten the whole thing.

Gran was sitting in an easy chair pretending to be engrossed in the newspaper. She made little attempt to converse with Mr. Hart except to ask him, as a polite matter of course, whether he wanted anything to drink. He had refused, tucked a pipe at the side of his mouth and was preparing to light up the tobacco. She did not like him at all, and had turned on the television minutes before he had entered trailing after his wife's breathless chatter and handbag smile (he had delayed to lock up the car and to inspect it again, as if inviting the secret approval of the world whose satisfaction he acknowledged with a practised, stiff gait and pencil moustache and the studied inattention of a half-successful, brooding man). She had hoped he would be tempted to watch, and he had indeed nestled (it was close to a programme of World News) into that thought-tidy, scrupulous sobermanliness with which he approached the tumult of every ungodly event, encapsulated and reported now in the satisfyingly grave tones of the local newscaster.

She thought he was quite unlike her son and glanced at him, photographed and framed on the piano. She had heard, however, that he was an impressive lawyer, given to colourful speeches on behalf of destitute clients. His English wife was much more the talker during social visits. She chirped solicitously, asked serious questions about quaint local customs and told hilarious anecdotes about other people which only foreigners to the island could relate with such peculiar zest, such human world-weariness. She had attended the Courts once and had said after, about Mr. Hart, that he displayed (Gran remembered her exact words) 'a poet's remarkable sensitivity to their unlettered terror of farcical procedure and legal rigmarole'. She was a lecturer at the university. Their marriage was the trump-charged hand of bridge players in the field, a contract of concealment, without child.

But he sat before the television and sorted out from all the screen intensity information about seemingly unstoppable upheavals in far-flung parts of the globe. He had grown familiar with the 'trouble spots', the 'psychopaths' to the left and right, and at weekends (often after strenuous afternoons of lawn tennis and over frothy beer at the club's bar) he turned his thoughts incisively on the 'painful absurdities' here at home.

Gran turned to the centre pages and looked through the windows half-expectantly. She wondered about Morgan, her grandson, who had retired to his room earlier that evening, and she feared an interruption, another display of bad manners which his mother had, after one unforgettable evening, spoken to the Doctor about, believing that his accident when still a baby had caused serious damage to his brain as well. Recently he had been given a chemistry set (his mother always returned home with an expensive gift; she felt it made up for her long absence and would help to *motivate* the boy).

It was when she caught the first vagrant whiff of an offensive smell that Gran knew the little demon was concocting gases or something. She rose to speak to him but heard at the same moment the sound of a car approaching the house which meant (she tensed in every patient muscle) the Doctor. The door of the bedroom had opened and Mrs. Hart came out still running her tale but preparing to leave. Mrs. Segree looked slightly agitated and glanced towards the door. But the car had stopped, the motor had gone silent, and shortly after (Mr. Hart was also slowly, and with visible regret and annoyance, detaching himself from the News) the Doctor came through the door. He was a smooth-shaven man of middle height, wearing an informal jacket, a neckerchief and flashing white shoes. His gruffness of greeting softened into tasteful silence as he found himself being quickly introduced, nodding politely at the English woman and shaking Mr. Hart's hand (the name, the name didn't register).

They seized a few moments of chatter, in a small impromptu circle in the living room. It was their rubber dinghy of sharing a rare warmth amidst the dark choppy waters of the island's disorder. And Gran hoped they would not notice the smell which had intruded and was becoming stronger. But Mrs. Hart, warming instinctively to a new island acquaintance, unwrapped a story about the day she arrived on the island.

"We had just left the airport," she was saying in confidential tones that promised intrigue, "and we had reached that stretch of road, you know, where you get your first marvellous view of the sea and the mountains. Well all of a sudden, there, right in front of us, was this positively revolting figure of . . . a black man. Absolutely stark naked!" The group perked up and shuffled. The Doctor folded his arms and waited. And Mrs. Hart, now feverish and inspired, rushed on up to the intimacy she had flagged down. "He just stood there, trying to stop our car. He was almost in the middle of the road and we were, oh, about fifty yards or so away, when suddenly he threw up his hands as if he were about to die or fling a curse at us or something. We had to swerve to avoid hitting the man. We might have run right over him."

(Mr. Hart had hissed, "My God! The mentality of these people . . .", as if passing a traveller's cheque of self-advertisement, or a scribbled note of apology to the flabbergasted witness of the world.)

"I turned to my husband and I said, 'Darling, are we really home?' I asked. Of course we all laughed and he said that for a moment he was not quite sure, that, maybe, we *were* home, back on the mainland somewhere. It really was the most incredible sight. I haven't met him since, the man I mean, though you never can tell where next he'll turn up."

Gran had slipped away while the introductions were being made. By the time she returned to the living room having spoken sharply to Morgan about his inconsiderate conduct (he had not even looked up at her), the Harts, to her great relief, were getting into their car. She seemed to recall a voice shouting farewell, hoping perhaps the sound would locate her wherever she was in the house and deliver its ringing good cheer. The Doctor was standing before the television, impatience beginning to swell in his neatly dressed figure; for Mrs. Segree was back in her bedroom attending to finishing details, but appearing to delay longer than was necessary. Gran was on the point of taking up the newspaper again (there was little she could say to the Doctor in that mood) when he swore and exploded with trembling anger.

The newscaster was reporting on army and police operations in the hills. Gran had noticed a similar report in the newspapers outlining new plans to combat disorder and crime. The operation was designed to smoke out criminals believed to be holding out in the hills. There had been rumours of secret training camps and an unearthed cache of weapons, and it seemed a big swoop and gunbattle had taken place in which three men had been fatally shot.

The face on the screen affected deep concern but there was just a hint of compensating triumph in the announcement which did succeed, however, in comforting the Doctor. He swore loudly again (Mrs. Segree was running to the bathroom, shouting an excuse and promising to be right out) and broke out in a tense perspiration. He fumbled for a handkerchief.

"Hooligans . . . morbid anatomy and laziness, that's what it is. And all these strikes, killings, all this *indecency*. Nothing but morbid anatomy. Damn lazy, hooligans, predatory on the hard-working. A heap of unhygienic rabble, look at them!" The screen was showing a small group of captured men being handcuffed and pushed into waiting jeeps by cinematically-clad troops, bristling automatic weapons. "And those other dreamers blaspheming our sight with their self-righteousness, polluting our ears with foolish lamentation and drums! I'd castrate the whole pack of them. Make all that innocence and holy rage into the impotence they conceal and robe in seediness and ignorant prophecy. It is the morbid anatomy of the victim, badly wanting insult and courting our complicity and reluctant hand in rituals of defilement."

He was wiping his face, fresh and wet and slapped from some coiled serpent sleep, and he was apologising to Gran as if she were a patient on a crowded hospital bed, staring at him through a film of bewildering pain; as if he had committed an irrevocable error, with his blunt authority of scalpel and stainless white jacket and hypocritical wedge of an oath he could not now renounce, like a cancerous disposition. He was sorry, he said.

Gran wished them a good night and waited until the car had taken off before rising to peer through the window. The darkness outside prowled away and assumed the stillness of a drowsy, half-attentive jury. She felt strangely soothed by its absence of stress, its accommodating ocean depth (there were lights up in the distance, of dwellings she could see clearly during the day). She turned off the television, lights in empty rooms, and decided she would speak again to Morgan before she retired.

He had never known his father, Gran's only son and bridge-head of an unexamined privilege of birth and the stolen right to make a name for himself. That was a self-made man, she always said. He had not gone abroad to pursue and fulfil an impossible island yearning, and to return shot down by treach-erous, doubtful homesickness. And ingeniously clever, he had shown an early interest in building model planes. On Sunday afternoon he went to a playing field nearby where scruffy, slum youth, fighting over football, stopped, squatted on haunches and watched as the model plane circled and dipped through space. And later in his life when his position in the insurance company allowed it, he had paid down for a private plane, the airship (it was his charming way of describing the Cessna), and flew around the island. On the day he died (Morgan was one year old then) she felt as if the light of day over the island had dimmed to an almost permanent state of mourning for the loss of his kind of daring inventiveness.

She had not attended the funeral (she was too weak, and the light seemed to hail her with a coded message she struggled, through deeply private sadness, to decipher). She had read a report in the newspapers (a vulgar piece, she thought, by some exuberant trainee) which reported a man from a distant village as saying that the airship had shot out, 'had come tumbling out' of the sky. There had been a photograph on the front page. The nose of the airship had lodged in the ground, one wing had tilted at a ludicrous angle. It seemed so utterly beyond repair. They had spared her details of the tragedy and had made arrangements for a quick burial (the doctor had been extremely helpful in making all preparations). Within one week he was buried and when Mrs. Segree returned that after-noon from the funeral, her eyes reddened with weeping, she found Gran studying a framed photograph of her son, handsome and in full vigour, almost indestructibly modest.

But calamity had struck again soon after. Mrs. Segree was giving Morgan a morning bath when the child slipped from her fingers and fell to the cold tiles. She had screamed, and was hysterical for several weeks. The doctor had been summoned and Morgan was taken to hospital. After months of what Gran imagined, with a sigh, to be the best in local consultative care, he was brought back home but it was feared he would grow up unable to walk. It was a year of unbelievable tragedy for the family but they survived the worst months quite well. Mrs.

Segree had taken this job with the Tourist Board, and Gran had assumed the responsibility of bringing up Morgan.

Above all, she was careful to educate him. She sat with him and watched television programmes which brought the troubled world into their living room; she read him children's classics, fairy tales (he was fascinated with stories of forests and monsters, and old men with white hair), and before he was ten he was coping with Dickens and even Shakespeare. She was honestly amazed at his quicksilver mind and imagination, and when one day (it was two days after his twelfth birthday) he appeared suddenly in the dining room, attempting bravely to walk, she stared at him and felt an oncoming dizziness. When she could see properly again and had focussed on Morgan, he was telling her about the first science fiction book he had just read but she was only half-listening. It seemed that the light had assumed a sharper edge, almost too strong for her ageing eyes. It was as if some trapped animal, after years of despairing waiting, had released itself; as if some shrunken leg and spirit had found its way back to a half-remembered lair. It was a miracle of forgiveness for which, it seemed, there was no one to thank amidst the vulgar confusion and foolish, strúggling human war with the tight-lipped patient of life.

When Morgan was moving around the house (not too steadily; he walked with a stick, an absurd prop to his natural brilliance, Gran felt) she watched him with even greater anxiety. She would wait for him to approach with some marvellous question about the island or the world (he was given, however, to uttering elliptical statements of late, and often stood gazing blankly into space as if hoping to catch a chance communication, or scribbled note dropped from the beak of some winged intimation).

Her life was the routine and blessed compensation of the ageing. She went through the regular motions of, first, unlatching the kitchen door for the maid to get in at five-thirty; of answering the phone and informing callers (frequently male voices that sounded alarmingly familiar) that Mrs. Segree was not in the city; and assimiliating the sounds of domesticity in their quiet neighbourhood.

She did not have much to say to the neighbours, hardly finding the occasion to meet them. Across the road and beyond their high hedge lived, she knew, a French engineer, his daughter and a rather fierce dog. She had glimpsed him several times, washing his car or reading on the patio, and could hardly avoid raising a hand in respectful greeting. She was more intrigued with the little girl with short blonde curls, who romped on the lawns with the fierce dog. She felt Morgan would find her interesting to talk with. She seemed incredibly happy. And charmingly wicked, for they waited (dog and solitary girl) many afternoons until a noisy dishevelled group of children from a public school in the area passed by on their way home, then the dog would be set to give chase, scattering the children screaming in all directions. At precisely three every day the girl practised on the piano, first rapid up and down scales, then simple melodies of left and right hand delicacy. And Gran, listening from across the street, forgot the dryness and heat, the dust and hill fires, the mad hammerstroke of the sun. She slipped gently into the reflective pool of the melodies. It was the soothing hand of eternity upon the withered brow of her years.

But on Sundays, each week and every month, there was a visitor at the gate. A woman who travelled from a village in the hills all the way down to the city to sell her vegetables, oranges, breadfruit and cane. Gran had stopped her once, had found her land produce cheap and her peasant manners quite pleasing. She had told the woman to reappear at six in the morning, not before and not much after, but as early as five-thirty the woman and her boy (she had taken to bringing him along to introduce him to the mistress, and to allow him a taste of the city) and a mule bearing two heavy baskets were waiting at the gate. The woman knew perhaps she had arrived too soon. Gran was careful to go out shortly after six, her greeting tones suggesting that the woman seemed to have no understanding of what time meant.

On this Sunday (two days after Mrs. Segree's birthday; she had flown off from the city), Gran went to the gate holding the collar of her dressing gown tightly against the morning chilliness. She enquired about the boy's health and inspected the baskets, all the while complaining to the world about the rising prices, the city problems of water and electricity, and her good fortune in conducting gentle transactions with the woman. When she was ready to withdraw (she never purchased very much but received, always as a generous offer from the heart, more vegetables and fruit than she could use) she listened as the woman spoke of her recurring illness. Recently she had received an injury which now compelled her to limp (she pulled up the hem of her long, plaid dress to display a stained bandage strapped around her left calf). Gran commiserated as best she could, exalting the woman's private distress to the battered, suffering status of the world. It was the poignant melody and game of lament played by the untidy island in the open, dark field of the world.

"Wha's happening to us, ma'am?" the woman pleaded suddenly, as if seeking a golden nugget of unearthed feeling, truth to take back from the city to her tiny village in the hills.

Gran felt a strange shudder in the morning light and looked up, as if a huge wing-tip had brushed by her heart, flying dangerously low and radioing its message and rhetorical plea for incredible salvation. The large markings of the woman's obvious disquiet lay folded and wet, jettisoned in haste upon the chilly dawn by some callous deliverer, or anguished victim of miscarriage.

"Our suffering is . . ." she was wrestling with a swelling irritation and sadness but she seemed to detect, in an infinite flash of sympathy, the ancient sigh nestling in the impulse of the woman's question.

"Our suffering," she tried again, "is like the rude loss of a treasured son, an emptiness . . ." (It was coming through, rushing up, plummeting down to an unmistakable clarity of disclosure) "I mean, the illegitimacy of such dank unfairness . . . it will be . . . unclaimed or reclaimed . . . Christ or Christophe . . . It will be, you'll see . . ."

But the woman and her son and the mule had reached a bend of the road where the curving hedge took them gently out of sight. Gran looked around her, thinking she had addressed some stray dog or an upstart wind panting at the back door of her heart for all that she had sown and gathered and stored away from all the hideous contemporary seriousness and frantic grope. It was (she hastened now to the house) the awesome, quivering bloodstain and issue of a dark wrong and amputation which no physician or magic healer from the sky could join, with all the skill aboard this grounded ship of an island, together again.

When she came into the living room she sat down in an easy chair to catch her breath. Her ageing heart was heaving with the thought of facing anew the intrusion of the world's curse and ugliness, its shoddy vagrancy and dropped anchor of innocence. And now, more menacingly than ever, this new insolence with which its wandering beggars, cast ashore and freed, dared to march into her island and boldly set up their shacks of human refusal to accept the logic and sentence passed over and upon them.

It was too much for her frayed soul (she wished her son were alive, he would know how to deal with this) and she lapsed into a troubled sleep.

It was the sound of someone hailing the Godharboured day of rest which brought her to her feet (each hovering sound was now a startling signal). What she saw when she looked outside almost felled her with its seeming lack of reason. Morgan was (What was he doing out there? And what time of day was it?) conversing with a strange man who seemed to be selling yard brooms. She recognised the man and shivered anxiously. He was one of the mad cultists. He wore a pouch of a hat, a thick, black beard, and a towel or rag was draped across his left shoulder.

"Morgan," she shouted from the door, "come inside at once. Get away from that man. You, sir, what do you want?"

The man had seen her peering the first time through the window. He smiled and replied, "Selling brooms, ma'am, yard brooms." He broke off knowing he could sell nothing here and, leaving a whispered prayer or password or sealed pact with the boy, he stalked off, tossing in the air the weirdest song and laughing lyric, or knife of a trick artist:

God is Dog / In-land is I-land
In and I and Out
I-land is I-world
God is Dog
in the spell of the Master
I-mind

Morgan was flabbergasted and stared after the man, his nose tracking the strangest aroma, receding breath of illumination, forbidden and outlawed from his steep diving hands until that moment, until the man selling yard brooms had approached the gate.

"Come in here at once," Gran called, "come away from the gate. That man is dreadful. They're dangerous. They kill."

Morgan turned slowly, paused and started forward uncertainly. (He seemed so brave and frail out there, Gran thought, confronting the unpredictable, the shocking indecency out there.) He started up the path to the house, prowling lion of a child, in a webbed lair of self-possession from which, on occasion, he pulled out or snapped the unfairest of sleeping questions. He was muttering to himself.

"No wonder," (she could hardly catch his words) "no wonder we take off in quest of new orders to sell, new orders to celebrate, or cerebrate. It is this obsessional hunting of a destitute prey. Foolish compensating raids on a praying community by legions of the saved, privileged to disdain or patronise as the dripping fat of profits or scandal decrees.

"An incensed, islanded love," (was he trying, the foolish boy, to balance the whole earth on his left foot? He almost fell) "and the suffocating incense of the dead dog in humanity."

"Gran, what have your eyes seen?" (He was looking, through uncountable trees of bewilderment, at her.) "Who piloting this damn airship? Chinee racehorse owner? Coat-and-tied Black? Syrian money eater? White grab 'n flee? God is Dog, see him there . . .?"

He pointed and knew, where the man selling yard brooms hailed songs to the heavens, his laugh and lyric looping back through the air like raw meat tossed from the butcher shop of his heart, whetting its patient knife for a humble sale.

Morgan looked at the gazing hills, then took the deepest breath to exhale its burning tremor of the future. Its hewn face of secrets, he knew, was the runaway spirit that once sought its green slopes for a refuge and forge of its angry breathing. Its smoke, curling in ascent, was the signal to a gloomy patient (refusing to grieve, planting new seed) finally free from the groping fingers counting the fee for a fumbled job or flight of mercy (commission of the sensitised doctor, rummaging an island wound for the beloved hem that dragged an unswept ocean floor; commission of the brooding lawyer, exhibiting the dried blood on a curious murder weapon to a jury convinced of the savage and unsalvageable in humanity).

It was growing dark, alarmingly dark upon the island, above the dog/shot kennel of the world.

Gran shuddered, turned, stumped a pealing toe, entered the house, shut and bolted the door.

Love Orange

by Olive Senior

Gold, 1974

Somewhere between the repetition of Sunday School lessons and the broken doll which the lady sent me one Christmas, I lost what it was to be happy. But I didn't know it then even though in dreams I would lie with my face broken like the doll's in the pink tissue of a shoebox coffin. For I was at the age where no one asked me for commitment and I had a phrase which I used like a talisman. When strangers came or lightning flashed, I would lie in the dust under my grandfather's vast bed and hug the dog, whispering, "Our worlds wait outside," and be happy.

Once I set out to find the worlds outside – the horizon was wide and the rim of the far mountains beckoned. But I was happy when they found me in time for bed and a warm supper for the skies, I discovered, were the same shade of china blue as the one intact eye of the doll. "Experiences can wait," I whispered to the dog, "death too."

I knew all about death then because in dreams I had been there. I also knew a great deal about love. Love, I thought, was like an orange, a fixed and sharply defined amount. Each person had just so much love to distribute as he may. If one had many people to love then the segments for each person would be fewer and eventually love, like patience, would be exhausted. That is why I preferred to live with my grand-parents then since they had fewer people to love than my parents and so my portion of their love-orange would be larger.

My own love-orange I jealously guarded. Whenever I thought of love I could feel it in my hand, large and round and brightly coloured, intact and spotless. I had moments of indecision when I wanted to distribute the orange but each time I would grow afraid of the audacity of such commitment. Sometimes, in a moment of passion, I would extend the orange to my grandmother or the dog but would quickly withdraw my hand each time.

For without looking I would feel in its place the doll crawl-ing into my hand and nestling there and I would run into the garden and be sick. I would see its face as it lay in the pink tissue of a shoebox tied with ribbons beside the Christmas stocking hanging on the bedpost and I would clutch my orange tighter, thinking I had better save it for the day when occasions like this would arise again and I would need the entire love-orange to overcome the feelings which arose each time I thought of the doll.

I could not let my grandmother know about my being sick because she never understood about the doll. For years I had dreamed of exchanging home-made dolls with button eyes and ink faces for a plaster doll with blue eyes and limbs that moved. All that December I haunted my grandmother's clothes closet until beneath the dresses smelling faintly of camphor I discovered the box and without looking I knew that it came from Miss Evangeline's toy shop and it would therefore be a marvel.

But the doll, beside the Christmas stocking, had half a face and a finger missing. "It can be mended," my grandmother said, "I can make it as good as new. 'Why throw away a good thing?' Miss Evangeline said."

But I could no longer hear, I could no longer see for the one china blue eye and missing finger that floated in my vision. And after that I never opened a box again and I never waited up for Christmas. And although I buried the box beneath the allamanda tree the doll rose up again and again in my throat, like a sickness to be got rid of from the body, and I felt as if I too were half a person who could lie down in the shoebox and sleep forever. But on awakening from these moments, I would find safely clutched in my hand the love-orange, conjured up from some deep part of myself, and I would hug the dog saying, "Our worlds wait outside."

That summer I saw more clearly the worlds that waited. It was filled with many deaths that seemed to tie all the strands of my life together and bore some oblique relationship to both the orange and the doll.

First to die was a friend of my grandparents who lived nearby. I sometimes played with her grandchildren at her house when I was allowed to, but each time she had appeared only as a phantom, come on the scene so silently, her feet shod in cotton stockings rolled down to her ankles, thrust into a pair of her son's broken-down slippers. Her face was flaky, wisps of hair escaping constantly from the scraps of someone's worn-out skirt tied on her head. In all the years I had known her I had never heard her say anything but whisper softly, her whole presence was a whisper, she seemed to appear from the cracks of the house, the ceiling, anywhere, she made so little noise in her coming, this tiny, delicate, slightly absurd old woman who lived for us only in the secret and mysterious prison of the aged.

When she died, it meant nothing to me, I could think then only of my death which I saw nightly in dreams but I could not conceive of her in the flesh, to miss her, or to weep.

The funeral that afternoon was at five o' clock. My grandmother dressed me all in white and I trailed down the road behind her, my corseted, whaleboned grandmother lumbering from side to side in her black romaine 'funeral dress' now shiny in the sunlight, bobbing over her head a huge black umbrella. My grandfather, also in shiny black shoes and suit, stepped ahead of her. Bringing up the rear, I skipped lightly on the gravel, clutching in my hand a new, shiny, bright and bouncy red rubber ball. For me, the funeral, any occasion to get out of the house, the confines of our yard, was like a holiday, like breaking suddenly from a dark tunnel into the sunlight where gardens of butterflies waited.

They had dug a grave in the red clay by the side of the road. The house and yard were filled with people. I followed my grandparents and the dead woman's children into the room where they had laid her out, unsmiling, her nostrils stuffed with cotton. I stood in the shadow where no one noticed me, the room filled with the scent of something I had never felt before, like a smell rising from the earth itself which no sunlight, no butterflies, no sweetness could combat. "Miss Mirie, Miss Mirie," I whispered to the dead old woman, for suddenly I knew that if I gave her the orange to take into the unknown with her it would be safe, a secret between the two of us. I gripped the red ball tightly in my hands and it became transformed into the rough texture of an orange, I tasted it on my tongue, smelled the fragrance. As my grandmother knelt to pray, I crept forward and gently placed between Miss Mirie's closed hands and her body the love-orange, smiled because somehow we knew each other and nothing now would be able to touch either of us. But as I crept away my grandmother lifted her head from her hands, gasped as she saw the ball. She retrieved it swiftly while the others still prayed and hid it in the volumes of her skirt. But when in anger she sent me home, on the way the love-orange appeared comforting in my hands, and I went into the empty house and crept under my grandfather's bed and thought of worlds outside.

The next time I saw with greater clarity the vastness of this world outside. I was asked to visit some new people who lived about a mile away and read to their son. He was very old, I thought then, and he sat in the sunshine all day, his head covered with a calico skull cap. He couldn't see very clearly and my grandmother said he had a brain tumour and would perhaps die. Nevertheless, I would read to him even as I worried about all the knowledge that would be lost if he did not live. For every morning he would take down from the shelf a huge atlas and together we would travel the cities of the world to which he had been.

I was very happy then and the names of these cities secretly rolled off my tongue all day. I wanted very much to give him the orange but held back, for I was not yet sure if he was a whole person, if he would not recover and need me less and so the whole orange would be wasted. So I did not tell him about it. And then he went away with his parents to England, for an operation my grandmother said, and soon he was back only as ashes held on a plane by his mother. When I went to the church this time there was no coffin like Miss Mirie's, only his mother holding this tiny box which was so like the shoebox of the doll that I was sure there was some connection which I could not grasp, but, I thought, if they bury this box then the broken doll cannot rise again.

But the doll rose up one more time because this time it was my grandmother who lay dying. My mother had taken me away when she fell too ill and brought me back to my grandmother's home, even darker and more silent now, this one last time. I went into the room where she lay and she held out a weak hand to me, she couldn't bear it. "Grandma," I said, searching for something more to say, something that would save her, "Grandma, you can have my whole orange," and I placed it in the bed beside her. But she kept on dying and I knew then that the orange had no potency, that love could not create miracles.

"Orange . . .?" my grandmother spoke for the last time, trying to make connections her tired brain couldn't see, "orange . . .?" and my mother took me out of the room and my grandmother died. "At least," my mother said, "at least you could have told her that you loved her, she waited for it."

"But . . ." I started to say and bit my tongue, for nobody, not then or ever would understand about the orange. And in leaving my grandmother's house, the dark tunnel of my childhood, I slammed the car door hard on my fingers and as my hands closed over the bones, felt nothing.

A Bargain

by Dorothy Bingham

Silver, 1974

It's not as if I have not experienced the feeling before. I have felt it several times during my life. Here it comes again . . . starting at the bottom of my abdomen, it moves up, up and out until my unsuspecting belly becomes a confused twisting mass of pain. Then it travels up to my throat, and there it stays . . . choking, strangling me.

Still feeling groggy, I open my eyes wondering what could be causing the discomfort. A sudden weakness attacks my knees, the pain in my belly becomes more demanding . . . opening the door, I rush out of the room and head for the latrine outside. Sitting there, my eyes fall on the torn page of a newspaper. Realisation, like a bolt of lightning, hits me . . . today is the day my sister's examination results will be published!

Convinced of her success, all twinges of anxiety, all pain, weakness, all choking leave me. The usual dismal feelings which used to assail me in this broken-down, ramshackle insult to human dignity . . . this latrine, infested with germ-carrying mosquitoes, flies, cockroaches, and reeking of human urine and faecal matter, are gone.

From there I hear a vehicle stopping at the gate. I run out hastily, thinking that it must be the van bringing the newspaper. As I run, heart pounding, I begin to have doubts. Suppose she doesn't pass? I reach the van to find that it is only the milkman! Observing my desperate hurry and shallow breathing, he asks jokingly, "Ah wheh de fire deh, dahter? Milk can't put it out, yuh know . . . too expensive!"

Smiling weakly, I take the milk, and walking around the house, I go into the kitchen. Mama is fixing breakfast, and leaning on the door. I watch her. "Come, chile, come. Come help me mek de dumplin's. A big woman like yuh, walking around like a living statue . . . bone idle!" she says gruffly. Smiling I reach for the flour pan. I am not put off by her rough tone. I know she isn't as mad about my not helping as she is about my watching her when, with all her defences down, she is just a tired, kind-hearted old soul.

"A living statue!" . . . this, of all my mother's phrases we, my father, sisters, brothers and I find most amusing; and when it's raining and we all sit inside, or my sisters and I might be under the tree outside, helping with the washing, or we might all be cleaning the house on a Saturday night, that is the phrase we tease her most about.

"Mama," I say to her, becoming suddenly serious as my fingers close around the satin-like flour, "yuh know that is today the exam results coming out, Paulette's exam?"

"Any fool would know dat by now, das all de young lady been talking about all week."

"But strange, yuh notice dat not a soul hear a word from her since morning? She mus' be fretting." The kitchen is beginning to get hot and Mama gets up and opens the window as she replies, "Paulette mus' get Religion, me love. She get up bright an' early dis morning – look 'pon de drum, it almos' full ah water."

I look and see that the drum is really almost full, the water is almost touching the last rim. Poor child. Now that I'm thinking about it I realise that she has been unusually helpful all week. I look out and see her coming, and marvelling at the innocence of her reasoning, I smile wryly. I watch her struggling to balance the kerosene tin on her head, the water keeps splashing out, she must have filled it right to the very top – Paulette, who has never yet been known to carry that tin even as much as half-full.

With all the feelings, all the sincerity I'm capable of, I look forward to the day when secure in the knowledge of my relatives' happiness, I will live without watching them in their distress and silently weeping for them. For this day, I will bargain with God. For now I watch my sister. Her dress clings to her, outlining the gentle swell of her breasts where the water has soaked through. I know her thoughts. Within her body which is just beginning to show the first signs of womanliness, is a heart which is still childlike in the simplicity of its faith. How can she not pass her examination after being so helpful and good? A Free Place has to be worked for, and this she knows, so having worked at school to please her Examiners, she now sets out to please God. If God is Just, and she knows Him to be such, then He will reward her good work.

I move away from the window and resume my kneading. As I shape the dumplings, rolling the dough around in my hands, I wonder . . . Is it like this with God? Perpetually He kneels by that legendary riverbank, shaping the earth into human forms. Does He make some rich, some poor? With the dough in my hand I am all-powerful. I have the power to make some of the dumplings big, some small. They, having being made by me, are powerless. They cannot change what they are. Is it like this with Him? If it is, then we as poor people should no longer hope for better. He, our Just God, has made us into what we are, and being from the dirt, some like us are dirt poor and should hope for no relief.

But where on earth is that van? I put the last dumpling into the frying pan and turning to Mama say, "Mama, yuh think Paulette going to pass?" Then before she gets a chance to answer I hurry on, "Ah just can't understan' dese newspaper people, ah mean . . ." Following my mother's gaze, I stop speaking and look out the window. I see my sister. One hand steadies the kerosene tin on her head, and in the other is the newspaper. Her steps are dragging, spiritless. I know those steps. They remind me of the days when for months after leaving school I walked home from the Post Office with letters which began, "We regret to inform you . . ."

I run to her as she empties the water into the drum. As I hug her she says in a dazed voice, "Teacher daughter pass, you know, Rose pass, Mama, she pass."

Granny makes one of her rare appearances, and from the door she observes the scene in silence. Mama stands at the kitchen door, cooking fork in one hand. My smaller sisters and brothers stand around, they do not yet know what has happened but they see enough to make them sad.

"OK, Paulette," I say, trying to cheer her up, "doan bodder to feel any way 'bout it, after all yuh can try again next year."

"But yuh doan understan'," she begins earnestly, "dis was de las' chance ah had, next year me too old to tek it over." It is then that she begins to cry, a sad, drawn-out wail.

Mama goes back into the kitchen, her eyes suspiciously shining, the young ones trailing after her. Granny, shuffling back into her room, puts into words what we are all thinking — "Jackass sey de worl' no level an' ah true." How could Rose, who has never done a single homework without Paulette's help, pass that examination, while Paulette fails? Don't they have any sense in Kingston? Rose's mother can send her to the most expensive school in Jamaica, my God, don't they have any sense at all?

Paulette cries on and in my heart I cry for her. I cannot allow the little ones to see me cry . . . I am the eldest. My father! How am I going to tell him this? Leaving Paulette I go to look for him. He is where he usually is, and seeing him, I do what I usually do.

I watch him. There is no joy in watching a man whose spirit has been completely broken, but there is a strange fascination. What I feel for my father is pity. It is an emotion which I find ugly and distasteful, still, I pity him. If only I could bargain with God. But where are you, God? The Jews have cried to you when often they have been victims of genocidal maniacs. The Christians have cried to you during years of persecution. Man has been calling to you throughout history. The Jews, Christians, Man are still suffering. Where are you, God, where?

Still I watch him. He leans on his shovel and flicks the sweat from his face. He stands still, staring into space, then absent-mindedly he scratches his crotch. He seems to be tired.

The gate creaks and my father looks around. From here I can see the expectant look on his face. I know he thinks it is me, but it isn't, it's only the dog, a sorry looking bitch. I feel sorry for it, and that's why I hate it. Ribs sticking out of an almost hairless body, ears flopping, tail between its legs, I know it wants to run and bark like dogs belonging to rich people but where is it going to get the energy from? Only its eyes look alive. Deep down within their depths there is a faint glimmer of hope which gives them a beauty not found in human eyes. Its other emotions are all human, though. I have seen it nosing around the high fences which enclose the houses of the rich people, and I have seen it longingly look at the proud Alsatians and haughty Siamese cats playing together. I have seen the envy in its eyes. A dog has human qualities.

Papa looks at the dog and I see the beginning of a smile on his face. He is probably, like me, remembering the day he brought the first dog home. That one had been a chubby, playful puppy, small enough to hold in a two-pound paper bag. I smile, there are still some good things left in life . . . memories.

I look at my father, he is no longer smiling. He is now probably recalling the fate of that first dog. I remember my sister screaming as she opened the gate on her way to church. We had all run to her. I'd stared sickly at the dog, its head split cleanly in two. Mama, Papa, all of them had cried. I had not cried, all day long I had gone about my business thinking . . . "What a clean job, whack! right down the middle. Not a swerve to the right, not a swerve to the left, whack! right down the middle." This mad verse had gone through my mind over and over until I had thought that I was going mad. There must be some good things left in life . . . memories?

But God, since you know all things I am asking you – should a man blame a thieving dog for being hungry? Does the fault lie in the dog or in its master? After all, You in Your wisdom did not see it fit to bestow on it the gift of speech. A dog cannot say to a man, "I'll watch for you, if you will give me food."

My brother could have worked, had there been work. He could have bartered also, had he had something with which to barter. But he had been shot through his head by the police, and all day long on that day also another senseless verse had gone careening through my head . . . "What a clean job, BANG! right through his forehead. Not a swerve to the right, not a swerve to the left, BANG! right through the middle."

When I saw the shame in my father's eyes, the grief in my mother and fright in those of the little ones, I had called out to You then, and I am still calling, but now I want to make a bargain.

My sisters and brothers have become quiet children, well behaved. Long gone are the days when they ran and shouted like normal children do. Mama does not have to go looking for them, shouting for one she might need to run an errand. She knows where they are, they are all sitting. All day long they sit, just sit . . . like old people.

I must tell my father that Paulette has failed her examination, but first You, God. God, they are young. They cannot understand the meaning of strikes, the blisters on their feet, the near empty plates in the evenings when the urge to eat remains long after the last bite has disappeared. Most of all they cannot understand why their once laughing parents have become quiet and withdrawn. It is their understanding that I want to bargain about.

I am the only one who understands. Mama thinks they're growing up, and my father thinks they're studying. Studying to do what? Studying to join picket lines? Studying to be laid off? Or probably they are studying so that they will be able to read those endless letters which begin, "We regret to inform you . . ." and blah, blah, blah, blah . . . "keep your application on file." Eh God, what do you think?

I am the only one who understands. I see the vacant look on gaunt faces, eyes staring unseeingly into books which are not being read. I hear the slowness in their steps, the guilty look on their faces when for some trifling reason, not being able to help themselves, they laugh. In the subconscious of their minds there is a sign which reads, "ANYONE CAUGHT LAUGHING WILL BE FINED. THESE ARE HARD DAYS." They do not know this but I do.

I am the only one who knows, that is why I must bargain with God. Let it always be like that. Let them be normal people, happy. Let them never know the hardships of life. Right now, let my father not feel any pain when I tell him what I have to. I will shoulder all the pain, anger, frustration, despair in store for them, You just let them be happy, please. And God, if You find it difficult to do, just imagine to Yourself that it's way back in history when You sent Your angels to destroy all the first-born of the House of Israel. I am the eldest.

Ascot

by Olive Senior

Silver, 1974

"That Ascot goin go far," Mama say. "Mark my words."

"Yes. Him goin so far him goin ennup clear a prison," Papa say. Every time you mention Ascot name to Papa these days the big vein in Papa forehead tighten up and you know he trying hard to control himself.

"Oh gawd when all is said an done the bwoy do well Jackie. Doan go on so," Mama say.

"De bwoy is a livin criminal. Do well me foot. Look how him treat him famly like they have leprosy. Deny dem. Is so you wan you pickney behave. Cho woman. Yu was always a fool," and with that Papa jam him hat on him head and take off down the road.

See here! I don't think Papa ever recover from the day that Ascot come back. This Ascot is a tall red bwoy that born round here. Mama and all the rest of the women did like Ascot who is Miss Clemmy outside son for Ascot come out with fair skin and straight nose and though him hair not so good it not so bad neither. And nobody know who Ascot father is, but is not Dagoman who Miss Clemmie living with all these years for you only have to look at Dagoman to see that.

Anyway this Ascot tall no langilalla and him not so bad looking though him have a mouth so big that when him smile him lip curl but all the women just melt when Ascot smile and say how him bound to go far.

But all that the men remember bout Ascot is that Ascot is a real ginnal and also that Ascot have the biggest foot that anybody round here ever see. Especially Papa.

One time Papa used to miss all kind of thing from the buttery. Now when Papa not looking all we children would tief in there and take like two finger ripe banana or some small thing but nothing serious. Papa would find out and accuse we and we would lie but none of we could lie so good because Mama use to beat the lying out of we and Papa would know the culprit right away so nobody would take it serious. Papa used to say he wouldn't grudge his own children nothing, but is the principle of the thing and he don't like to have his authority undermine and that sort of thing.

Well, anyway, one time a whole heap of big thing start disappear from the buttery – a brand new cutlass, some yam head, a crocus bag and finally, a big bunch of banana that Papa was ripening for the church Harvest Festival. Well sah, all we children used to run in the buttery and look at the bunch of banana till we eye water but none of us would bold enough to touch it for is the most beautiful thing that we ever see in our whole life.

So the Saturday morning before the Harvest Festival one bangarang no bus at the house! Papa go into the buttery and find the whole bunch of banana no gone way clean. Jesus. You should hear the noise he make. Then him calm down and he just stand there a look at the ground for a long time and is sad we think Papa sad for is the best bunch of banana that ever grow. But finally him say, "All right. Is Ascot do it. See him guilt there plain as day. Is Ascot one have foot that size." And is true for we all look at the footprint on the ground and we know is Ascot do it.

Papa say to we, "Doan say a word," and him send off to call Ascot while him close the buttery door and tell all of we to go sit on the verandah like nothing happen. So Ascot come grinning as usual like him expecting food and Papa say, "Come Ascot me bwoy, Harvest Festival postpone and we gwine nyam banana caan done tidday."

As Papa say the word "banana", Ascot not grinning so wide again and he say as if him deaf, "Wha Mass Jackie?" and we all start giggle for him voice come out squeaky like muss-muss and Papa say, "Yes bwoy feas tidday." Then we all walk round to the buttery and Papa throw the door wide open and the first thing that everybody see is the hook where the banana was hanging up empty as night.

"Oh gawd where me Harvest Festival banana gaan—o," Papa shout out. "Ascot look ya me banana no gaan."

"Wha Mass Jackie," Ascot say but you could see that him hanging back. "Nutten could go so afta nobody bol' nuf come in ya an walk weh wid yu banana."

Papa just stand there for awhile as if him studying the situation and then him say, "Ascot me bwoy, yu an me gwine have to play poleece an search fe clues."

Meantime Papa there looking at the ground and then he make as if him just see the footprint and he say, "Ascot look here me bwoy," and by now Ascot look like shame-me-lady macca that just done step on. Papa say, "But wait Ascot. Puddon yu foot ya."

And Ascot bawl out, "Laaad Mass Jackie, is nuh me do it sah."

Papa say, "No? Den puddon yu foot ya, yu tiefing brute," and make to grab after Ascot. But Ascot jump back so braps and fly off like streaking lightning. And from that day on, Papa swear that him wash him hand of Ascot.

Ascot stay far from the house for a good while and anytime he see Papa him take off to bush for Papa walking bout and threatening to shoot him for him banana though you know after a time that Papa enjoying himself so much telling everybody how him frighten Ascot that you can see that him don't mind bout the banana so much after all. But Ascot really have no shame at all and little by little him start hang round the kitchen again when Papa not there and Mama would feed him till finally him round the house almost as often as before.

Anyway my big brother Kenny did come up from May Pen one Sunday and Ascot come up to him when Papa back turn and ask if he couldn't give him job as gardener. And as Kenny don't know bout the banana – and he must be the only person Papa forget to tell – Kenny say all right. And although Papa warn Kenny that him taking up trouble Mama say that at heart Ascot is really a decent honest boy and that all he need is opportunity so when Kenny read to leave Ascot arrive with him bundle and seat himself off in Kenny car please no puss!

"No matter how hard yu wuk an how much money yu make yu will nevva find shoes for dem doan mek dem in fe yu size," was Papa's last word to Ascot.

Well sah, as Papa predict, Ascot don't stay long with Kenny. Little after Ascot gone there we get letter from Kenny say he sending Ascot home for Ascot don't want do nothing round the house and all he do all day is jump behind the wheel of motor car the minute people back turn, and make noise like say he driving. The letter arrive one day and the next day we get another letter say Ascot take his belonging and a few other things that didn't belong to him so maybe he on the way home and good riddance. Anyway, Ascot never turn up at all and Miss Clemmie getting ready to go out of her mind that he is in trouble till she get message say Ascot in Kingston learning to drive. And then one day bout a year after who arrive but Ascot. He wearing a shirt and tie and pants that too short but is all right because it allow you to see Ascot shoes better. Ascot no get shoes! See here, he wearing the biggest pair of puss boot that ever make. It big so till everybody from miles around run to look at Ascot foot in shoes like is the eight wonder of the world. Ascot tell we him driving in Kingston though most people don't believe him. But mark you, from Ascot small he used to tell me how him life ambition was to dress up in white clothes and drive a big white car.

So Ascot stay round for a while doing not a thing and he not smiley-smiley so much and in fact Ascot get very quiet. Then one day him no announce that him get paper to go States as farm worker and the next day him leave us again dress up in him big brown puss boots.

Well, it look like Ascot dead for true this time for nobody hear from him till government send a man down to Miss Clemmie to find out if she hear from him for he skip the farm work in Florida and just disappear right after he reach. Poor Miss Clemmie frighten so till and crying the whole time now for Ascot for the man say that they going to prison Ascot if they find him for he does do a criminal thing. But still not a word from Ascot and everybody give him up for dead or prison except Papa who say that the cat which is the incarnation of the devil have nine life and that is Ascot. About three years pass and Miss Clemmie no get letter from the United States. She beg me read it to her and it say:

Dear Ma wel I am her in New York is big plase and they

have plenty car. I am going to get one yr loving son Ascot.

And he enclose one dollar and no return address. About two year pass and then Miss Clemmie get another letter from the USA which she beg me read. Is from Ascot and it say:

Dear mother, wel here I am in Connecticut. Connecticut is big plais. I driving car two year now but is not white yr. loving son Ascot.

And he send two dollar. Then about a year later she get another letter that say:

Dear Mother Chicago is big plais I drivin white car for a wite man but he don make me where wite is black uniform so I mite leave yr loving son Ascot.

And he send three dollar. "Hey hey," say Papa to Miss Clemmie, "by de time yu get fifty letter yu nu rich." But Miss Clemmie don't laugh for she say she sure Ascot leading bad life. And that the last time she get letter from Ascot.

After that so much time pass that all of we almost forget Ascot. One time Papa did get a little banana bonus so I go to town and come back with some nice meat and Papa go and dig him good yam and the day after that we cook a backra dinner. Papa just sitting on the verandah making the smell kill him and telling me and Mama to hurry up. Next thing we know a big white car no draw up at the gate and turn into the yard. "Eh-eh, is who dat?" Papa say and we all run to the verandah. All we can see is the front door open and two foot stick outside.

"Jesus have mercy, is Ascot," say Mama. "Is Ascot one have foot big so."

"Ascot me teeth. Whe Ascot fe get big car from," Papa say.

But lo and behold. No Ascot! Ascot dress in white from head to toe and though him plenty fatter him teeth kin same way. And a woman get out of the car with him and you can see she foreign from the clothes she wearing and the colour of her hair though I swear afterward is wig.

Eh-eh, Ascot him no rush up to my mother and start hug and kiss her. "Aunt Essie, Aunt Essie," he crying.

"*Aunt* Essie," Papa say, "since when she anyting but *Miss* Essie," but Ascot rushing to him a-cry, "Uncle Jackie," and next thing we know he hugging Papa who turn purple he so vex. "Cousin Lily" – that's me he talking to – and he there hugging me too before I know what happening. Papa stand there with him mouth open like him seeing rolling calf but Ascot so busy a chat don't notice.

"An' this," he say, "is my wife Anthea," and the lady say hello in the American accent.

"Ascot then is really you," Mama saying and she look like she almost crying.

"Yes Aunt Essie is real wonderful to see you," Ascot say and him American accent so thick you could cut it with knife.

"Cousin Lily," he say, taking my hand, "can I speak to you for a minute," and he haul me off into the parlour. "Cousin Lily, you are my friend for a long time now. Right?" So I say "right." "Okay, so just pretend that you is my cousin and this is my house, right?" Eh-eh, I don't know what Ascot playing but this whole thing sweet me so I say OK and call Mama and tell her. Of course she don't understand what really going on so I keep my finger cross.

By the time I get back to the verandah Ascot is there like a man that make out of nothing but energy, is not the Ascot that leave here at all. He just walking and talking and moving his hand up and down the whole time. Then he say to the wife, "Come let me show you around my birthhouse," and next thing he leading her through the whole house as if is him own it. Mama just stand there with her mouth wide open and Papa mouth set while the vein in him forehead beating hard. Then Ascot take the wife into the yard and he there waving him hand and telling her, "And this is my property and this is my coconut tree – you ever see coconut tree with coconut before – and this is where I does bathe when I small and this is our water tank that I did help build."

See ya poppyshow! Well that was bad enough but next thing he gone to Papa cocoa tree and he there saying, "And this is a cocoa tree from which you does get chocolate. Bet you never see that before," and he grab up Papa cutlass and chop off one of the cocoa pod and start cut it up to show her the seed.

Papa start to get up but Mama say "Jackie" and he just sink back down into the chair as if he defeated. Then Ascot and him wife come back on the verandah and sit down and Ascot cock up him foot on the railing. He start chatting away but Papa not opening his mouth and so Mama and me there carrying on conversation. Ascot say him driving him own big white car and he work in a garage but he like one of the boss man now and he so happy that he had to bring his wife back to show her the birthplace where he spent his happy childhood. He also say they staying in hotel in Kingston and they going back that night and is rent they rent the car they driving. That was one thing but next thing I go ask the wife what she do and she announce that she really is a teacher but right now she just finishing up her Master Degree. Master Degree? – Ascot marry woman with Master Degree and he don't even finish third standard in school. See here Lord. We all speechless again.

So Ascot there chatting and chatting and we all getting hungrier and hungrier and the food smelling better and better and it don't look as if they out to leave so finally Mama say in her best speaky-spoky voice, "Would you like a bite to eat?" and I know is show off she showing off on Ascot wife who have Master Degree that she have good food in the house.

"Yes thank you, Aunt Essie. Is long time since I taste you cooking," Ascot say and cross him leg. Papa give Mama such a look that thank God none of them did see. Mama never see either she so please that she entertaining somebody with Master Degree for the highest qualified person she ever meet is Extension Officer and that don't count because is only agriculture him did learn. So we put out all the food that we did cook and Mama take out her best crockery and send down to Miss Melda to borrow the glasses that she did just get from her daughter-in-law in the States and everybody sit down to eat – everybody except Papa who say he not hungry and he don't want anything to eat and we know better than to argue with him when he vex like that.

Well sah. Ascot put down a piece of eating there that I couldn't describe to you and when he done the table clean as a whistle. As soon as they eat done, Mama say, "Well Ascot, I suppose you want to spend some time with Clemmie," and Ascot say, "Clemmie – Oh yes, soon be back," and drive off to see Miss Clemmie. I tell you that was the biggest piece of extraness I ever see because Miss Clemmie live in the next bend in the road and if we want to call her all we do is lean out the kitchen window and shout. But Ascot drive gone and he stay away a long time and I believe is to confuse him wife that Miss Clemmie live a long way away.

About half an hour afterward Ascot arrive with the car full with Miss Clemmie and Dagoman and all the children dress in their best clothes. Ascot say to him wife, "And this is Clemmie and Dagoman," and Dagoman lift his hat and bow and I swear that Miss Clemmie drop a curtsy.

"Oh and do you live nearby?" say the wife to Miss Clemmie.
"Yes ma'am, jus roun de corner."
"And are all these your children?"
"Yes'm. Hascot is the heldes but is not de same faader."
The wife give Ascot a look to kill and is plain she never realise that is Ascot mother.
"But I did almost grow with Aunt Essie," Ascot say quick but you could see him turning red.
"Clemmie," my mother call her inside. "Look here, Clemmie," she tell her, "is you daughter-in-law that. What you calling her ma'am for? Don't keep on saying yes ma'am, no ma'am to everything she say. You hear me?"
"Yes ma'am," say Miss Clemmie and while I inside clearing the table all I can hear is Miss Clemmie saying "yes ma'am no ma'am" to everything her daughter-in-law saying.
Miss Clemmie keep on looking at Ascot as if he is stranger and Dagoman sit on the bench outside as if he too fraid to come near the lady. The children start play round the car and make as if to open the door and Ascot snap at them so till my mother had to say, "Hi, Ascot, is your own little brothers you treating so."
"Half-brother," Ascot say.
From then on things just get from bad to worse. Ascot look like he vex can't done at Clemmie, and the wife and the step-father look like they vex can't done with Ascot. So finally Ascot say, "Come let me take you all home for I have to get back to Kingston tonight." But by this time Dagoman face set and he say he prefer to walk and Miss Clemmie and the children get into the car alone and even though Miss Clemmie look like she going to cry you can still see that she feeling proud to have her son driving her in car. But as they drive off all we can hear is Ascot a shout at the children to take their dirty foot off the car seat.
By the time Ascot get back he grinning all over again like old time but you could see that everybody feeling kind of shame and just waiting for him to go. So he finally jump up and start kiss us goodbye only when he put out his hand to Papa, Papa wouldn't take it though he shake hands with the wife and talk nice to her for he say afterward that she was a nice mannersable woman and is a shame that she mix up with a criminal like Ascot. So at long last Ascot and his wife drive off the way they did come with plenty horn blowing and hand

waving.

Mama was the only one that wave back though, and long after the car out of sight she there waving and smiling. "That Ascot," she say. "Fancy that. A wife with Master Degree. I did know he was goin' get far you know."

"Well he can stay far de nex' time," Papa shout out and walk out of the house.

Next day it all over the district how Miss Clemmie have daughter-in-law with Master Degree and how Ascot proper, and hire big car and staying at hotel in Kingston. But is only me one Miss Clemmie did tell how there was not a bite to eat in the house that day and Ascot never even leave her a farthing. This vex me can't done especially how he did gormandise up all Papa food. So right then and there I start tell her what kind of good-fe-nutten Ascot is. And is only afterward that I realise that Miss Clemmie not listening to a word I saying.

"Dat Hascot. I did always know he wudda reach far yu know," she say almost to herself and her eyes shining like ackee seed.

The Art of Kite Flying

by Michael Reckord

Silver, 1977

Flying kite not easy. You got to know a lot of things if you want to be successful at it.

Them boy think the hardest thing about flying kite is making the kite. Them say you have to get bamboo, which not easy nowadays when them cutting down all the bamboo trees to put up housing project, and you have to get kite paper, and paste and cord. And you got to cut everything right and paste and string up right.

But for me that's the easiest part. In fact, I don't worry with making the kite at all. I just buy it.

I say to myself, what's the use of spending days making kite when the first time you fly it a gust of wind catch it and rip it up, or the kite string bust and the kite fly away to kingdom come, or the tail drop off and the kite go crashing into your neighbour coconut tree?

No, the hardest thing is not getting the kite – is keeping it. To be able to keep it, you got to study the wind; you got to study the whereabouts of the light-posts and the trees; you got to study the strength of kite cord. But even after all that studyration, the kite still can end up in the neighbour coconut tree. And you will have to go get it; nobody going get it for you. That brings me to the hardest study of all: to keep your kite, you got to study people.

You with me? I mean, what will happen if you don't know your neighbour, or you on bad terms with your neighbour and you kite end up in them yard? You kite dead, right? Cause what? If you and you neighbour not talking, and you go into them yard and climb them tree without permission, them will set them dog on you. Or shoot you.

So my policy is know your neighbour and act pleasant towards them, even if you can't love them in your heart. For I admit it hard, even impossible, to love all the whole heap of people next door, and for all of them to love you.

After all, them dog come into your yard and dig up your rose bed; and you can't keep the hedge between you as neat as them want it. And them mango drop and rotten in your yard – the common mango that you don't want, not them Bombay which you wouldn't mind. And the man quarrel with the wife every Friday night when him come home drunk; and even though you don't want to hear, those Mona houses so close together that you can't help it. So you get to know all them business, and no way somebody going love you when them know that you know all them business.

You see what I mean? Neighbour can't love each other; them is natural enemies. But you can get along, and you can have a friend in the enemy camp. I have Mrs. Ferguson. She is my key, even though me and her son, Freddie, not talking.

Right now the reason me and Freddie, who is a year older than me – that is fourteen – not talking is because of the same kite business. Him make the kite last week and I buy it from him for a dollar. That is, I promised to pay him a dollar; but as I had only fifty cents at the time, I give him that and say that him would get the rest later.

I did really mean to give him. But after I take the kite and look at it good, I see that it never look as pretty and as strong as when him had it in him yard. So I tell him that I change me mind and would only give fifty cents for the kite.

"Fifty cents! You mussi mad."

"It not worth more. Look pon the flimsy paper. The bamboo look like it will break any time. And it don't glue together good."

"Give me back then."

"You lucky I give you so much."

"Give me back me kite." He made a grab for the kite over

the fence, but I slipped him.

"Your kite? I bought it from you. Is mine now."

"You said you'd pay a dollar."

"It not worth a dollar."

"Well give me back. See your fifty cents here."

"That's your fifty cents. And this is my kite. And I not selling."

"You damn tief."

"Like you relative."

"Give me back me kite."

"You want come for it?" I walked casually to the gate and squeezed the padlock shut – I'd open it later when Daddy was due home – and went inside with the kite. Through the curtain I saw that Freddie was still at the fence. He was staring at the fifty cents, and I thought he was going to throw it over into the yard, which would suit me, but then he pushed it into his pocket and went into his house.

The phone rang. "I'll get it, Mama," I shouted. "Hello."

It was Freddie, wanting to speak to my mother. "She not here." I hung up. I waited, but the phone didn't ring again.

"Who was it, Jim?"

"Wrong number, Mama." Fortunately, she hadn't come out of the kitchen. In my room I tore my old pyjama pants into strips for a tail.

Daddy brought home some cord for me next day and Sunday I climbed on the house top and cast off into the wind.

Flying kite not easy. The wind was strong, but it was ten minutes before I could get the kite mounting up into the air. It was just thirty yards up when it started drifting towards the electric lines. I jerked it away and a down current must have caught it for it dipped suddenly and – guess what? – the cord caught in the Ferguson's lime tree. The kite spun around a few times, twisted in a figure of eight and fell . . . just beyond the lime tree and hung there, halfway to the ground.

Feeling sick, almost crying, I stared at it. What was I to do? Where was Freddie? The picture of him coming through his door and seeing the kite in his lime tree loomed large in my mind. He'd be sure to grab it, and my kite and fifty cents would be gone forever. Or had he gone out? Could I risk sneaking over into his yard and rescuing my kite? No, the Alsatian would be sure to start barking and attract attention, and if Freddie came out I'd be sure to get a lick in addition to losing my kite.

Should I ask Mama to come watch while I went for the kite? That way even if Freddie came out he wouldn't dare hit me — not with Mama watching. But whatever I did I had to do quickly — the longer I delayed the greater the chance of Freddie finding the kite.

I cut the kite cord with my penknife and stuffed the ball in my pocket, then I climbed off the roof and went to stand by the bougainvillea hedge. I kept hidden as best I could while checking on movements next door.

Fifteen minutes passed without anyone appearing. Then Freddie came out on the verandah with the Sunday paper comics. He sat on the ledge and read for about ten minutes. I prayed he wouldn't look up and see the kite or the kite cord which stretched from our telephone line to his lime tree. God must have heard me for Freddie finished reading and went inside without even glancing upward.

Ten more minutes passed. The sun was hot on my neck; ants kept crawling into my sneakers. Then Mrs. Ferguson appeared, my spar, with a pruning scissors in her hand. She headed for the rose beds.

Now, what should my approach be? I was pretty certain that Freddie hadn't told her about my owing him money for the kite; he was getting to the secretive, rebellious age. But then again he might have, and I couldn't just ask to be allowed to get my kite without knowing exactly what the position was. On the other hand I didn't want to tell her straight out that I owed her son fifty cents. I had to be subtle.

"Mrs. Ferguson. Good morning."

"Oh, good morning, Jim. How are you?" She thinks I'm cute.

"Fine, thanks. Is Freddie inside?"

"Yes. You want him?"

"No, no. I just wondered if he said anything to you about fifty cents."

"For what?"

"Oh, it have to do with my kite."

"Your kite?"

"Yes. That kite." I pointed upward to the kite cord. Her gaze followed the cord to the lime tree. "It met in an accident with your lime tree."

"Oh dear."

"I wonder if I could come and get it."

"But of course. You want –"

Without waiting to hear more I ran through my gate and into hers. The Alsatians were lying there and I said, "Hello Monty, Buster," as I walked carefully around them. They looked toward Mrs. Ferguson, wondering if they should bark; but as it was such a hot day and as she was there they must have decided against it. They'd need all their energy for their nightly two-hour barking session.

"You want me to call Freddie to help you?" Mrs. Ferguson asked.

"No thanks, I can manage."

I couldn't climb the tree, too many prickles, so I used the picking stick leaning up under the mango tree and started pulling at the kite cord, drawing the length from over our telephone line towards the lime tree so that the kite would fall – gently, I hoped, and without hitching in the tree to the ground.

Mrs. Ferguson cut roses while I carried out my task. I kept one eye on her, for I didn't want her going inside before I finished. She'd be sure to tell Freddie I was outside.

"Mrs. Ferguson."

"Yes."

"You're taller than me. I wonder if you could use the stick and get the kite tail free from that branch for me. Is only keeping the kite up there."

"All right."

She put down the roses, came over and took the stick from me. She's getting plump now that she's middle aged, but she's still active and handled the picking stick better than I did.

All the same the operation was taking longer than I'd expected and I was nervous about Freddie coming out again.

As she poked at the kite tail I started telling Mrs. Ferguson about how much Mama admired her roses. What Mama had really said was that it seemed as if Mrs. Ferguson was still watering her plants even with the water restrictions in force, but I didn't bother mention that part.

Mrs. Ferguson was telling me about pruning and fertiliser when the kite tail got free and fell towards me. I pulled at it while keeping an eye on the front door for Freddie.

Then at last the kite came low enough for Mrs. Ferguson to catch hold of it. I pulled the cord from the tree, rolled it up and took the kite.

"Thanks very much for your help." I gave her my sweetest

smile.

"Oh, don't mention it."

"Bye."

"Bye. And be careful of those power lines."

"I will." I headed for the gate.

Then in a just-remembered-something-voice she called: "By the way, Jim, didn't you say something about fifty cents."

I turned. "Oh, that. It's just that Freddie had promised to sell me this kite for fifty cents. I gave him a dollar and he promised to give me fifty cents change yesterday. Maybe he didn't have it."

"But he got his allowance yesterday. I'll remind him he owes you the money."

"No, don't bother. He was selling it too cheap anyway. I showed it to a friend of mine this morning and he said a dollar was just right."

I walked around the Alsatians and through the gate. I closed it behind me and raised the kite in salute to Mrs. Ferguson. "Please don't even mention the matter to Freddie," I said.

She smiled and waved back. My key. I tell you, in this life you have to get along with people.

The Horse Doctor

by Nova Gordon

Gold, 1979

The blue eyes at the top of the wall vanished. They appeared again between the rust red rails of the gate, the pink stub of nose pressed hard against the lower cross rails. Above the tousled waves of pale auburn, the upper iron rails had been bent and painted bright silver into the outline of a lion's head, the mane flying far back to where it became a shimmering mass of green vine which snarled the length of the stone wall. Above the lion's head the gate rails continued upwards, spear-tipped, one or two bent slightly and twisted inward.

"Give it . . ." I held my palm open wide, the fingers straining. "Give it back!"

I edged nearer to the gate.

Lee held the peppermint stick, rainbow striped, up to his nose and sniffed. The glass blue eyes shot an arrow of jest my way. He laughed and put the peppermint between his teeth.

I pushed a hand between the rails. He jumped back. "Give it back!"

I tried to shake the gate . . . tried to shake it down on him.

"Come in and get it back . . ."

He was sitting cross-legged on the pebbled driveway, the peppermint hanging from his lips and glistening with saliva.

I pulled my hands away from the gate, my palms sore and a

dirty red.

"Close your eyes and open your mouth . . ."

He was standing now, face pressed into the lion's silver mane, his shorts pulled far up into his groin, baring the trim muscles of his thin, pale legs.

I put my fists over my eyes and opened my mouth wide until the corners hurt.

"Here!"

I choked. Dry dirt stung my face and slithered down the back of my tongue . . . Lee laughed . . . The dirt kept coming, dirt and pebbles burying themselves in my hair and nostrils . . .

. . . I screamed.

The outhouse door was jarred into place and the heavy iron bolt shoved into position outside. The scream petered out, fading into painful whimpers which themselves waned into a hollow silence.

The beam from the oil lamp which had seeped in where the outhouse door had cracked down the centre, retreated, leaving a refuse of stifling darkness.

I squirmed through the darkness as far as the water barrel where two rough walls met in a narrow corner and the wood floor had become coarse and splintered.

I pulled my knees up to my chin, burying my cheeks between them and watching the darkness hang around me.

Faceless shadows squeezed themselves through the crevices and wavered about in the corners waiting for me to move so they could lunge at me . . . They were outside too, hovering in midair or crouching among the yam hills and in the pea trees alongside the house.

I crossed myself. "Red cloth . . ."

The shadows dissipated. I closed my eyes in case they came back. They always did.

Dried leaves and twigs snapped among the pea trees outside and a sharp bark punctuated a low growl . . . The shadows never growled. They only whispered and muttered . . . The growling continued, muted but near enough to the outhouse to sound loud.

Ma had forgotten to give me a candle and I had not had time to bring my shoe box. He had come earlier than usual . . .

. . . He used to come late in the night, just after Ma had bathed, rubbed scented cream on her thighs and rolled her hair up on top of her head and pinned it there with bright coloured combs.

She used to put me on the back steps to cut pictures out of newspapers while he was there.

Then the shadows had appeared, scurrying through the darkness, hunchbacked, grinding their teeth. One night one had come right up to me and flashed past my face in a cold breeze which kept my cheeks tingling. I took my pictures back inside.

They had been together, talking in low, strained voices, the bunk grating the floor, the springs groaning.

I dropped the scissors.

Ma had come out to me her hair plastered around her wet face, the combs hanging on to thin strands and a blanket wrapped loosely around her, shoulders bare and shiny wet above the collar bones.

I was put in the outhouse that night, and locked in there every night when he came . . .

. . . A low whistle called the growling away from the door of the outhouse. The harsh grate and whine of an engine preceded the crumble of dirt and stone under heavy rubber tyres. He was going back up to the big house.

One night his jeep had broken the standpipe in the front yard and there had been puddles . . . mud and brown puddles . . . all around the house the next morning . . . Lee said I looked like mud, all half-breeds looked like mud. . .

The beam from the oil lamp returned slicing the darkness and settling in a warm puddle on the floor. . .

She was a silhouette in the corner by the washstand where the lamplight barely touched the darkness, making a thin wash of grey. She slid into her nightgown slowly, pulling it down gently over her curves and around her wide hips and protruding buttocks. The lamp flickered and she looked up.

There were matchsticks strewn all over the floor, used matchsticks burnt almost halfway down the stems. She moved into the light, bending low to sweep the matchsticks into a corner with her palm.

"You finish?"

She straightened, the thin blue straps of her nightgown sliding below the deep, black ridges of her shoulders.

"Bedtime." The voice was soft, deceptive, like that of a woman invulnerable to anger.

She took the mug of partly drunken wash from me and disappeared behind the chenille spread which separated the bedroom from the rest of the house.

The house succumbed to darkness and I was aware only of Ma's soft breathing as she bent over me to push open the windows and settle down in the bunk beside me.

I lowered my head to her full warm bosom. She smelt of cheap talc and rum. There had been an empty quart bottle of white rum on the floor by the bed. She had carried it out with my mug.

The faces hung in the moonlight on the chenille, huge faces twisted and distorted, staring sombrely at me and moving a little when the wind came in through the open window.

"Red cloth . . ."

I buried my face in Ma's armpit. She was warm and damp, her bosom heaving, and her breath coming in whistles.

"Is not dat ah don't want him to see you, Seanie . . ."

There was effort to make the words come. She squeezed a finger into the soft of my arm. "Is jus dat when he is here we got things to talk about. . . We got things to talk about an yu is a chile. . ."

The faces smiled.

"An yu don't have to stay out dere long either. . ."

I thought of the matchsticks swept into the corner by the window. I would collect them in the morning . . . Collect them and put them in my shoe box.

"He know you out dere. . ."

I wanted to tell her about the peppermint . . . about Lee. . .

"I always remind him. . ."

She would have to get me some more, Lee had taken my last one. . .

"So he try not to stay long. . ."

The faces grinned widely at me as they merged into one gross face. I winced.

There were caterpillars on the front wall of the house. They had been sprinkled there from the orange tree and clung desperately for life on the nog. There were dozens of them, soft, green larvae wriggling and contracting into themselves.

Ma kept an eye on her pepper tree by the porch. She did not want the caterpillars nestling there and eating off the leaves.

I picked a caterpillar off the wall and examined it between

my fingers. Ma slapped me. She made me put it back on the wall and wash my hands at the standpipe with brown soap and lime . . . "next thing" I would be getting "bumps and sore all over . . ."

The gully narrowed into a maze of bush and dirt infested with prickles. It was a good place to hunt lizards or mongooses if you could keep clear of the cowitch.

The floor of the gully was hard, the dirt parched dry by the sun. Meagre common mango trees bristled crisp green leaves in the heat while clumps of rough scrub and bushes gnarled their way down the gully slopes.

"Want to catch lizards?"

Lee fixed his slender body in front of me. "There're a whole heap of them in the bush. . ."

There were bright red patches on his cheek and forehead. I shook my head and tried to push past him. He put all his weight into the foot that came heavily down on mine. One thin arm circled my waist and flung me backwards into the dirt.

"Sorry. . ."

He scuttled off on all fours, his slingshot in his hand, looking back over his shoulder to smile.

"Sorry. . ."

The pipe gurgled and spat.

"Got to give you some bitters. . ."

Her hands emerged from the metal basin and plunged in again fiercely, tiny white suds flying. "You rompin up in di dirt gettin all kinds o' things."

I had ringworm once. . . on my left ankle. Ma had rubbed some bush on it until my leg became a pale green. Pa brought some medicine in a tube. The ringworm went away.

"I been tellin him to get you into a good school. . ."

I examined my mangoes. I had picked them in the gully.

"A real good school like the one Massa Lee goin to. . ."

One was burst and bled orange-coloured pulp.

"He said he can't send you there. . ."

It was flecked with black. It was not good.

"Can't send you and Massa Lee to the same school. . ."

She was standing straight now, her palms flat against her buttocks, her eyes taking me in in short, swift movements. She had turned off the pipe but water still dripped into the basin.

"They ripe?"
She lifted the basin from under the pipe, her fingers pinched white, the knuckles a soft grey.
"Not yet. . ."
I could wrap them in brown paper.
"They not fit. . ."
She rested the basin on her hip.
"Not goin ripe good. . ."
I threw them away.

I scouted among the yam hills and pea trees for bits of twig and leaves for my shoe box. There were two deep gaps where Ma had dug up yams. She always said I should learn how to do it myself. I would not have her around forever. She never let me do it in the end however. She did not want me catching anything from the dirt. . .
"Hey, Caroline, das yu likkle bastard man?"
The one-eyed man selling fish from a large icebox closed the lid of his one good eye and opened it again quickly, his face wrinkled like crumpled bread paper.
Ma's hand closed in around mine. I was dragged roughly alongside her.
"But Caroline, he not growin, man. . ."
The man's collar bones jutted out like weals beneath his neck.
The people were laughing. I could see the wave of white teeth and convulsing black bodies from the corners of my eyes.
"Yu bes get he Papa to sen him to one o' dem fancy doctas in Kingston, Caroline. . ."
"Black shit!" Ma whispered fiercely, her market basket clutched closely to her in the crook of her arm.
The smell of fish, pungent and rank, filled my nostrils.
"Wha di hat for Caroline. . .? Eh, wha's it for?"
My hand moved defensively up to my sun-bleached straw hat.
"Yu ent want him gettin black like me, eh, Caroline. . .?"
The fish man had been swallowed up by the crowd and only his voice seeped through the minute spaces.
"Cover he up good, Caroline. . ."
The stench of fish and stale sweat was stifling.
"Shouldn' bring him down here, Caroline. Yu shoulda lef him up wid him Papa. . ."
A fat woman selling yams hid her lips behind a large, white handkerchief, her body convulsing and her black eyes wide and

sparkling.

"Missa Thomas wouldn' mind tekkin care o' him eh, Caroline?"

The crowd around us had gotten thicker. The heat and the noise surged.

"You goin be raisin a brood wid Missa T, eh, Caroline. . .?"

Stale sweat and the smell of fish. . . heat and the smell of stale sweat. . .

"Dem odas yu give some o' Missa T's estate boys. . ."

A heavy feeling like hard phlegm settled in my chest.

"Yu hide dem now das yu got yu likkle mulatti, Caroline. . .?"

The crowd loosened and a man in a bloodstained merino and khaki shorts rushed through holding a goat up by its fore-legs, the stomach split open and dripping. I shrieked.

The fish man now restored to view pointed a long knife at me. "Po lil ting, eh, Caroline. . .?"

The smell of blood and raw meat persisted long after the man and the goat had disappeared. I became sick all over the market ground.

There was not much candle left, only an indented disc of melting wax from which the wick burned pale blue . . . I set out my houses on the outhouse floor. There were six of them . . . matchsticks tied together with strong thread and covered with cardboard. . . The candle flickered and a stream of hot wax crept across the floor . . . my houses needed trees . . . sweet orange trees . . . I tied two matchsticks together with a clump of green leaves between . . . I would need a bottle cover . . . a bottle cover filled with wet dirt in which to plant it.

Rex was scratching at the door, growling and scratching. Two black furry paws squeezed in through the space beneath the door and raked at the floor . . . I needed more trees, big trees . . . big common mango and orange trees . . . Rex whined.

I hit my fist against the door. He barked loudly, powerfully. I put my hands over my ears . . . The candle went out.

"When you see the mongoose, you fire quick before he gets away."

Lee's eyes were focused on the bush, his sleek form stretched out on the ground, his hair lapped wildly out of his face by the breeze into a waving mass behind his ears.

The thick red rubber of his slingshot was pulled far back between the thumb and forefinger of his left hand. His right arm trembled, his breath audible.

Before us the gully sloped gently downwards among a thick snarl of bushes. A trail of sugar-coloured ants poured out of a hole in the dirt and passed by a few inches from my nose. I watched them, barely moving my eyes to follow their course. They disappeared in a clump of weeds and reappeared some distance away in a ring of dull brown around a mound of putrid green mango.

"There it is. . ."

I did not look up, afraid to move.

"See it, Sean. . .?"

I held my breath and closed my eyes.

I heard the stone buzz through the air and the dull thud which followed.

"You pushed me . . . Goddamnit, you pushed *me*. . ."

Lee's elbow dug into my side. "You made me miss. . .!"

I spun onto my back. All his weight was on top of me squeezing the breath out of me. . .

"Dammit, you made me miss . . . Goddammit!"

The pale arms tried to lift my head, tried to slam it down against the ground. I felt ants all over my face, creeping slowly up my cheeks and digging their stings into my flesh.

"You – made – me – miss!" He counted the words, his face flushed red and full. I struggled.

His fingers dug into my arm and raked the skin there. Terror drained the strength from me and numbed the pain. Lee's teeth met fiercely into a white grille of anger.

Behind him the sky was lost in a blurry haze in which his sobs and curses resounded. His blows weakened and, as they became fewer and less frenzied, I felt the pain rising with the water in my mouth.

He rolled off, his slingshot hanging from his lips by the rubber band. I did not move. I watched the sky and tree tops take shape again out of a chaos of swirling blue and green.

Lee stood up. The redness had left his face and the smile broadened into a grin. He stared hard at the bush before him.

"You ever been down here in the evenings?"

I did not answer. The water was dribbling out at the corners of my lips.

"I've been down here . . . twice. . ."

I spat out the last drops of water.

"I've seen the cowherds down here after working hours, they

and some women lying around. . ."

He laughed.

He had told Pa, he said, and Pa had sent Tom, the headman, down to chase them out. . .

The orange tree spread sparse branches over the zinc eaves of the house where it had spattered dead leaves and twigs. Some of the branches hung as low as the porch rails where the tomato vines trailed.

The bird seemed to be asleep on one of the lower branches from which the round, green fruit hung in loose clumps. It had come into the yard with the flocks of pigeons which fed on the coconut trash Ma flung into the back yard.

It was not like the other birds. It was bigger, and the brown feathers never lay smoothly on its back but in ruffles and as far apart from each other as the bright orange toes stuck closely together. Its head was grotesquely larger than that of any ordinary pigeon and the sound it made, when it did make a sound, was something of a croak.

It did not fly away either, like the other birds, when I descended on it with my slingshot. Its only response to one of my bottle stoppers on its broad side was a harsh croak and a solemn stare from the blue pellets in its large black head.

The others pecked at it sometimes when Ma flung the coconut out. I chased them away.

The bird slept either on the roof of the outhouse or in the open yard, its head flung back from its breast, the white of its throat absorbing the moonlight. Ma said it was some 'ole ige' in disguise. She chased it out of the yard.

"He beat you like dat?"

Ma removed the cover from a black iron pot and almost vanished behind a curtain of steam. "What you do him?"

I did not answer.

"Mus' have been something real bad."

I scuffed my toes in the dirt floor of the kitchen and watched the small red eyes peeping out at me from the cluster of black coal beneath the pot.

"Don't want yu fightin wid him, Seanie. . ."

The eyes glowed brighter.

"Massa Lee's a good boy."

There was a whole pile of used matchsticks beside the coal

pot. I scooped them up.

"Goes to a good school too."

I would ask Ma for some more string later.

"Wish I could get you there. . ."

She replaced the pot cover and wiped her hands in her skirt. "Mama's dolly baby." She slid a warm forefinger under my chin and stared at me sheepishly with silent pleasure.

Around us the kitchen simmered in a pale grey blue while the charcoal crackled gently.

"Goin talk to yu Pa bout Lee." She passed her thumb over my cheek. "Can't have him thumpin yu up like dat."

I pressed my face into the warmth of her cotton blouse and she nestled her chin in my hair.

"Can't have him thumpin yu up like dat none 't all. . ."

The tamarinds had not yet ripened. The hard shell would have to be scraped off to get at the tart fruit inside . . . green tambrin' was good with wet sugar. Ma had wet sugar at home in a pail but not much. She had not stayed long enough in the market to buy more from the bald-headed Syrian man who sold sugar-head and hair ribbons. I would take some tamarinds home anyway. . .

They had swarmed down on the tamarind tree just outside the pasture lands with stones and sticks. They were estate children, anaemic and dull-eyed in their fathers' cast-offs or their mothers' frocks tied at the waist with ribbon or cord.

Their legs were black spotted, and here and there the black spots ruptured into sores on their knees and ankles or bled and formed soft scabs.

They filled old baskets and paper bags with tamarind, chattering and swearing as, with expert aim, they brought the fruit down.

I moved closer to one of the smaller boys.

"Is not mine. . .!" He held his bag away and scanned me with wide eyes.

There was defiance in the sudden silence and the stares. I was aware of the sticks, of the stones . . . Bags lay half-filled on the ground and a girl held the edges of her skirt up to receive more fruit . . . I had seen black men, black women fight. I knew their hellish anger. These were their children, the offspring of their flesh and their manners, their fingers readier to release the fruit than the sticks or stones. . .

"Stop picking my father's tamarinds. . .!"

I tried to meet the stares equally. "I goin tell him you pickin dem."

Lee said all the land belonged to Pa. All of it.

"He don't want nobody pickin his things. . ."

They shuffled and a few stepped back disassociating themselves from their companions.

"Give him a bag!"

The huge negro, khaki clad, strolled up from the direction of the pasture leading a bedraggled mule.

"Give him a bag!"

He shouted fiercely, this time prodding a small boy, the smallest in the group, with his black boot.

The boy handed me his bag of tamarinds before turning beseeching eyes on the man, and scratching a hairless patch in his head timidly.

"Can deh go now, baas?"

The man was smiling, his arms folded over his chest. "Deh won't be foolin on yu property nex time, baas."

He pushed a tongue between the space in his front teeth. "Tell yu Ma Tom'll be seein her, y' hear?"

He winked. "Seein her some time early tomorrow mornin."

The children were still there, staring and picking the scabs on their feet.

"Git!"

The man pulled his belt from his waist and cracked it in the air over their heads.

They fled.

"He beat him real bad . . . real bad. . ."

The two figures were silhouetted in the darkness about my bed.

"Lee need a lil talkin to. . ."

Ma's voice was strained and anxious. "He complainin . . ."

He was there. I could smell the strong sweetness of his scent and the richness of tobacco.

"I don't wants no trouble. . ."

What little I knew of him I heard from Lee.

"He scratch up bad real bad. . ."

He had a gun, and a whole trunk of bullets. He had killed a man once. He would shoot me too if I gave any trouble, Lee said.

"You sleepin, Seanie?"

Ma spoke gently.

"Roll up yu shirt. . ."

She pulled the pajama from over my stomach.

"See dem dere, a whole heap of bruise. . ."

A strange hand found its way to my stomach, the fingers moving roughly over the tender bruises.

"Ma!"

The same terror which Lee's frenzies injected into me seized me now.

"Ma!"

"Hush, Seanie. . ."

The hand went away.

There were retreating footsteps. They had gone away.

The faces sneered at me from the chenille and outside the shadows tapped at the wall trying to get in. I crossed myself twice. The faces frowned.

"Red cloth . . . red cloth. . ."

Ma came to bed shortly. She lay silently on her back until the grate and whine of his jeep had subsided.

"Yu not to get into no more fight wid Lee. . ."

Her face was close to my ear and the warm breath tickled.

"He start it!" I dug my fingers into the sheets.

"Yu Pa seh yu not to get into no more fight wid Lee!" A frantic ire flew into her voice.

"He start it!"

"Yu want me doin yu up worse dan Lee. . .!"

I turned my face to the wall.

"He lef some money to get some ointment fo yu. . ."

The moonlight made fine patterns on the wall.

"Two pound. . ."

The pattern was like a thin web, all intricate and delicate. . .

"An yu not to get into no more fight wid Lee!"

. . . A thin web all intricate and delicate. . .

"Mawnin, baas. What yu doin out so early?"

The negro leaned over the rails of the porch, his shirt hanging open. "Yu might ketch a draught, yu know. Yu good folks is delicate."

The tip of his tongue wagged at me from the gap between his teeth. "Enjoy your tamarind, baas?"

My fingers tightened around my mug.

"Whas dat, baas . . . Red wine?" He put a finger on the edge of the mug and tipped it towards him. "Man yu shouldn' be drinkin chocolate, it not good 'nough for you. . ."

A flash of mock gravity swept across his face.

"Yu want something?" Ma appeared in the doorway, one half of her hair in plaits, the other left free.

"What a question!" Tom whistled.

"Yu don't answer yet." There was a smile at the corner of Ma's lips.

"Sure I want something, but it seems mightier powers beat me to it . . . eh, baas?"

His yellow eyes, red-veined, met mine and he laughed powerfully.

Ma looked down and finished buttoning her housecoat. A weak giggle escaped her.

"Yu beggin food, Tom. . .?"

"No missus . . . no missus. . ."

I took a quick sip from my mug when his eyes left me.

"Don't got no time to chat dis mornin." Ma did not look up.

"What yu doin mek yu so busy. . .?" Tom hoisted himself over the rails.

Ma laughed openly this time. "None of yu business. . ."

"Well if yu need any help. . ." He winked at Ma and laughed.

"No thank you."

I sipped.

"Enjoyin it, baas?"

I started. Some spilled.

"He shoulda been a girl, Caroline. . ."

Ma met his eyes questioningly. He nodded.

"He should been a girl . . . Dem kinds look better when deh is girls. The kind o' colour look better on girls and di hair would a look better plaited . . . in long plaits. . ."

Ma smiled. "I have to cut his hair plenty. . ."

Tom grinned. "Fine boy, though. . ."

Ma put a hand on my shoulder and squeezed it hard. "Dem boys up at di big place . . . dem . . . well I not sayin nuttin. . ."

Tom folded his lips. He pulled me to him. He smelt of cattle, but predominantly of goats. The negroes raised goats . . . mainly for their food . . . Lee said they ate all of the goat . . . every part. . .

"Dis likkle baas here gettin good food effen nothing else, eh, Caroline?"

I struggled free.

"All he need now is a good black nayga pappa fi warm he hide now and then when he gets up to trouble. . ."

Ma's hands were on her hips. She shrugged.

"Should really take him up to the big house to meet the missus, Caroline. . ." He broke into peals of laughter. "She woulda please, eh, Car?"

Ma smiled.

The white pickets, thinly laced with large green-leaved creepers, cut across the pastures sealing off a square of shredded emerald dotted with large purple umbrellas, the silver stems glistening and winking above round tables porcelain white.

They sat, they talked, they laughed, they played, fat men with bulbous red noses and cheeks the colour of stale porridge, pale women iced with sweet talc, their hair swept up beneath silk scarves which fluttered in the wind, and children, pink-faced and red-cheeked, scampering over the green, their shrill voices above the glassy laughter of their elegant mothers.

He sat with them, powerfully angular, one thick leg flung over the knee of the other, his head thrown back to make the laughter come. Rex, shiny black and white chested, was stretched out at his feet.

The 'stinkin' toe' tree hung its fruit low over the pickets. I picked two of the long pods and broke one open. Ma did not like me eating them so I did not take any home. I ate them right there by the green.

A child screamed. One of the pinkest of the lot, a boy with bright ginger hair, raced across the green hiding his face in his hands. A bigger boy sped after him, his brown hair flying. The small boy fell. The bigger boy was intercepted by another boy, a taller boy, carrying a cricket bat.

Lee said something and the taller boy let him go. The ginger-haired boy had retired to the lap of a woman in a yellow scarf to stare petulantly over her shoulder at me before sticking out a wet, pink tongue.

"Going to catch one . . . going to catch one early and take him up to the house."

Lee dug a neat round hole in the ground with his finger. "I alone goin do it too. . ."

He spoke to the hole and the spray of dirt that his finger

brought up.

"I caught one once . . . over by those bushes. . ."

He indicated a clump of fine-leaved weeds.

"He didn't even get a chance to bite me. . ."

He dug furiously at the ground.

"When I have a whole heap I'll sell you one. . ."

He looked up and grinned. "I'll sell you one for twenty pounds . . . You'll have to feed it grass . . . mongooses like grass."

"They don't eat grass."

His smile disappeared. "How do you know that?" The hair fell in his face.

"They don't."

"Orville knew you, fore you were born." His eyes narrowed as he spat the words at me. "He was out with his air rifle. . ."

He closed one eye and held his hands up, head cocked to one side, shouldering a rifle which only he could see. "I'm going to get one . . . use it to shoot a few cows . . . Pii . . . Pii . . . two cows down. . ."

He laughed. "Going to get one from England . . . Pii . . . Pii. . ."

He cocked his head back and aimed at the sky. "My Pa's from England . . . Pii. . ."

He watched his victim fall. "Your Ma's from the jungle . . . Pii . . . Piii. . ."

He discarded his rifle and stared at me. "An you's from nowhere. . ."

He rolled onto his back and laughed kicking his legs up at the air above him.

"Orville saw your Ma and Da down by the store-rooms. . ."

He rolled over onto his stomach. I used to hide from Nan down there . . . used to hide behind the barrels and fire-dried peas at her feet . . . she was lucky she was black or else she would have had red bumps all over. . ."

Lee shrieked. Then, as suddenly as it started the shriek stopped. "He saw Pa and your Ma down there mating . . . like how dogs mate . . ."

He shrieked again. "And that was you being born!"

I spat.

The white blob settled beneath his left eye. He returned the offense spitting madly. Then he stopped. We sat up, our faces dotted with little watery white beads.

A line of small black faces peered over the gully ridge. Lee spat in their direction. They did not move.

"Ma!"
I pulled aside the chenille and stumbled into the bedroom.
"Ma. . .!" I climbed onto the bunk.
"Ma. . .!"
"Wait a minute, baas!"
I was lifted roughly from the bunk to the floor.
"Ma!"
"Hey hol on a likkle dere, baas. . .!"
There was something about the blackness of his bare body that repelled me. The pitch blackness like that of the outhouse when I had no candle . . . a blackness rank with fish . . . fish and raw meat mingled in sweat. . .
"Didn hear yu come in, baas. . ."
I tried to wriggle free from his hold.
"You dancin wid me, baas, eh?"
Ma lay on her back staring blankly at the ceiling, her lips slightly parted.
"Cool yu foot, baas . . . cool yu foot. . ."
His palms were sticky wet and he still smelt of goat. His thumbs dug into my wrist . . . I tried to bite them . . . He pushed me an arm's length away.
"Pa!"
I kicked my feet out at him. "Go tell. . .!"
Ma sat up. Her fingers gripped the edge of the bunk. Tom released me. I felt the blood flow back into my wrists. Tom remained unabashed in his black nakedness, his face twisted in grim restraint. He spoke between his teeth, the muscles of his stomach tensed. "Yu shut yu bloody mout or deh fish yu god-damn body outa a bloody pit latrine. . ."

I made a gun.
I wound a piece of thread around three horizontally placed matchsticks and tied them on near to the ends of four vertical ones . . . Ma had given me a new stub of candle which burnt yellow . . . My houses were spread out all over the floor . . . The biggest one, the one with the cork roof was mine . . . I lived there . . . I had a huge horse pen too . . . some of the houses had collapsed but none of the horses had gotten out . . . two small caterpillars made fine horses, except that they were green. . .

I made a bridge too. . . I had enough matchsticks. . . I made a bridge for the horses to get to the waterbarrel. . . Anybody else who used my bridge had to pay twenty pounds . . . twenty pounds to use my bridge. . . They knew I had a gun . . . they would have to pay.

There was movement outside. . . The wild people were coming to attack my houses . . . the wild people . . . they were so black you could not see them . . . you could hear them though . . . I fired . . . they screamed and some of them ran . . . they were wild, wild and naked . . . I fired again, one of them fell . . . a one-eyed wild man fell. . . I fired more bullets . . . another one fell . . . a big one with a space between his front teeth. . .

"Seanie. . ."

The door opened.

"Come. . ."

I put my houses back into the shoe box, one by one, carefully fitting them in. I blew out the candle.

"You buil' house for Ma?" She was tired. Her voice was weak. "I told yu Pa yu buildin big fine houses out here. . ."

"Yu Pa seh he been talkin to someone. . ."

The bunk was in disarray.

"Tryin to get yu into a good school. . ."

Ma whipped off the top sheet and rolled it into a bundle. "One o' dem good school where deh learn yu all dem good tings. . ."

I stood half dressed between Ma and the dressing table holding my shirt in my fists.

"A lot of good people go dere. . ."

Tom had threatened me.

"You be goin to a fine school. . ."

Ma had let him threaten me.

"You be a good docta, eh. . ."

She hit the pillows with her fist.

"You be a good docta like Docta Benson, eh?"

"I not goin!"

Ma's face froze in a stupid grin.

"I not goin. . ."

I let the words sink in.

She pulled off her housecoat and stood for some time staring down at the bunk before she sank into it. Her shoulders slumped, rounding over until her breasts sagged on her stomach.

"Yu want a whippin?"

She looked at my feet. "Yu want a fine strippin tail whippin?" Her eyes hardened like smooth, round stones. "Yu gwan jumpin outa yu likkle short pants wid me an yu see what yu get!" Her voice rose. "Yu jus mind yu damn likkle tongue!"

I had not realised how swollen Ma had become. As she sat her stomach jutted out above her thighs.

"Yu gettin big for yu pants, eh?" Her movement up from the bunk to her feet was full of effort. "Yu gettin big!"

I barely saw the blurred pink of her palm before it landed full force on my face. Another quick blow followed the first. . . I scrambled for the bunk and pulled my knees up to my face. She tried to wrench them down. . . The scream stuck in the back of my throat. . . I gasped.

She moved towards the dresser where she kept the switch.

I rolled off the bunk to the floor.

"Go tell my Pa!"

It was a plea and a threat.

"Go tell my Pa!"

Ma turned on me with unrestrained fury. The switch tore into me. I writhed, kicking madly at her.

"Yu go tell yu Pa nuh?" She grabbed my hands and pulled me to my feet. "Yu go tell him, eh. . .?"

She shook me, then let me go.

I dived for the floor and squirmed beneath the bunk. She took hold of my feet and pulled me out.

"Yu tink him know yu?" She flung the switch behind her.

"Yu tink he know yu? Yu not nuttin weh he have use fo. . . He only know yu wen he come here . . . when he want me!"

She beat her chest with her fist. "Gwan go tell him see ef he don't set him dog pan yu. . . gwan!"

She was overcome. She sank slowly to the stool by the dressing table. Her lips opened and closed silently, her eyes focused steadily on the bottles of cheap, sweet smelling water.

"Deh'll learn yu all dem good tings . . . all dem good tings. . ."

" 's for you. . . I don't want it. . ."

Lee flung the paper bag at me, did a quick handstand, then stared at me blankly, feet in the air.

"What's it . . .?" I held the bag cautiously, apprehensively.

"Something I don't want. . ." He righted himself, did a cartwheel then another handstand. His shirt fell into his face, exposing his stomach, the red patches dotted with bumps.

"Mosquitoes?" I felt obliged to be considerate.

"Yup!"

I opened the bag.

It was made of hard china, hard white china, and its belly had been chipped away in places. The brown eyes where flecked white where the paint had chipped off. Bits of the ears had cracked too.

"The foot broke off . . . I don't want it . . ." He bent his arms at the elbows until his head touched the ground.

"Thanks. . ."

I put the horse in my shirt pocket and pinned the pocket shut with a rusted safety pin Ma had used to pin my shorts up.

"Yu can go to Doctor Benson to get the foot fixed . . ." He came gracefully down on his knees. "Pa says he's a pig doctor . . . I think he's a horse doctor . . . He's got a big nose like a horse. . ."

Lee laughed and did a backward roll, landing clumsily on his stomach.

I had vague memories of a man in white slacks and a bright red open-necked shirt who had come to the house once when Ma had had sores and rashes all over. All that I could remember distinctly was that Ma had propped me up in her lap and had combed my hair so I would look presentable when he came.

Lee said he drove the Black Buick which was parked occasionally by the barracks. He looked after the estate hands . . . He did not 'born' their babies though. The old women did that . . . He looked after Pa sometimes too, Lee said, but Pa had other doctors . . . better doctors who did not have big noses. . .

I crept further down the gully away from Lee. He followed me. "You smell something?"

He crept close to me. "You smell it?"

I nodded.

"It's your brother . . ." He laughed. "Girl up at the estate had him. . ."

Lee shrieked. "Don't care wedda is Missa Thomas or anybody else . . . Ah don' want it in here . . .!" Lee was mimicking, his voice high-pitched and nasal. "Her mother made her throw it out. . ."

Lee's shrieks soared through the gully and seemed to rattle the leaves of the mango trees. "She drowned it in the outhouse and carried it down here . . . where Mamma wouldn't hear about it. . ."

Lee had wandered away from me and was creeping amidst the nut grass and bushes, laughing and imitating negro women screaming at each other.

I would put the horse in the horse pen when I got home.

"Sean. . ."

I would get some more matchsticks and put a roof over one part of the pen so the horse wouldn't get wet when it rained.

"Sean!"

I could do away with the caterpillars then . . . they had become motionless, hard and useless.

"Sean!"

I turned slightly. Lee had a long stick in his hand. He waved it at me.

"Look. . ."

He pushed the stick into the bush and pulled out a towel-wrapped bundle. A cloud of black rose, dissipating into buzzing black pellets. Lee flicked open the towel with the stick.

I retched.

The china horse was in pain . . . He was the best in the stables . . . he had had his left foreleg bitten off by a dog . . . I shot the dog and took the horse home to the pen. I wound a long piece of thread around three matchsticks . . . If the china horse died all the others would die too . . . He was the best in the stables.

Ma had gotten some glue for me . . . glue and toffees . . . I did not like peppermints anymore . . . I kept the toffees in the pocket of my shirt and used the glue to paste the matchsticks on where the horse had no leg. . .

. . . The rumble of his jeep moved away from the yard.

"Ma . . .!" I stood up and shouted.

"Ma . . .!" I hit my fists against the walls.

"Ma!"

"The door's not locked!" She was shouting from inside the house. "The door's open . . . Come."

I put one palm lightly on the door. It creaked open.

"Come inside now, Seanie!"

The shadows snickered from the pea trees. They were waiting for me to come out into the yard, waiting to attack. Their eyes glowed with every twisted movement of their shapeless bodies.

"Ma. . .!"

I was about to pull the door back shut . . . I wanted Ma to come as she always did . . . I wanted her to come and bring the lamp. . .

"Ma!"

"Get yuself in here now fore I bring my switch to you!"

"Red cloth." I kept my eyes straight, crossing myself.

"Red cloth . . ." The shadows slunk alongside, muttering.

"Red cloth . . ." Ma waited on the steps.

"Red cloth . . . red cloth . . ." A frantic spurt took me to her and the open door.

There were white flakes from the soles of my feet, where the skin was lifting, up to my stomach in a sore round patch about my navel. There were flakes on my palms and wrists too.

Ma gave me bush baths twice a day and sopped the sore parts with bay rum and pepper leaves. The itching became a persistent burning and the white flakes continued as far up as my nose and lips.

She told him. He was concerned, she said. He brought a pair of boots and a bottle of yellow medicine. Ma made me wear socks the whole day and the boots he had brought.

The stripping persisted. Long, thin ribbons of skin tore away leaving the skin beneath a tender, rich brown. Ma kept me indoors for two days. He said I should be kept in.

I was given the yellow liquid and put to bed, wrapped in a huge blanket from nose to toe.

On the third day I hid the blanket under the bunk and fled in pajamas and bare feet to the gully. Ma was waiting for me when I returned. She whipped me.

I spat all over myself and screamed. I screamed until long into the night, wetting myself as soon as I felt the heaviness in my stomach.

The bush baths ceased. The socks and boots were abandoned.

It rose up from the matting of rich green lawns, a mass of brick and stone breathing through open glass windows and wide archways from which poppy-red drapes billowed out into the sun, and delicate ferns and potted plants skirted sun-splashed flagstone courtyards.

The white pebbled driveway parted the carpet of green lawn as far as the latticed front porch which jutted out to meet it from behind a shimmer of green vine that twined itself between the intricate spaces and nosed its way up the outer walls to the brown shingled eaves.

Clumps of palms and heliconias flanked a shallow stone pond from which the water glistened clear and clean beneath a topping of pale green lily pads and the iridescent wings of dragon flies.

A plump negress in a white apron which the breeze swelled out around her shuffled out from one of the archways, carrying a tin watering can. She stopped, stared towards the wall then made a few quick steps forward. She stopped again by the palms, shading her eyes with one hand.

She put the watering can down by the palms and skittered across the lawn, her white scarf blown forward into her face.

"Get down from there. . .!"

She flashed the backs of her hands furiously at me. "Get away from there. . .!"

I had wanted to see Lee . . . I had wanted to find out if the dead baby was still in the gully.

"Get down!"

I was astraddle the wall, the woman bearing down on me. My foot caught in the vine on my way down. I tugged at it desperately.

Pieces of vine came away and clung around my ankle.

Behind the wall the woman exclaimed. She could not stand all these likkle bitches takin set on di place. . .

I would not go to the gully . . . not until I knew if the dead baby had been removed.

"You . . . you . . . get away from here!" The negress pointed a sharp finger through the rails of the gate, her nostrils flaring open. "Get away from here . . . y' hear me?"

The cows came down the slopes in a flood of dust and lowing mingled with the harsh, imperious voices of the cow herds. I knelt behind the low prickly hedge that hemmed the pastures . . . There were lizards there . . . lizards and wasps. The men came down on mules, the boys running alongside the herd, coconut fronds flaying and whipping the ground.

The women had come down early. They squatted beneath the thatched shed, their wood fires puffing grey smoke into the morning. They bent over large iron pots, their skirts pulled up to their thighs, their faces shiny wet at the cheeks and forehead.

A lizard scooted by amidst the bushes. I aimed a metal bottle stopper at it and fired. The stopper plummetted into the bushes. The lizard disappeared.

One of the men had joined the women beneath the shed, a stub of a man with huge wet lips. He put a hand on a carton box, looked down into it then looked up at the girl with long snake-like plaits who was sitting nearest to it. The girl smiled and wiped a stray plait out of her eyes with the back of her hand.

No more lizards appeared, only a few wasps which darted about some distance from me.

"Breakfus smellin good." The mule drew up by the shed.

"Yu eatin here, Tom?" The short man grinned and pushed his hat further back on his head. "Thought yu was goin to eat wid one o' yu gals dem."

"They don't want him." It was the girl with the long plaits who spoke.

"Yu runnin joke wid yu headman now gal?" Tom dismounted.

The other women stared solemnly at the girl.

"Headman?" She stared defiantly up at Tom.

"We gotta be watchin those calves today. They lookin real sprightful. . ."

Tom fumbled in his pocket for a cigarette.

"Gimme a smoke Tom?" The girl had not given up.

"Not good fo yu." Tom lit the cigarette from one of the fires.

"Who sch so?" The girl tossed her plaits.

Tom mounted his mule again. "Ah gotta be watchin dem calves today. . ."

He rode off, the mule twitching its tail at the women.

The wasps danced nearer. I aimed. They darted around dodging each other. One flitted near me . . . I fired. . .

"Is what dat?" The girl with the long plaits started. "Is what?"

I stood. "Is mine. . ."

The women's eyes settled on me.

The girl with the long plaits beckoned to me. "Come fo it."

I hopped over the bushes.

"Yu playin' war?" She handed me my bottle stopper.

"Yes . . ." I reached out to take it.

"Whas yu name again?" Her hands closed around mine. "Sean."

"How you spell dat?"

The short man regarded me with interest.

"S-e-a-n." I tried hard not to smile.

"Nice name." The girl with the long plaits let go of my hand. "So how is you?"

"Fine." I could let the smile come innocently now.

The man scooped up a chunk of yam from one of the fires. He passed a penknife beneath the charred black skin.

"Like yam?"

I nodded. He held it out to me. I took it.

"Yu Ma give yu yam, eh?" He picked his teeth with his penknife.

"Yes. . ."

I bit the yam. The women's faces were wreathed with smiles.

The big carton box seemed to move a little. I rose onto the balls of my feet and peeped in.

"Like 'er?" The short man had taken off his hat and was fanning himself.

"Yes. . ."

The green eyes stared up at me from the box, the tiny brown fists clenched, small knots of brown curls scattered on a pale head.

"She name Vicki." The girl with the long plaits drew me nearer to the box.

"She go have long plaits?" I was having a hard time finishing the yam.

"Yes." The girl ran a hand through my hair. "She go have nice hair . . . good hair like you."

"Love 'er?" The short man tilted the box to one side. The baby squealed.

'Yeh . . ." I passed the yam from one hand to the other to cool it.

"Yu mus come play wid er some time." The mother caressed the tiny brown curls as she spoke.

"Yu lookin some likkle fair 'kin gran-pickney, Elsie. . .?" Another man had appeared, a scrawny youth with a shadow of a beard on his chin. The girl with the long plaits flashed him a warning glance. He laughed.

"Pa go set his dog on her. . ."

I dropped the yam.

"What you say?"

Elsie leaned back on her heels.

"Pa go set his dog on her. . ."

I bent to pick it up.

Elsie stared at me, hard, cold, and shocked.

"He set his dog on you?"

I thought of Rex scratching at the outhouse door.

"He ever do that to you, Sean?"

A number of children had gathered. The smallest boy regarded me coldly.

"He ever set dog on you?"

His right hand was twisted into his shirt and his left thumb buried between his thick lips.

"They ever bite you?"

He was the boy who had given me his tamarinds.

"Eh, Sean?"

His stare was bitter.

Elsie's face dropped. She fumbled with her fire, nudging two fat fingers of banana back into the glowing wood.

The short man stood up. The women straightened, pulling their skirts down over their knees. The skinny youth scurried away back to the open pasture.

"I don't want these children down here."

The black stallion pawed the ground.

"They should be up at the barracks!"

It was strapped over his shoulder . . . just as Lee had described it . . . sleek and shiny . . . silver at the butt. . .

"Get them off. . ."

The pair of hard blue eyes swept around the shed. They rested on me momentarily before they swerved back to the women. The straw-coloured hair streaked with silver was swept back from the pale forehead into solid looking waves. The two blue eyes expressed dominance over the chiselled ridges of his face, flashing a stubborn arrogance wherever he laid them. He fit fully into his clothes, swelling out firmly beneath the rough work suit and exuding a rank aggressiveness beneath a cloak of indifference.

He tugged at the reins and the horse turned and trotted off. The sun glinted from the rifle on his back.

"Yes, baas. . ."

The women's broken whispers came long after the black stallion had been engulfed by the wave of brown that moved steadily across the pasture.

The boy's stare returned to me. This time it burned with interest. The left thumb appeared, wet and shiny, coming out with a thread of spittle.

"Go off to yu Ma, boy." Elsie whispered to the clump of burning wood. "Gwan."

"Yu sleepin dere. . .?"

My face was buried in my pillow. I did not look up.

"Yu gettin too big to sleep wid Ma?" Her hand moved over my bare back. "What is dis, eh?"

She moved away. I turned onto my side. The chair at my feet slid. I grasped the edge with my toes. There was a stool beneath my stomach and another chair and a pillow at my head.

The lantern flame flickered wildly behind the sooty blackness of the glass shade. Ma hovered about the room, stopping to pinch my side and watch the spot go red or to look at herself in the mirror of the dressing table.

She was going to burst.

I shivered. She was going to explode. Her stomach had rounded out like a tight balloon. One day she was going to burst and there would be blood everywhere. . . She sat by the dressing table scraping white stuff from her scalp with her nails. She was going to burst . . . there would be blood . . . blood and pus everywhere, her stomach would rip open . . . rip open like the goat in the market . . . there would be blood everywhere.

Her eyes drooped heavily with sleep. She ran a palm over her stomach, felt my gaze on her, then stood up and went towards the bunk. She lay down like a wounded animal, slowly, laboriously. She stared at me, her lips open, breathing loudly. "He been talkin to some people. . ."

I closed my eyes. He had not been here for weeks.

"Bout gettin yu into a good school. . ."

I bit hard into my lower lip.

"Yu go be a fine docta . . . like Docta Benson . . ." She flung an arm over her forehead. . . . "Like Docta Benson . . ."

The bird came back into the yard. It lay among the pea trees, a damp ball of feathers, the eyes closed. I touched it. The feathers fluffed out a little and one of the feet was pulled in.

I shouted for Ma. She hurried out down the steps, the straps of her nightgown peeping out from beneath her dress. "Lef it, Sean . . . you lef it dere!"

I picked up the bird.

"Yu put it down, y' hear me?" She tried to hit the bird from my hand. "Put it down, please, Seanie. . ."

I kept the bird in another shoe box stuffed with strips of brown paper in the outhouse. It lay on its side still warm, ruffling its feathers to let me know it was still alive.

I put pieces of cabbage, thinly shredded, among the brown paper. When he got hungry enough he would eat . . . if he liked cabbage.

There was a cover for the box too, crudely perforated with my fingers to let air in. I punched two holes in the narrow sides of the box, ran a thin piece of wire through, out through the holes in the cover and knotted the two edges together.

I carried the box hung over my shoulder when Ma had to clean the outhouse.

Lee screamed.

I dug my fingers into the sides of his neck and pinned down his outstretched arms with my knees. He screamed again and again until his screams became breathless gasps. I released him.

He squirmed away from me and curled up by the clump of nut grass. The redness filled out his face again before it became light shades of blue around his eyes and cheeks.

He wheezed, drawing in his knees and grasping at the hard ground with tense fingers. He wriggled onto his back and lay still, his eyes closed. He had called Ma a whore . . . a black whore. . .

Bloody foam seeped through the corners of his lips and trailed down his cheeks as every fibre of him twitched and shook suddenly as if each member of his body had a life of its own.

There was a foul smell gathering around him. The front of his shorts had become wet. He made wind and trickles of watery faeces flowed down his pale legs into the dirt.

The foam had become a large white bubble covering the lower half of his face, until the convulsions ceased and he lay motionless and reeking like a stale corpse.

"What is it?"

The thick black eyebrows lifted. "Eh?"

The negro came towards me preceded by a huge paunch which hung over his belt.

The line of negroes shuffled uncomfortably before the murmur subsided. They lined up every Monday outside the hospital, an old stable transformed for the purpose, to make appointments or just to be first when the doctor arrived.

There were a few benches on the porch, but they were reserved for people whose legs were bound between pieces of board and old women who leaned precariously forward as if their grey plaits were dragging them down.

"Yu made a likkle mistake here, sah." The fat negro put a swollen finger on the bird. "We treat people not pigeons. . ."

One of the men in the line commented gruffly that time was going.

The fat man smiled. "Don't even look like a pigeon to me, either. . ."

The bird fluttered.

"What kind o' bird is it?"

I shook my head.

"Don't know effen Docta Benson treat birds. . . He not here now and I's not docta. . . I just tekkin names an mekkin appointments. . . So if yu want to wait yu can join di line. . ." He indicated the line of about thirty people at the end of which a grossly fat woman had her fists on her hips. "An yu can give me di bird's name. . ."

The negro was bent low, his palms on his knees as if to whisper, but he spoke loudly enough for the others to hear. He turned and went back up the steps to the hospital.

"Lee says he treats horses. . ." I moved forward, "so he can treat birds then. . ."

The fat man stopped and turned around, pushing his stomach out further. "They look like horse to you?" He indicated the line of negroes with a huge forefinger.

The negroes met my glance with something between a scowl and a smile. The fat man laughed.

He was stretched on his left side, his shirt open and pulled away from his stomach, his lips folded. The small red patches on his stomach and cheeks had become huge red blotches. I examined my bare stomach and arms. The white flakes had gone away and left a deep, golden brown like wet sugar. I smiled . . . wet sugar . . . I chuckled.

Lee rolled his stare towards me. There were men coming, he said . . . men who lit their pipes with ten pound notes . . . Lee was sick. . . Ma said he was sick. They were going to lend Pa money. He had fits . . . a whole heap of money. Ma said he was not as strong as I was. He had fits . . . bags and bags of money. He burned too . . . sun burnt. I did not burn . . . I never burned . . . they were bringing a whole pile of money. . .

A slight breeze sprinkled mango blossoms into the gully where they scattered like bright pebbles.

. . . And Pa had to get a new headman too. . . Maybe Lee would die. . . He had sent Tom away . . . sick people always died. . . Tom had been foolin wid Pa's women.

Lee was grave. His brother had told him. . . He rubbed his chin in the ground. . . Orville had told him that Tom had been fooling with Pa's women.

Something moved in the narrow end of the gully. The familiar gleam returned to Lee's eyes.

"I saw a mongoose that looked like you. . ." He grinned. "A large ugly one with six legs. . ."

The skies broke.

It rained for days. Puddles formed on the roof and seeped in leaving dark water marks on the ceiling. The yard became soft mud, and then a basin of brown water which flowed between the pea trees and settled under the house.

I dropped stones and stubs of old pencil through holes in the floor and listened to the splash they made in the water beneath.

Ma stayed in bed on those days. She insisted that I stay with her. I sat on the floor and pasted matchsticks together. I made more houses . . . more houses and a school. I made a church too. . . I made a church and coloured it red with wax crayons. . . The china horse watched me from the pen. It could stand now . . . I had many trees now too . . . orange trees. . . I kept my gun in my pocket in case the wild people came back . . . tamarind trees. I had made a fish pond for my house . . . sweetsop trees . . . I filled a bottle cover with water and surrounded it with leaves. . . June plum trees. . .

In the evenings, the women came, dishevelled figures dripping wet, dragging boots caked with mud. They carried covered tin pans and damp paper bags with bush.

They cooked. I was fed. They huddled around Ma in a crude circle of which I was not a part. They talked and they sang. They drew the sweet smelling bush and they all drank.

I watched them from my 'bed', creatures of sagging black behind the veil of pale smoke spat up by their lanterns. They sang strange songs from deep down in their throats or through their noses, their faces distorted like the face which hung about in the dark . . . like Lee's face distorted in anger. . . I closed my eyes . . . closed out their faces. . .

The rains had made the rich green damp, and drops of water glinted on the sleek blades of grass. The umbrellas had all been closed except for one at the far end of the green where one of the porridge-faced men sat brooding over an empty glass, the buttons on his shirt straining at his belly. A slender honey-haired young woman sat opposite him, legs crossed, running a palm along her calf, one black leather slipper dangling from her toes.

The black Buick was parked a few yards away from the pickets, the driver's door flung open. The driver leaned against the boot, one foot propped on the pickets, a cigarette, lighted side turned in, hanging from his lips.

Tight dull brown curls clung to his head and trailed down the length of his smooth milk chocolate cheeks into an unruly clump of beard on his chin.

The honey-haired girl had diverted her attention to her fingers, sprawling them out wide, palms down. She said something, smiled, and attempted to get up.

The porridge-faced man looked up quickly and locked a fist around her small hands, leaning so far over that the umbrella tipped dangerously.

The brown man laughed. The clump of beard jutting out before him, he laughed loudly. He saw me and the laughter became a curious smile. "They taste good?"

I nodded and stuffed the remnants of my 'stinkin' toe' into my pockets.

"Used to eat them myself." He leaned sideways on the car, facing me. "Can't see what I saw in them. . ."

Above a broad, fleshy nose, the liquid brown of his eyes seemed held together by the solid white. "Come here often?"

His gaze had wandered back to the porridge-faced man who had pulled his chair round next to the honey-haired girl.

"Yes. . ."

The bird fluttered in the box at my side.

"Oh. . ." A wide grin cut into his brown face.

The porridge-faced man was whispering something to the girl, his lips close to her ear.

"I come here in the afternoons myself . . . some afternoons . . .

if there aren't many cases up at the hospital. You have seen those lines, haven't you?"

I nodded.

He was big . . . much bigger than Pa, with a chest that protruded strongly forward beneath his white shirt and thick, powerful limbs covered in smooth, dark brown hair. . . His neck began where Pa's head stopped.

"Whose bastard are you?" He put a heavy hand on my head and rocked it gently. I dug my toes into the ground and watched them swallowed by the dirt. "Eh?" He lifted my face with the back of a finger.

I searched the brown eyes for mockery. It was not there.

"Thomas." I looked past his face to the leaves of the 'Stinkin' toe' tree.

"Me too. . ." He let my face down gently and pinched the chin.

"You?" It shot out from me. I looked away quickly to the green where the honey-haired girl was hurrying across the grass.

He chuckled. "Not your Thomas. His Pa. . . You wouldn't have liked him . . . fat old drunkard . . . went bankrupt . . . only left your Pa with the house . . . and a few cows. He's done well off them anyhow."

The porridge-faced man waddled in pursuit of the girl.

"My Ma did her share in bleeding the old sponge dry anyhow." He smiled and passed a finger over his lips. "She was a blessed soul anyhow. . . God rest her. That's why I took her name. You come here often you say. . ."

One thick arm encircled my shoulders.

"They don't mind you once you stay out here. . ."

His smile hardened and he nodded. "That's true."

The bird fluttered more vigorously this time and the cover of the box lifted a little.

"What's that?" He indicated the box.

I untied the wire knot and opened the box.

"Why do you have him in there?" There was a slight frown which rolled his forehead into chocolate ridges.

"He's sick."

"Sick?" The brown fingers lifted the bird from the box. "Sick?" His fingers moved gently over the feet and wings. "Healthiest creature you'll ever see."

"He looked sick!" I held the box up for the bird.

He smiled broadly, sympathetically. "His kind may just do

strange things normally . . . must have been sleeping when you picked him up. When I say strange things I mean he may just be different from other birds." He put the bird back into the box. "You keep him locked up like that he will get sick. You give him a chance to fly and he'll fly."

"What is he. . . .?" I put the cover back on the box.

He shrugged. "Don't quite know . . . but I've seen his sort before. Must be some kind of bast . . . some different specie I suspect."

Lee went away.

The men who lit their pipes with ten pound notes did not come. The cows stopped coming down to pasture and fresh beef was sold cheap to the negroes before they were turned out of the barracks.

An old Scots woman was left in charge of the big house along with her two flea-bitten collies that growled at anyone who passed the gate.

Ma watched the jeep roll away down the slopes. . . He would come, she said . . . he would come before he left. She waited out in the yard, her shawl wrapped around her shoulders watching the jeep and the two large cars that followed it melt into the evening darkness about the hillsides.

A strong wind tore the shawl from around her and it flapped out violently behind her like wings.

The bolt of the outhouse had broken away during the rains and it swung loosely from one screw, grating against the door, scratching the wood away into fine dust.

The box in the outhouse was empty save for a few warm feathers and bits of stinking cabbage. I turned the box upside down and pulled out the wire. . . I would use it on my horse pen. . .

I told Ma the bird had gone.

She pulled the sheets up between her legs and bit into the edges. . . Maybe she was glad it was gone. . .

She watched the rain moths circling the lantern, her lips folded, and her eyes wide. She kicked off the sheets and lumbered across the room to the dressing table, the back of her nightgown caught in the waist of her drawers.

She wiped cream all over her thighs until they shone like polished mahogany. She moved her hands, still flecked with cream, up to her hair, pulling it away from around her face and knotting it on top of her head.

She lifted the nightgown away from her stomach and stared at the mound in the mirror.

"Deh'll learn yu all dem good tings. . ." Lucid tears gathered on her cheeks. "All dem good tings . . . like Docta Benson. . ."

"Come boy . . . You get up. . ."

I awoke, startled. The faces leered at me from the chenille.

"Yu get up now, boy . . . get up. . ."

The women had returned . . . all three of them. "Not no place for a chile now. . ."

A full moon cut through the darkness and the faces on the chenille unfolded into large painted flowers . . . roses . . . pink roses. . .

A buxom wide-hipped woman led me from the bedroom to the door. "Wait out dere. . ."

The door closed behind me.

The shadows lunged at me from the darkness of the morning. I froze, watching their twisting movements across the yard as they melted into and rose from the pea trees and the yam hills.

Ma screamed.

The shadows melted. . . The twisting gyrations of their bodies became the quivering of the pea trees in the moonlight, their eyes the transient flicker of fireflies.

I leaned back against the door. It creaked open behind me . . .

Ma sat up. The whites of her eyes were bared at the ceiling. A hoarse groan forced its way between her teeth while drops of water oozed out from her forehead and shone around her nostrils.

The women forced her back into the pillows. She screamed.

The scream hung in the air and echoed in my head until it was cut into by the wail of a young child. One of the women turned away carrying a bundle in her arms and muttering.

Someone pulled me roughly through the chenille, into the next room and back onto the steps outside.

I flung the outhouse door open and kept it back with a stone so I could see the moonlight spreading along the yam hills, and the ribbon of clear silver that hung from the eaves of the house, tearing away in long strips which splattered in glistening droplets on the steps.

I tried to find the shadows . . . tried to pick out their macabre substance somewhere in the night. They had disappeared . . . had lost form . . . they were merely dark spaces among the pea trees . . . harmless dark spaces. They had lost all power to frighten.

Ma had scrubbed the floor of the outhouse clean with beeswax. I stretched out on it, my cheeks pressed to the cool wood.

The old water barrel had sprung a leak from far up, almost just beneath the cover. Cold drops of water trickled down my nape and lodged behind my ears. . . A cool wind bent the pea trees and carried dead leaves in a mad scurry across the ground uncovering a rat, its head eaten away to leave the red blood and bone exposed, just outside the outhouse. I put a hand out and pushed it away.

There was another sharp gust which brought with it a sprinkle of rain and the cry of a woman. I closed my eyes. The cry of one woman became the cry of two, and then three. The ribbon on the eaves had been torn away by the wind and the undulating zinc edges left raw and naked.

The flood of sunlight rushed in, blinding, before it settled into a thin, transparent haze. I sat up. My clothes stuck damply to me and my head and cheeks were wet.

The water barrel had leaked still more and a membrane of clear water covered the floor and made soft ridges in the dirt outside the door.

Beneath the membrane of water I saw him . . . rustic brown . . . staring back up at me through pale brown eyes and shivering against the water as if at any moment he would emerge in a bubbling foam of white.

The black men came, sober-faced, red-eyed, the women following close on their heels past the yam hills.

They carried an old spring bed. They had ripped away the chenille, leaving it in an untidy clump on the floor, and stretched her out on the bed springs with the small black creature turned face down on her bare stomach. They covered them with white sheets, from her gaping lips to her cold soles.

They went back down the steps and past the yam hills, the women beating their breasts and invoking divine mercy for the seed of sinful man.

The grey Morris stopped beyond the standpipe.

The driver, a bleary-eyed negro in shoddy overalls, dragged himself from his seat and made his way across the yard, favouring his left foot as he came.

The white-haired Scots woman waited in the car, one of her collies under her arm, her sharp nose perched over a slit of mouth cut into the papery whiteness of her face.

The driver took my case, heaved it onto his shoulder and led the way to the Morris, his free hand swinging wildly at his side.

The rains had washed the eaves clean of dead leaves, and the oranges, a burnished gold, pulled the branches to the eaves. The pea pods had ripped open and the dry pods curled upwards away from the ripe seeds. Blood-red tomatoes glistened on the green vine beyond which yellow peppers filled out between the leaves of the pepper tree.

Swarms of tiny yellow and blue butterflies converged on the treetops and drifted low across the yard like sprays of coloured dust, darting between our feet and flitting by our faces.

The Scots woman watched through rheumy grey eyes as the driver helped me into the back seat beside her. She said nothing, her lips trembling and her fingers buried in the discoloured white coat of her collie. . .

The vine had torn loose from the iron gate and trailed dejectedly down the side of the wall while bits and pieces still clung uselessly to the curved metal of the lion's mane.

The gates had been flung open and small chunks of white wall had splintered away where the gate rails made deep, red gashes in its side.

They had sent a letter to him. He did not want me staying 'down there' alone.

"Stop yu by the front porch, Massa. . .?"

The driver glanced over his shoulder at me. I looked up at the Scots woman. There was a smile playing around her pursed lips.

"Eh, Massa Thomas?"

The driver was getting impatient.

"Drop yu by the front porch?"

I nodded.

In These Our Sunshine Years

by Trevor Fearon

Silver, 1979

Edgar Reflecting
The child is ill. Angie carefully spoons out the prescribed liquids. I myself a little while ago went into the bedroom for a fatherly chat. Now I lift my head periodically from the magazine I am reading – whenever she passes – in fair exhibition of solicitous enquiry: the article is an interesting one and I resent losing concentration, but the action is one that makes for a peaceful life.

I am not inordinately fond of that child. I have just impressed upon it the inevitable results of wrongdoing. I gave it the benefit of the doubt as to whether the look on its face was that occasioned by pain or whether it was an impertinent scowl. It (he, really) is not, I grant, fond of me either. "That child," I have said to Angie, "does not even pretend to like its own father. It pissed on me the first time that I held it and it has been doing the same thing since." In former days this would have been taken as (albeit poor) witticism. Now, she's likely to shrug – something she's been doing a lot of lately – saying: "And you have been holding that against him ever since"; shrugging her way into the kitchen where she shrugs the dishes into the sink, to reorganise them with audible displeasure.

And she's wrong there. I concede to not being the perfect father. Who is? But I *have* made the effort. The years it spent on my knee, the hand-holding excursions, the patient explanations – who remembers these things?

Besides which, if fair be fair, some amount of blame resides with Angie, who, short months before the birth, went home to her father in one of her by then ever-increasing departures. She, heavily pregnant and not being able to stage her fits of anger effectively (blood rushing from face as she stands, falling for me to support), had me drive her home. It was, as I recall it, a beautiful day. We chatted amiably, and I was quite attentive to her, stopping every half-hour or so as we drove through the countryside. Subsequently she refused to see me whenever I came to the house, leaving the father and myself to sit in the garden, drinking beer and talking about politics and women: interrupted only, as the birth grew closer, by Angie who invented errands for her father so as to leave me alone. Not that I minded, as her father and myself had never liked each other much. The fact is though, that I was not allowed to see the child for several months. By then it was as disagreeable as it is now, graduating from selective pissing to the biting of my hand whenever I patted its head. Should I have fought her? "You deserted me in my hour of need," she now says. "Not so," say I. "You merely wanted to do more than empathise with your feminist and proletarian causes. You wanted to identify with the ethos of male abandonment – heroic woman single-handedly bringing up child at breast." Depending on whether this is prelude to war or peace, I might add, "nice breast."

Introducing Angie

He first saw Angie at Devon House where he and Valerie and CJ, his guests for a week, had taken the table across from her. He had noticed her because Valerie and CJ, a very together couple (as they would undoubtedly have put it, he thought), seemed to be, out of consideration for him, only just able to restrain themselves from devouring each other over their fruit punches. Out of courtesy on his part he studied the other patrons. She was sipping a drink and tapping her well-shaped legs – in gaucho pants – and appearing pleased with the evening's entertainment, a band whose clangour he had first resented but now welcomed as it drowned out the cooings of his guests.

He stared at her profile. Through the corner of his eye he saw Valerie and CJ diverting their lust by watching him and nudging each other. He pretended to be caught up in his study, which was why, when she lifted her head, she caught him staring. ("Do you always stare?" she asked months later when they met.) Trapped, and annoyed by the giggles of the couple, he periodically resumed his observation. She was later joined by a tall woman and they both went into a low-toned conversation with her looking across every now and then. Within a year they were living together and a few months after she had already left him the first time.

Angie Accuses

"You don't know how to enjoy yourself," she says, "because you put up all kinds of barriers. Everything is too *simple* for you. Everything has to be *meaningful*." He admires her ability to speak in italics. "You don't know how sorry I am for you. You can't even express tenderness, affection." Can't I? he rages silently. Have I not burned, been consumed, even *cried?* (Sometimes he thinks in italics.) Has not my muted cry of anguish at love inexpressible been as real as any other's? I who have felt pure agony (well . . . pain then) at the glimpse of the unattainable? What do you know of the moments when the beauty of symmetry, the completeness of things, the all – the being, the seeing, the unseeing? Besides which, how can I when I am afraid of embarrassment, of being made to feel like a fool? Who can protect me from that? People scare me. They hover, calculating my weaknesses. Familiarity breeds rudeness. Let me be alone then, cocooned in self-pity.

Angie Leaving, Edgar Desolate

Angie leaves regularly. He is sometimes silent, pleading with his eyes ("You have really nice eyes though," she had said that first meeting), sometimes openly distressed, wondering what to say ("Must you go?", "We can't go on leaving like this", "Need some help with your bags?"). He stares at the page headed: *The Nuances of Disaffection.* He types: "You know she is leaving you when . . ." Angie bears her suitcase firmly to the door. No nuance that. The dilemma usually leaves him stretched out on his back on the floor.

He phones her long-distance. The split-second gaps are disconcerting. "You try to negate feelings," she begins, "to pretend that there is nothing that matters, nothing that you love. It gives you great pleasure to deny everything."

"Come home," he echoes, giving the lie to his rehearsed words.

"The feeling of independence is a vital one for any artist," he types furiously. At the same time though, he thinks later, isn't there something to be said for a little dependence? Angie, tutored, badgered into independence, becomes a stranger.

He wakes, hearing the radio – the early night's accompaniment – hissing. Norma, she of the fat thighs, the liquid mouth, sleeps. Under the sheets, he touches his penis. Tender, it feels caked. Norma sleeps slackly, hands outstretched, making stars on the sheets. Her face, turned towards him, is open, trusting. He realises that the newness of the experience is already fading. He longs for the mutual and long-lasting afterglow, the merging (so to speak) of mind and body. He sees himself briefly, defenceless, tucking his head under a pillow, remembering a baby, remembering warmth.

A Judgement Is Called For

(This, you might well suspect, is mere posturing on his part: a performance for his and your attention. Imagine him then, leaving the bedroom quietly, holding his head, eyes half-closed, heading for the living room where he slumps naked on the settee, making choking noises as he attempts the ease of tears. The futile spasms, the delicious half-tasted agony, fade too quickly, and, feeling silly, he reaches for a magazine. This too will pass, he thinks. But the family periodical is a betrayer, and page after page features beautiful women radiating sincerity into the eyes of handsome, unconcerned men. Jealous, he selects the most promising and heads for the bathroom.)

He Thinks Of Angie

"How many women have you had in your life?" she had asked. After discussing the semantics of 'had' and whether or not she was to be included, he ashamedly confessed, "I do not remember." She sulked. That night he tried to add up. When he returned to bed her face was turned to the wall. "Forty-eight," he said, "I think." She said nothing the rest of the night. In the morning she asked sharply, "Can you remember their names?" "Most," he said guardedly, but eager to please.

He could not say, the way things are these days, whether that could be considered a small or a large number.

He reviews her past men. No clear pattern emerges, except an inclination towards artist-types. He dislikes them personally, but stronger yet is the feeling of retrospective jealousy, which, however, he cannot bring himself to discuss with her.

The Return, Palisadoes

To tell the truth, he had forgotten what she looked like. Any of three women in the procession from the plane could have been her. One he had ruled out after she waved casually – reluctantly, he thought – at some country types to one side of the waving gallery, who for the past minute had been screaming "Pat! Pat!". Her response triggered off a thunderous celebration. He gave them the evil eye, but already, grandmother and all, he thought sourly, they were streaming downstairs to, he knew, press their faces to the glass, giggle and nudge, with "see har dere", and "she dress pretty eh?".

That left two. They had both disappeared underneath the gallery. It would take them half an hour to clear Customs and Immigration.

Her brief moment of arrival had come at the end of a long letter. She had told of her activities in a dispassionate manner, and he, reading closely, had detected boredom. She would be coming for a couple of weeks. Date, time, flight number. But she hadn't specifically asked him to pick her up.

Downstairs now, he tried to see through the glass. Jostled by the more obviously eager, he returned to the car and sat smoking. A little while later he returned to the building and leaned against a column that afforded a good view of the exit door.

He saw her as she came out. She was pulling a big-city collapsible trolley, trailed by a laden porter. Her headscarf was almost like a skullcap – she's cut off her hair, he thought – and her long dress, more a long skirt tied under her arms and leaving her shoulders bare, was enchantingly feminine. He waited until she was halfway down through the barriers before he straightened. She walked unhurriedly, glancing around calmly without any of the shock of return in her eyes. She saw him and smiled. A beautiful smile, he thought. They kissed briefly, and as she directed the porter to deposit her luggage he went off for the car.

Why hadn't she asked him to meet her? She hadn't said either, whether she would be with him for the duration of her stay. There had been a coolness – no, a strange self-assuredness in that kiss. He started the car.

He remembered the day she had left, over ten months earlier; the relief and the loss. At the airport that night he had sat in the car, his mind chasing resolutions, attempting to arrive at long-lasting conclusions. But he had been unable to concentrate. It was then that he had broken down: not the self-surprising half-coughs that had crept up on him, leaving him wondering, until the experience itself had become more fascinating than the reason – which was her announcement that she would be leaving. This time he had not cried. His mind had reeled, forcing him to lie across the seat where he remained for several hours, falling asleep and waking up in the dark.

He drove her home and they made love. She asked what he had planned for them to do over the next several weeks, and he eagerly drew up a schedule.

A Little Note

(This had been, in the two years since they had been living together, her first departure. At that time they were both twenty-four years old.)

Edgar Thinks

Why? Well, for one thing, their bodies had grown too familiar. There remained no more secrets. Their bodies, grown accustomed to each other's nuances, interacted unthinkingly. Why didn't women get as tired of men's bodies as easily? Or did they? When the man's body ached for new discoveries they lay there, the moist-eyed crucified, pleading silently.

Another Departure

Edgar applies for, is granted, and leaves to take up a two-year post overseas. Angie writes: "I don't believe in long-distance relationships." He writes a long, bitter letter. He castigates his tutorial students. Angie responds: "Maybe." Overjoyed, he jokes with his puzzled students. He and Angie over most of the two years repeat the routine, sometimes by letter, sometimes by telephone.

Edgar Returning. A Scene Is Set

The comfortable-looking apartment is fairly large. Straw and wood dominate the living area – the suspended and floor lamps, the magazine-filled basket, the bookshelves, the chairs, the carvings. Otherwise the predominating colour is beige, except where the colourful spines of books project. In one corner the turntable, tuner and amplifier, flanked by the speakers. Angie lying on a cushion surveys the room, disinterest and anticipation flickering across her face. The beers are cold, the *vin rose* is chilled, the crackers and cheese ready.

Angie Ponders

The times I've been with Edgar have been some of the best and worst times in my life. In fact I've never been so happy as when it was going well with me and him. Whatever happens I'll always be grateful for that. Possibly that's as much as can be hoped for.

But I wish I knew if he ever loved me, if, as he says, he loves me now.

Edgar Thinks

Angie. Angie. Angie.

They Meet

He had intended a firm kiss, but feeling her body unresponsive, he brushed his lips across hers. So no magic, eh? "You look sweet," he smiled, seething. "You too," she said. He professed tiredness, so she closed the bedroom windows, cutting off the sunlight and leaving him to sleep. When, hours later, he woke, he found her entertaining guests downstairs. He knew them all but felt their visit an intrusion, so he affected strangeness, shortness, sarcasm and frank rudeness. He bit the hands that he saw snaking out to pat him. They left soon after.

Some Conversations The Day After

"Do you think that when people – particularly former lovers – ask you how you're doing, that they want to see – happiness? That they want to see the glow for someone else? That they want to hear, for instance, about the children? Nothing is more pleasing than to hear that the other person couldn't make it in your absence, that the other person is

shattered. We want to know that we'll be remembered."
"I've never felt that way. You're sick if you believe that."
"Yeah – well . . ."

"You haven't changed much. You still flaunt your cynicism. Don't you realise how narrow that makes you? Last night you and those people . . . it's really sad."

"What did you tell your friend – what's his name – Peter?"
"I told him I wouldn't see him for some time."
"Did he like that?"
"I didn't ask."

Edgar, in the bathroom washing his face, asks: "So – are you going to explain things to him?"
From the kitchen, Angie asks: "What?"
Towelling his face in the bedroom, he asks: "It doesn't bother you – I mean having to explain things to him?"
Silence.
"I mean at some stage or other?"
She has prepared him a drink, and handing it to him before returning to the kitchen, asks: "Why does that interest you?"
He lies on the cushion in the living room and says: "Oh I don't know – it's just that, y'know, what one says in such a situation is bound to be interesting."
Angie arranges the dishes. She questions: "What's the matter – you short of material?"
Edgar winces and says: "That's a nasty thing to say."
"Well . . ."
She looks in on her way to the bedroom. "What you'd really like to hear is that I told him that everything comes to a dead stop whenever you're around."

A Serious Exchange
"Angie, let's get married."
"What? Hah! I don't know about that at all, boy."

Another Serious Exchange
"Edgar, I really don't know if you are ready for a thing like marriage."
"But I need you."

And

"You really think it could work?"

Conclusion

The child is ill. Angie spoons out the prescribed liquids. I have gone into the bedroom for a fatherly chat. Angie shrugs.

Maria

by D. Maria Corwill

Silver, 1982

"Maria, is how you grow so? You turning big girl!" Old Joe said, not recognising me. I just turn eight, and I feel big when people notice me.

The coal bag getting so heavy since I leave the noisy market (with too much people); and through I running like mad man after me I stop in the cemetery to catch some breath. I like coming here because there's no one to worry me, or pick fight with me or tease me about school. Is just me and some stray goats enjoying the peace and planning revenge on the one Shirley. She's not like Patsy. Patsy nice, unlike other fatties bullying little children. Shirley live near me. She's always tidy and wearing shoes. Her parents work at the factory and they can give her everything. She don't play with me cause she go to school and can read and write. But is only Grannie I have and she don't work at no factory, and although school free I don't have bus fare or uniform to go.

"Dirty Maria!" Shirley say. "Don't come back down my school again, you hear? I going to see that Patricia don't play with you, cause I going to tell teacher!"

She think I fraid of that. Bully! Go on! Do that! See who listen to you, Miss Bighead! Serve her right, her head really big for true.

"Dirty Maria, dirty Maria!" she sing-song.

But I stay silent, because I know that is fight she's looking. I know, cause Shirley hate me.

The sun hot like fire and the pavement burning my bare foot. I wish I was down by the bridge splashing in the cool water, feeling it hug me like cool breeze on Sunday nights. Playing water fight. Wowee! Digging up worms and crawlies in the marshes and catch tadpoles and fool the little children them that is fish you catch. And forget about the one Shirley.

"I wonder, where Maria is so long?" I hear Grannie saying to Miss Piggy (I call her that cause she look so), before I reach inside the yard.

"The children nowadays so unruly," Miss Piggy say, rubbing her pot belly. "Is romping she . . ."

She don't finish for she busy pointing me out as I try to sneak past them. I planning what to say as Grannie take the coal from me and push me inside. She take off her glasses and wipe them. But she only ask if is Old Joe keep me. And I see the relief in her face that I come back safe. I glad.

Grannie give me the rag from her skirt pocket to wipe my black up self. Then she take down her old straw hat. Is church she going. So she wipe up too and put on her socks and slippers and I pull out my sandals from under the old rickety bed. I glad cause we'll soon go down by the Station to sell *Star*. The afternoon train soon come, and shake the board hut like how breeze shake cotton tree.

Then things change suddenly the day Miss Myrtle come to our yard. She come in a yellow Volkswagen car, parked by the break-down gate. Clip, clip, sing her high heels on the hard road to die away in the muddy yard. She is a pinched-out reddish looking lady with a thick head of fluffy brown hair, where she wear her glasses.

It was only last week Sunday that Miss Myrtle come to look for my Grannie. Although Grannie send me round the back to play I could still hear what they saying, cause at the side of the house (near the kitchen) is a hole in the old boards and is there I decide to play. Grannie sound vex, so vex that she just letting Miss Myrtle do all the talking. I can imagine how hard Grannie biting into her bottom lip, if she don't talk soon she going to really bite her lip hard. And I can feel the vexation hanging heavy inside the house, while the old rocking chair creaking its anger. I suddenly feel sorry for Miss Myrtle.

Miss Myrtle talk like one of the teachers them I see down at Patsy's school and I feel good all of a sudden cause I would be so glad if is come she come for me to go school at last.

Then I hear Grannie swearing, and I jump thinking she spy me hiding round the corner, but I listen still, and find out that is Miss Myrtle she cursing. I can't understand some of the things Grannie quarrelling about but I hear she call my mother name (is a very long time that I don't hear she say 'Icilda') saying she's a worthless gal. I wonder if is my mother send Miss Myrtle here to take me away from my Grannie. How she can do a thing like that after she leave for foreign all these years since I born, and she never come back or even write. A wonder.

I feel fraid. I don't want to leave my Grannie, of course I want to go to school but I want to stay with Grannie.

"The child will be brought up properly in the home, Miss Brown. And I am sure the society will be able to provide the necessary education she needs. You won't have to worry about food for her and all that. I'm sorry, Miss Brown, but if the child's mother requires . . ."

Like lightning I reach back down the cemetery. Almost out of breath. Yes, that is what I going to do, I going to run away. I hate Miss Myrtle! And I don't want to go to no home, what my Grannie going to do without me? Miss Myrtle don't care bout that, Grannie is such a old woman now and she need me more than ever. I don't care about school then if it mean I going to leave my Grannie all alone. They don't care, (I feel so foolish how everybody passing and looking at me crying) but I don't care . . . I mean . . . yes, I care bout my Grannie. She is the only person I have in the whole wide world. And me is all she have.

But soon after (Miss Myrtle never come again), Grannie call me one Saturday morning and give me a good rub down. She make me put on me church dress and slippers and she give me twenty cents to take the bus and go up to Vineyard Town to Miss Myrtle house. All the while Grannie singing 'Rock of ages cleft for me' and trying to hide the sadness in her voice, but when she give me a smudgy air mail envelope I could tell that she was crying over it. I wonder what it say. Serve that Miss Myrtle right if is 'no Maria not leaving her Grannie'.

Is a number 26 bus I take to go to Vineyard Town, I can't read the big writing but I ask a bus conductress and she show me where I must get the bus. Then I ask a lady on the bus for Antrim Crescent and she show me where to come off. I see the big houses them with them marble verandahs and them green lawns and pretty flowers at the gates. But somehow it remind me of the cemetery cause not a soul is there. No children playing hopscotch on the road, no drunken men or old people idle and chatting this and that, only a few dogs barking at you as you come too near them gateway. The place so silent you can even hear the wind blowing even though it not blowing hard.

Miss Myrtle live in a pretty white and blue house, I see her in the yard looking on some flowers. She look just like a lady in a picture book. She in her shorts and she is so skinny and before she see me I call out.

"Miss Myrtle! Miss Myrtle, ma'am, is me Maria!"

She turn and give me a big smile, her teeth just like white lime. Her fluffy brown hair peeking out from under a red polka-dot tie-head and her glasses at last perched on her straight nose. She grab me inside quick and hug me. It feel so strange cause I don't even know her and I don't even like her. All the while she grinning and chatting how she glad to see me, and how I find my way, and if I hungry. But my Grannie tell me not to eat from people you don't trust so I shake my head, no. Then I give her the crushed up envelope. Now I smiling cause I hope is bad news that will just wipe the grin off Miss Myrtle face. But she laugh out loud and hug me and say "Welcome home, Maria."

I don't know how I can run so fast, but I running and running. And I crying bad. I hate Miss Myrtle, I hate her cause she want to take me away from Grannie. Last thing I remember is Miss Myrtle screaming out me name, but I never look back I don't want to, I want to go home to my Grannie.

Two days pass and every time Miss Myrtle come to the yard I run down the cemetery to hide. Everybody in the yard get to hate her too and as soon as they see the yellow car come rumbling down the lane they know is she and before she reach the yard Miss Piggy or Girlie from next door done tell us and I run like pickpocket to hide. And for days we keep up this game.

One Sunday long after, rain fall and fall like God a come. Thunder roll. And not a sky in the black clouds and the day look like midnight, with the lightning flashing like street lamp.

Grannie wasn't well, she had the flu. So I had to go down to the Station to sell the *Star*. I never like that day. It was as ugly as death.

I never wanted to go sell *Star*, but Grannie needed the money to buy bread and tinned mackerel so I take up the papers and run down to the station before the other sellers them reach. The rain stop fall now and it just drizzling and not even the old coat that Grannie say was me dead grandfather's can keep the cold from finding me. And I hug the papers to me stomach and call out *"STAR"*. People all wet and trembling buying *Star* as they wait for the train to go home. I wish I was them so I could take a ride on the train, me and my Grannie, and leave this place and so Miss Myrtle won't be able to find we.

It was late in the night when I come back, with the stale bread under one arm and the tin of mackerel in me coat pocket, to see a whole heap of people in the yard. Some covering them face with them hands from the drizzle. Miss Piggy like a mother hen ordering everybody including her nine pickneys round the yard. She at the doorway and she crying. And the yellow flame belching up from the tin lamp on the table making frightening shadows round the room. Then I hear Girlie telling a man that is somebody dying and the man asking if is the little old lady.

Grannie on the bed like grass withering away, and she calling, calling for me. I push past Miss Piggy who trying to keep me outside and rush up to the bed. I hold the shrivel up hands and squeeze them gently and Grannie open her eyes and her voice like the rustle of dry leaves when wind blowing. I hear her asking, "Maria," she say, "Maria, Grannie sick, sick bad," (and then she just go out like a light bulb and I squeeze her hand again) "Maria, go to Miss Myrtle, love, go home to Miss Myrtle."

Then her eyes like they turning over look at me, then she call for Miss Piggy and I can't hear a thing they saying cause tears just rolling down my face. Cold fear clutch my eight-year-old heart and all the things I remember me and my Grannie used to do come to me. The rain start to pour again like judgement come to take my Grannie. Far away in the black night I hear a dog howling. And the little body, like a baby, suddenly go stiff, stiff on the bed and Miss Piggy start bawling like a frog in her throat and she grab me head in her soft round stomach and me bawl too.

The night blacker than ever and nobody hear the sound

of the yellow car, but me hear it and me know is Miss Myrtle come (is like her appointed time) for me and I can't run now. I don't have nowhere to run. No one to run to. I have to obey me Grannie and go home.

Land of the Purple Evening

by Diane Browne

Silver, 1983

Joshua Morgan thought about the meeting with grave misgivings. He knew it would not go well. But Adele had said, "Go! Go and tell the old red man that you won't work any longer unless you get the land at the bottom side of the hill."

"Adele, is too soon," he had replied. "Miss Miriam not dead a month yet."

"Then now is the time," she had said. "Now is the time, before the children come and tell him what to do with the property."

"But Adele, a jus' can't tell Maas George to give me the land. A not entitle to it."

"Not entitle to it! After you work all you life with the family! You 'fraid of him? You a man or a slave? Besides," she added coaxingly, "him always say him would give you a piece of land one day. Him not using the land. Him depend on you, you know, man. Ask him."

So Joshua had dressed himself in his suit shiny with age. The early morning dew dampened his shoes as he walked through the thick grass. At the bottom of the hill he stopped and gazed affectionately at the large old house with its verandah running along three sides. He had worked on this property from he and Maas George had both been young men. He remembered the day Maas George had returned from his trip to England with Miss Miriam, a tall thin English girl with a figure like a boy and straight stiff brown hair. The family had been pleased, as had the servants. But Joshua had averted his eyes when he was introduced to her. There were so many pretty Jamaican girls around. Why had Maas George chosen this foreign woman, who to add to her lack of beauty would no doubt lack understanding of their ways?

Miriam, however, had learnt quickly and she understood many things. Many misunderstandings between Joshua and George were made smooth by her intervention behind the scenes; and with the years she had even ceased to be ugly.

A week before she had died, when she had been taking her usual walk through the orange groves, she had stopped beside Joshua as he stood gazing at the fungus-covered branches of the trees. He had noticed then how her transparent white skin barely covered the veins of her face and hands.

"Old trees, old house, old people, eh, Joshua," she had said in her dry abrupt way. Then she had added, "You know, Joshua, I have greatly appreciated your help all these years, and I know I can count on you to look after Maas George when I'm gone."

"Gone, Miss Miriam? You not going anywhere, ma'am. You stronger than me."

"Stronger than you, eh? Of course I am," she had laughed, pulling her old blue sweater around her even though the morning was already warm. "Just remember, Joshua, George is a stubborn old man but he really cannot do without you."

No, thought Joshua as he walked slowly up the hill. He did not see how this meeting could go well, and there was no longer Miss Miriam to set things right.

George Long grumbled to himself as he hurried to fix his morning tea. He wanted to be done before the new housekeeper came in to manage him with her concern. His grey eyes, now cloudy white, watered as he thought of quiet mornings with Miriam. Damn it! Where was Joshua? He was just about to call him loudly when he remembered that Joshua had gone home last night to Adele. Long ago he had offered them a place to stay in the servants' quarters but Adele had refused. Her father had left her a house and she would live in it, she had said. And besides, she had a little pastry business in the town.

So Joshua had stayed on the property sometimes, and sometimes in town with Adele. He did not really work any more. He would just walk around the property, then he and George would sit on the front steps – George at the top and Joshua on the bottom step – and smoke, making never-to-be-executed plans for the land long into the purple evening.

But now that Miriam had gone, thought George, Joshua would have to stay with him. There were no other servants living there. Joshua and Adele could have the entire servants' quarters to themselves. And he would give Joshua the piece of land at the bottom of the hill. Joshua was too old to work it but he could pass it on to his and Adele's children. George pictured Joshua's reaction. Joshua would pull himself up to his dignified full height and say, "A will pay you little by little for it, Maas George." George smiled as he mouthed his reply. "Pay! No, man! You have earned it by your faithful service. This is your pension." He would not say, but Joshua would know that it freed him from dependence on Adele and her father's house and her pastry business.

George's hand, speckled yellow-brown with age, shook as he walked slowly onto the verandah, and the cup rattled in its saucer. He lowered his tall angular frame into the old cane chair. A man was coming up the hill in a suit. In the morning sunlight he could not make out who it was. The man was at the bottom of the steps before he recognised him.

"Joshua, is you, man. But what happen? Why you in you suit? Anything happen to Adele or any of the children? You grandson sick again?" George trembled, death was still so close to him, misfortune waiting all around.

"Everybody fine, Maas George," Joshua laughed nervously. "Is jus' a little business a come to talk over with you."

"Ah," sighed George, "what is Adele up to now? She is a real business woman, eh! Well, man, what is the problem?"

George leant forward from his seat. Once he would have stood up to talk to Joshua on a serious matter of business, but now he was tired. He did not ask Joshua to come up on the verandah. Joshua did not expect him to. He remained standing at the bottom of the steps.

Joshua shifted his weight from one leg to the other. He did not have the words to say what he had to say. He did not want to say what Adele had told him to say. He began to get angry.

"What has happened to Adele now, man?" said George in his booming voice. "That politician lawyer of a landlord giving her a hard time with the cake shop?" It surprised him to discover that secretly he hoped Adele's business was in trouble so she would be more willing to accept his offer. Then he and Joshua would walk over the property in the mornings and evenings just as they had done when they were young. Joshua was his friend – more than his friend, really – his second self.

At last Joshua found the words. "Well, a come to tell you a can't work any longer. A too old now." The words came out more roughly than he had intended.

George's face went pale. His bony hand gripped the arm of the chair. He did not understand. "Eh, man? Eh, what you say, Joshua? But you don't work, man. You come and go as you please. You don't do a stroke of work here. A don't expect you to."

"All these years a been working with no reward," said Joshua, his voice rising. "No reward!" he repeated, but he could not bring himself to mention the land at the bottom side of the hill.

"No reward!" shouted George. He was on his feet. "You have made a good wage. Your children were schooled by us. Who lent Adele the money to set up the shop?" He stopped, out of breath. He had not meant to mention the children.

Joshua's eyes shone white with rage in his black face. "Days of slavery done! You think I am a slave? I am a man. You don't own me."

"What the hell are you saying, man?" replied George swiftly. "Days of slavery! Why, you ungrateful . . ." and he stopped himself, his face red and blotched. Never had he spoken to Joshua like that; never had he thought he could. He turned and walked into the house.

George lay in the bed he had shared with Miriam. He had wanted to give the land to Joshua – it was his due. But even if he could take back the things he had said he could not give him the land now. Joshua would feel that he was doing so only because he had been forced to as a result of their quarrel. Moreover, he could not believe that Joshua had felt such bitterness for him all these years when he, George, had looked upon Joshua with such affection.

George Long turned his face to the wall and cried. Not only

had Miriam left him, but so had Joshua.

Joshua entered Adele's father's house. Adele was baking. He could smell the rich strong ginger. She did not look up as Joshua sat on the stool by the kitchen door.

"What happen, man?" she asked. "You get the land?"

"A tell Mr. George Long that a leaving the work."

"Good!" said Adele. "So what him say? You get the land?"

"Land!" grunted Joshua. "Land! I am a man. A don't need his land. A leave the job."

"How you mean you leave the job?" she snapped, swinging round on him, hands on her wide hips. "What a tell you to say? What you tell him?"

"Woman," he said loudly as if she were in another room, "a tell him just what a tell you."

There was something in his face that Adele had never seen before. Without another word she turned back to the kitchen table.

After a while she said briskly, "Well, that is fine, then. A really glad, you know, because now you don't have to hassle up youself to go up the house any more. You can come and work with me in the shop. A jus' feel that chile a have in there thiefing me. A will jus' fire her."

Joshua did not answer. He gazed through the back door past the scratching chickens, the banana trees and the dry cane in the yard. In his mind's eye he could see the rolling hillsides of the property where he had worked all his life. He and George Long walked through the orange groves in the crisp morning just as the mists lifted ahead of the streams of sunlight. He and George Long sat and smoked on the front steps and made plans for their land in the purple evening.

9 789766 101589